40 SHORT STORIES
OF HORROR
AND
THE SUPERNATURAL

BRIAN WRIGHT

CONTENTS

FAT MAN

After Gilbert moved to New York to take up his new job, the novelties had come thick and fast. Meeting his work colleagues, finding a place to live, acclimatising himself to the maniacal pace of the city. Above all, the gratification of seeing people being themselves - big people, fat people, *enormous* people, who seemed content to be larger than life, proud even of their adiposity.

Like them, Gilbert became accustomed to walking happily through crowds, his head held high, looking directly into every face. Things he hadn't done before in his twenty-eight years.

His colleagues included other fatties, who told him about the specially reinforced equipment in the company gym. It was another pleasant shock to the system - big people who exercised! Soon he was walking the treadmill as enthusiastically as anyone and happy to observe that, while not losing much weight, he was definitely adding tone to his flab.

He quickly fell into a lively social scene. His existence back home in London had consisted of work and train-spotting, standing around ice-cold railway platforms with the other misfits, endeavouring to fill the hole in his life with rows of digits. His evenings now, though, were packed with numbers of a different kind, the music which thundered out of the sound systems in the clubs he visited with his new friends.

Everywhere around him would be other big people enjoying themselves to the full. The city even had clubs that catered specially for them, where ninety percent of the clientele were fat. Then it would be the few scrawny ones who looked freakish, desperate to atone for their lack of avoirdupois by attaching themselves to plump partners.

One club quickly became his favourite, the Purple Porker, owned by the largest people he had ever come across, Courtney and Mamabelle Cooke. They were metropolitan sophisticates down to their pudgy fingertips, an aggregate of more than seven hundred pounds testifying to many years of spectacular over-indulgence. Since the club was close to his apartment, he began to go there almost every night.

Gilbert was no judge of women, had never even had a girlfriend - his female co-workers always intimidating scarecrows, no such thing as lady train-spotters - but he believed Mamabelle to be the most magnificent creature imaginable. Standing over six feet in her high heels, draped in yards and yards of tulle and satin, resembling a ship's figurehead with her painted face and abundant bosom.

She was matched by her husband, a behemoth in evening dress, every one of his many jowls always polished to a shine and exuding the delicate fragrance of expensive aftershave. He was a wisecracking, backslapping presence at the heart of the club.

Once only, Gilbert saw the man lose his temper, savagely bawling out an errant waiter, and for a second had the impression of a wholly different personality lurking behind the affable exterior. Telling himself a cuddly teddy bear could never have built such an empire, he ordered another whisky.

With the guilt factor much reduced - if not removed altogether - Gilbert was eating and drinking with abandon. Breakfast at his local deli followed by a giant submarine sandwich or two for lunch and some international cuisine in the early evening - Greek or Mexican or Chinese - and then more food washed down with beer and Scotch at the Purple Porker.

Doubling his efforts on the treadmill, he was content to maintain his weight at the same level while adding a healthy-looking sheen to the vast acres of his skin.

The Cookes, though, were the undisputed eating champions of the Big Apple.

Compared to them, he was on a diet. He had seen Courtney swallow a thirty-six ounce steak, accompanied by an avalanche of vegetables, and then complain of being hungry within a couple of hours. And Mamabelle was trampling on her husband's heels, metaphorically speaking (physically it would have been impossible).

Courtney and Mamabelle were at the peak, but many others were climbing to be with them.

And so the restaurant area was always the busiest part of the club, the sounds of gastronomic activity sometimes threatening to drown out the loudest dance beat. To satisfy the demand, the club employed several highly-trained chefs to churn out delicious food in vast quantities, but Gilbert heard it was like the doling out of soup at Dotheboys Hall compared to the dinner parties thrown by the regal couple in their penthouse home.

Anchored at the centre of their universe, the Cookes were like mighty twin suns encircled by a host of planets and satellite moons, irresistibly drawn into their orbit by the promise of a word and a smile, a slap on the back from Courtney, a dance with the surprisingly nimble Mamabelle. Above all, there was the hope of an invite to dinner, granted only to the lucky few.

The call would always come unexpectedly, the fortunate person taken to one side by Dragan Fleischer, the Cookes' factotum and fixer, as stern and spare as his employers were smiling and obese, and handed an embossed invitation card. Only an unusually favoured guest would be summoned a second time.

The dinner parties were intimate and yet elaborately staged affairs, so he was told, never more than a half dozen guests dining off exquisite French china arranged on the finest table linen. Beautifully cooked, the food came in amounts that threatened to overwhelm the most capacious stomach. There would be at least three meat courses, the lamb in particular being of a melting quality that haunted the palate for months afterwards.

His informant, Chastity deWan, was a professional Big Beautiful Woman (BBW) on the internet, making a living from selling advertising space on her website, which basically consisted of pictures of herself in various stages of undress. Having hit the site on several occasions since first meeting her, Gilbert was very close to putting his friend above Mamabelle in his affections.

Astonishingly, Chastity also seemed fond of him. It helped that she, too, was on her own in the big city, an out-of-towner from the Midwest. She sighed again at the memory. "They're having another one tonight," she said, "which is why they've left him in charge. They say that *thin* man would do anything for the Cookes."

She tilted her several chins contemptuously in the direction of Dragan Fleischer, stalking grim-faced around the club. As ever, Gilbert was reminded of a hunting dog on the prowl through an over-fed grazing herd.

He had spoken only once to Courtney and hadn't yet summoned up the courage to ask Mamabelle to dance, but occasionally got the feeling they were watching him through the noisy throng. Chastity told him the dinner invitations only ever went to people who stood out in the crowd, who were in shape under their corpulence, healthy in spite of their size.

They began to attend fitness classes together, both wishing for the same thing. Hoping to gain an additional edge, he dyed his hair peroxide blond.

The club reflected the city outside, in a state of perpetual flux. It was a swirl of familiar and unfamiliar faces, people disappearing off to other clubs or other lives, newcomers taking their place on the dance floor and at the bar. That all added to the excitement.

But the truth of urban living, its capacity to devour its own, its collective amnesia, was brought home to them when human remains were discovered in a rural corner of Long Island. They were traced, through a distinctive prior injury to the skull, to a 280 pound security guard from Queens, a bachelor without any close family. He had been shot in the head and dismembered.

FAT MAN

Other remains were soon found close by; the bones and last vestiges of at least three people, their bodies cut up with varying degrees of skill. They had been put into the ground in the space of a few months and had lain undetected for two years or more. The news media, of course, was in its element, trumpeting that a serial killer was on the loose, speculating whether other death sites might be scattered around New York.

The shock was really felt at the club when forensic tests revealed the new finds also belonged to fat people, none of whom had apparently been reported as missing. Thinking they were being targeted by a madman, many of its patrons stayed away from the Purple Porker for a week or two. But they gradually drifted back as the sensation died down.

Chastity, in touch with other webmasters on the internet, where every rumour was fuelled as it flew through cyberspace, reported one gruesome fact. The slicing up of the earliest corpse had been amateurish, but the murderer's skills had improved to the point where the last body had been dissected with almost surgical precision.

"Practice makes perfect, I suppose," Gilbert said with a smirk, and was relieved when Chastity's playful but beefy slap just missed his head.

But her good humour was gone a few days later, when she told him that a black limousine with tinted windows had been seen cruising around her apartment block. "It's probably nothing," she said, "but there's still a serial killer out there."

Gilbert, who couldn't help thinking she lived in a fantasy world in more ways than one, was taken up with his own news, still thinking about the ornate white card that Dragan Fleischer had slipped into his hand earlier in the evening.

The next week, gazing out on the luminescent towers of Manhattan while savouring mouthfuls of a wonderfully fragrant meat, his former existence had never seemed so far away.

The one disappointment was not sharing his big day with Chastity, who had stood him up at the gym that afternoon. Still nervous about possibly being stalked, she had talked of going back to visit her relatives in Grand Rapids. In spite of her apparent defection, he had never been happier, he realised, looking at the glowing faces and ample stomachs of his fellow diners, staring with wonderment into Mamabelle's deep cleavage.

It was a joy to be fat in New York.

Courtney was the perfect host, his customary exuberance toned down for the occasion as he drew out his guests with tact and charm. Gilbert, flattered by the attention, found himself talking freely about his life before coming to America - the bullying at school, his estranged family, his newfound sense of freedom.

His host seemed to be evaluating every word. They went on to discuss the benefits of introducing a computerised payroll system at the Purple Porker. Gilbert decided it was the last word in mixing business with pleasure, his attention diverted once again to Mamabelle's décolletage.

After that evening, he wanted nothing more than a return visit. Chastity still wasn't back from Grand Rapids, but he had already decided there was only room on the pedestal for Mamabelle.

He knew he had arrived in the inner circle when she asked him to dance; he saw the envious looks of other men as he led her onto the floor. He tried out several of the moves learned at the dance class he now attended, feeling like a more generous version of John Travolta. Mamabelle laughed as she matched him step for step.

She gave him an admiring glance afterwards and ran a long fingernail down his forearm. "You really are a fine figure of a man," she said, "healthy as a prize animal on a farm." She fluttered her eyelashes. "We must have you back for dinner one of these days."

There seemed to be an invitation inside her invitation, and he wasn't sure which prospect excited him the most. Mamabelle in her fleshy glory or the glory of lamb flesh. A recollection on his tongue serving as the answer, he joined in the long queue for food.

An almost unprecedented second invitation!

He didn't mention it to anyone in case of bad luck, but was even more encouraged when a day or two later he saw Courtney and Dragan Fleischer deep in conversation and casting glances in his direction.

Earlier on that evening he'd spoken once more about the advantages of computerisation to Courtney and got the impression the club owner was definitely interested. How could he refuse, Gilbert told himself, if the job was offered to him? He fervently hoped it would be done over another glorious meal.

When the black limousine came slowly alongside him as he walked to the subway station the next morning, he couldn't help thinking about Chastity's fears and lengthened his stride.

"Gilbert, over here." Dragan Fleischer's voice. Surprised, he walked across to the car. "Get in." Although the man looked as saturnine as ever, his lips seemed to be approaching a smile. It unnerved Gilbert, but he obediently slid into the front seat.

"What is it, Dragan?" he asked. "I'm on my way to work."

"Don't worry, I'll get you to where you're going." He looked Gilbert over appraisingly. "You know they want you back?"

Gilbert laughed out loud at the confirmation of his wildest dream. "I can't wait," he said. "That meat!"

"They're cooking up something pretty special for you," Fleischer said with a sly grin.

Gilbert, at ease now they were on his favourite subject, laughed at the pun. "I never thought of it before, the Cookes who love eating."

"My name is like that, very appropriate in the circumstances," the thin man murmured.

Gilbert looked at him, puzzled, and said, "Fleischer?"

"It means butcher in German."

"Sorry, but I don't understand." The man reached across him to shut the passenger door with its tinted window, before accelerating out into the traffic.

"You soon will, Gilbert, you soon will," he said.

BLOOD

I've seen a ghost.

The whole of my recent history, in fact, has been a farrago of shocks and mysteries that I can't even begin to explain. Which is a tad surprising, given that I'm an investment banker, at the dull end of a dull profession, and my chief ambition is to open a book store specialising in first and second editions of classic Victorian novels, preferably somewhere nice like Greenwich Village.

And the ghost? To be truthful, it wasn't in any way scary at the time. But the memory of it still pops into my head now and again. In particular the one detail.

But to begin at the beginning.

Talk is cheap, but time is money, as are air fares; and so the preliminary meeting of a proposed task party to investigate the bank's staffing levels was held via video-conferencing link between our Boston and New York offices. It was then that I first met Brad Chandler.

The meeting was even more disorganised than these things usually are. That was entirely down to the Chairman, Marty Rainier, Vice President in charge of Internal Finance, but without management or any other skills save the complementary abilities to put across other peoples' ideas with persuasive bluster and then to claim them as his own.

Now he chuckled at his own jokes while everything around him went to hell. People on both sides wandered in and out without a word of explanation, to take a leak or catch a coffee, safe from any reprimand. There were competing voices and constant interruptions, breaking all the rules of video-conferencing.

As if by accident, the guy in charge of the remote control at the other end kept zooming in on the prominent cleavage of an attractive blonde colleague. The majority of female attendees in both locations were *not* amused. One latecomer in New York, distinguished by red hair and sloping shoulders, strolled blatantly in front of his colleagues to an empty seat. As with several of the others, his contribution after that was non-existent.

Brad Chandler stood out even in this shambles. He said little at first, seemed ill at ease, more on edge than I was ever to see him again, shaking his head every so often as if unable to believe what was going on around him.

Then, gradually, he took control both of himself and the meeting; and I quickly realised that here was a complex personality, with enough ice on the surface to sink the Titanic - he later told me he'd put himself through college with his poker-playing - but burning inside with ambition and other less obvious emotions. It was clear he hated his boss Marty Rainier.

When order was restored, largely because of Brad's crap-cutting comments, we soon ran through the agenda.

He proposed a smaller sub-committee should be set up to run the day-to-day affairs of the task party. Surmising that this was where the power and eventual rewards would lie, I strongly supported his idea, and sensed rather than saw the look of appreciation he directed me across the ether. Brad and myself were both voted onto the sub-committee.

Marty, following his usual tactic of maximum kudos for minimum effort, decided it was enough for him to chair the video-conference meetings of the full task party to be held once every couple of weeks. In actual practice, these would do little more than rubber-stamp the decisions of the sub-committee.

Realising this was the case, people lost interest or found better places to be, which meant that attendance at the video-conferences rapidly dwindled to the inner core. The big blonde and the red-headed nonentity, for example, were among the first casualties and I never saw either of them again, lost among the thousands of drones in our Manhattan beehive.

A few days after the first video conference, I flew to New York with a colleague to spend some time with the other members of the sub-committee. Up close and in the flesh, the coldness in Brad's eyes became apparent, but his dynamism and quick intelligence were similarly accentuated.

Our relationship was defined from the moment I showed pleasure at his throwaway compliment on a piece of work I'd done. Since, however, I have always slipped easily into the role of acolyte, and here was a man clearly going places, that suited me. I decided he was someone who would stick with me if I stuck by him. The next time I visited headquarters, he invited me out for a meal and it felt as if I'd been given some sort of award.

Brad's wife came along too. Trish, dark and petite, a third grade teacher, a carer and embracer of good causes, seemed different to her husband in every way.

While she was voluble and self-dramatising, he was as buttoned-down as his shirts; she loved Mahler, he listened to Nirvana; she supported Greenpeace, he was a fan of Green Bay. Yet they seemed fond enough of one another.

We ended the evening in a noisy Irish bar off Times Square. By midnight, I was gone, awash with the black stuff, and ready for my hotel bed. When I made my excuses to leave, Brad gave me one of his unblinking, unnerving stares, which seemed only slightly diluted by the alcohol he'd consumed.

"What do you think of Trish?" he asked. I guessed this was another defining moment in our relationship.

BLOOD

"She's OK," I replied. "Very nice, in fact, but not my type." He said nothing, but I knew my answer had been just right.

Something strange happened at the next video conference.

One of the New York attendees, Arch Flugelmann, was another of the nobodies at whom the task party initiative was directed (its ultimate aim being to shed staff, preferably - but not guaranteed to be - the sick, the stupid and the grossly incompetent).

He was the sort of guy who wouldn't say boo to a very small duckling, let alone a goose. He didn't even have the nerve to stop coming to the meetings like those others who felt they had nothing useful to contribute. He wasn't much to look at either, which was why I was doubly amazed by the thought that entered my head when I saw his balding pate on screen.

He's an adulterer.

And thereafter the words crossed my mind every time I looked at him. He was always a nervous person, fidgety even when just sitting and listening to others talk, and he didn't look so very different then, but the thought kept coming until I had to make a conscious effort to edge him out of my vision.

Although puzzled and not a little disturbed by my reaction to Arch, I decided that I couldn't do much about it. At the following video conference, he wasn't in his usual place and there was laughter at the other end, led by Marty Rainier, when I commented on the fact. "Arch is having a few problems at home," someone said.

"Seems his wife discovered he's been playing games with his secretary. Too embarrassed to show his face, I guess."

More laughter.

I thought long and hard about it afterwards, yet there seemed no rational explanation for what had happened. I've always been able to empathise with other people, I suppose, to sniff out how they are feeling and to respond appropriately - it's one reason for my small success in the business world - but this had been different, even a bit frightening. I hoped it was a one-off.

On my next trip to New York, I went to the theatre with the Chandlers and then for dinner afterwards. Trish began to tease me in the restaurant. "Why aren't you married?" she asked. "Don't you like girls?"

Although he was lounging back, I could tell that Brad, too, was interested in my answer.

"I like lots of girls," I replied. "For a start, there's Edith Wharton, then there's Mrs Gaskell, George Eliot."

BLOOD

They looked at me stupidly for a moment before Trish burst out laughing. Brad, however, remained expressionless even when she explained the joke. Later on, after we'd consumed a lot more wine, Trish began rubbing her foot against mine under the table. I moved my leg and looked towards her husband, but he appeared not to have noticed.

Another video conference, another happening.

The target this time was the buffoonish Marty. He was more subdued than usual, even making a feeble attempt to impose his authority on the meeting, and the thought came to me without any warning.

He's hiding something.

Luckily, the meeting was a short one as the life of the task party was coming to an end and we were simply sharpening up on the final proposals. Yet when I looked at my notes, the word MONEY, always in upper-case, appeared several times in the margin of every page.

This time I was more perplexed than worried. Deciding to utilise my new-found telepathic skill, I phoned Brad to ask if he suspected any sort of financial irregularity in connection with Marty Rainier. He was immediately interested. "No, but what have you heard?"

I was expecting that one so had my answer off pat: it involved a mysterious contact who had gotten a whisper. I could tell Brad wasn't overly impressed, but he said he'd get on to it. As I knew he would. You know, for a moment, I almost felt sorry for Marty Rainier.

Within a week, he was escorted from the New York building by security men, never to return.

It seems that some of our sales people had been running a scam involving heavily padded expense accounts. Marty had recently gotten wind of the fraud, but held off taking action for fear that, as Vice President in charge of Internal Finance, he would be expected to take his share of the blame.

Now financial institutions like ours will tolerate just about any kind of impropriety or negligence - so long as it doesn't involve the loss of their own money. From the moment Brad, regretfully, placed his evidence in front of the Management Board, Marty Rainier didn't stand a chance. So Brad took the huzzahs and approbation, the most manifest sign of which was promotion to the position recently vacated by his boss.

And my recompense? Well, apart from virtue being its own reward, I was only too pleased to accept Brad's offer of a post as his deputy, especially since it meant coming to live in New York on a substantial wage increase. Greenwich Village was getting closer in every way.

On the day we started in our new jobs, Brad and I went to his favourite bar to celebrate. Trish joined us there. As the spirits were lowered and spirits got higher, Trish started to stroke my calf with her foot. Although Brad was drunker than I'd ever seen him, I could tell he knew what was going on. He didn't look pleased.

I decided to get my message across once and for all. As her stockinged foot reached towards me again, I scraped my shoe very hard down her shin. She drew back with a yelp of pain and Brad laughed.

"Fuck you." Trish stood up and stared at her husband until he looked away. I suddenly had the feeling that what bound these people together was closer to hate than love. She turned to me. "And as for you, you smug bastard, why don't you ask him what his last slave died of?"

She left us sitting in an awkward silence.

Brad must have read the question on my face. "She's only kidding," he said. "We're buddies. You do right by me and I'll see you alright."

I could see him debating whether to go on. Drink finally won out over discretion. "It's just that some people can't resist temptation. Not everyone's like you."

This was high praise indeed, from Brad, and it emboldened me to put the question into words. "And what *did* your last slave die of?"

The inner fires were on his cheekbones, visible even in the dim lighting of the bar, but there was a deep chill in his voice. "Let's just say I have a way with a baseball bat." Then he dug me in the ribs. "C'mon, you boring old bastard, don't you know a scam when it's run at you?"

We both laughed and raised our glasses to the memory of Marty Rainier. And all the time I was thinking, I'm going to do everything in my power not to cross this man.

I soon learned exactly how Brad's last slave had died. It was no secret.

The guy's name was Dean Sirkowski and he'd worked directly to Brad in Internal Finance; until he had been found in his apartment one night with his head beaten to a pulp, apparently the victim of a random break-in. The perpetrator or perpetrators had never been caught. Mark it well, this had happened two or three days before that fateful first video conference.

"Such a sadness," said a middle-aged secretary, cornering me by the water dispenser to peddle what was already stale news. "They were very close, you see,

Dean and Mr Chandler, socialised out of work and everything. Poor Mr Chandler was so upset."

I bet he was.

Now I may be dull but I'm not stupid, and my initial instinct was to get the hell out of there and open a book store in Kansas City or somewhere suitably far away.

However, Brad shows no sign of remembering our conversation in the bar and anyway, given his new high-flown status, has far more important people to socialise with these days.

On the few occasions we do hit the town - I generally try to ensure other people from the office are also there - Trish is notable by her absence. Brad has hinted that she doesn't want to be in my presence ever again. Suits me. And so I grind it out, counting my money and the days.

My fear of Brad has diminished to the extent that I'm almost looking forward to the video-conference with some of our Chicago people next week, my first since moving to New York. It'll be interesting to find out if I still have my strange new gift, and maybe the opportunity for another step up the ladder. At the very least it will bring some excitement into my banker's life.

Oh, you were wondering about the ghost?

Well, I was looking through my secretary's desk one day when she was out to lunch, searching for a clean disk for my computer. She isn't the best organised of people and in one of the drawers I came across an out-of-date hard copy of the bank's internal telephone listing, containing colour pictures of every employee in the building.

I still don't understand why, but I turned to the index and looked under "S". And there he was, Dean Sirkowski, wearing a buttoned-down shirt in the style of his erstwhile boss. Although I felt sure I'd seen the face before, it was the physical peculiarity that clinched recognition, the shoulders plunging away from a long-stemmed neck. What *is* the term for it? Ah, yes, slope-shouldered.

Now some people might think it's cool to see a ghost, especially one that appears at a distance of several hundred miles and does little else but sit still for an hour. You could even argue that it was nothing more than my telepathic powers converting Brad's disturbed and disturbing brain patterns into an hallucinatory image, scarcely counting as a ghost at all.

I have sympathy with both those viewpoints, in fact. And yet there was the shock of coming across his photograph and recognising him. Then, on top of everything else, the difference in his appearance. The devil in the detail.

BLOOD

It's the one reservation I have with regard to the upcoming video-conference. I can only hope that no-one in Chicago is harbouring a secret that's *too* dark and nasty.

Because it still disturbs me, sometimes, thinking back to that first occasion. Sirkowski being Polish-blond in life ... and recalling that red, red hair.

LA WOMAN

Miki Thrust was in a spin. Back to where he'd started. Nowhere.

Jesus Christ, when and how was he going to get his break? He'd done all the right things, followed up hundreds of ads in *Variety* and the other show biz papers, attended dozens of auditions all over the Greater Los Angeles area and beyond, cold-called production companies, even found himself an agent, one Ramon Sifflis.

It was Ramon who told him - as if he needed telling! - that he was in a competitive profession.

It didn't seem fair. After all, he was an all-American boy, who'd been taught to honour the Flag, give thanks to God and love his mom. He hadn't seen his family in four years, but wore Old Glory briefs and said Jesus Christ a lot. Two out of three wasn't bad. He was also a hot-blooded male, ideal for the work. And, anyway, wasn't it the right of every citizen of the USA to be a porn star?

But the only jobs he'd found since landing up in LA had been short-term and short on class. None had been remotely appropriate to a film-star lifestyle. Not one had lasted more than a few weeks.

He worried, too, about the animal theme running through his life. He'd been an assistant rinser in a poodle parlour and a helper in a pet store, even done a TV commercial dressed as a rabbit.

A particular foul-up had been his time with a dog-walking firm that carried out loads of business in Laurel Canyon and other places where the rich and famous clung together.

Thinking there were bound to be some adult video producers among the clientele, he pictured himself making an instant impression, all lean body and white teeth, when he took charge of their beloved pooches at the front door. But the only people he got to meet were Filipino housemaids and the occasional snotty butler.

He resigned the job in his own way, letting loose an over-pampered and fractious Yorkshire Terrier on Rodeo Drive and watching it scurry across the road, yelping for its mother as a Rolls Royce threatened to squash it like a bug.

In spite of that small victory, he couldn't help wondering if his recurring involvement with furry creatures pointed to a future at the bottom end of the blue movie market. Story-lines involving a man, a woman and a German shepherd.

Twice, he'd been close to achieving his dream.

The first time his leading lady-to-be went down with a dose of the clap only days before the start of filming.

More recently, he'd been waiting to go on set and mentally going through his part - third lead in a video feature to be called *Stick It To Me, Baby* - when the male star got bitten in the balls by a parrot that belonged to the owner of the house where they were doing the shoot.

The woman producer, who happened to be married to the leading man, immediately called a halt to the proceedings while her screaming partner was carted to hospital. The guy couldn't have been that bad, though, because two days later his old lady had caught him screwing a nurse in his private room at the hospital.

Business is business but pleasure has to be paid for - and the ensuing bust-up ended with both the production company and their marriage going into liquidation. *Stick It To Me, Baby* was never made. Miki cursed all animals.

Now he was reviewing his life.

He was twenty-two years old and without work, without a regular girlfriend, and living in a dump in a not-so-good part of North Hollywood. At least he could try to change one of those things. There was a singles night coming off at one of the supermarkets in his neighbourhood; he'd heard they were great for picking up chicks. He could even kill two birds by asking if they had any jobs going.

"Hoping to come across some porn producers, too, uh?" Ramon, ever the joker, said.

That Saturday evening found Miki cruising the aisles in his tightest jeans. It was about midnight and he'd been around so many times he was starting to get dizzy.

The only interest shown in him so far had come from a pair of forty-something twins, who'd eyed him in unison and then wolf-whistled simultaneously. He was flattered, but decided they were too old. Anyway, they probably did everything together. He shuddered at the thought.

He'd already finished two tubs of Haagen-Dazs icecream during his wanderings - well, it saved on having to pay for them - and in a fit of depression was reaching into the freezer cabinet for another when a bright female voice said, "Hullo."

She was the chick of his dreams, streetwise and smart-looking and with a great figure. OK, perhaps her lips were a touch too thin, but who was perfect? Not even him. He felt suitably humble at the thought.

The girl had gone silent and Miki realised she expected him to say something. That was the trouble with working in the porn industry, all your manners with the opposite sex went out of the window. "I'm sorry," he said. "My name is Miki." He decided to leave his last name - not real, but the industry insisted on handles that were *dangerous* - until they got to know each other better.

LA WOMAN

"Hi, I'm Candi."

They shook hands and Miki couldn't help thinking, if this was a film we'd have our tongues in each other's mouths about now. But there was a half-smile on her face that, perhaps, promised a good deal. He felt sure she liked him.

They went for a coffee and were soon chatting like old friends. Miki struggled to remember when he'd last done this with a girl, and felt sad when he realised how long it had been. After they arranged to meet again, he walked her to her car as they laughed and joked together.

"Candi," he joshed. "You could be a stripper with that name." Wanting to bite off his tongue as soon as he said it, he was relieved when Candi only gave another of her mysterious smiles.

It wasn't until their third date that Candi told him exactly what she did for a living. Before that, she'd simply said she was in computers. Knowing rather less about that subject than he did about thermonuclear physics, Miki preferred to discuss the green specks he claimed to see in her eyes.

They still hadn't slept together. He wondered how he'd managed to keep his hands off her; even more perplexing was how she'd kept hers off him. Then Candi invited him back to her place for a meal.

"Have you told her you're a virgin yet?" Ramon teased him.

She picked him up in her Toyota sports coupe and took him to a spacious ranch-style bungalow in the hills behind the Hollywood sign.

"You're in computers?" he asked in wonder.

"I have my own business," she said.

Over dinner he brought up the subject of her money. "How did you get to own all this?" he asked, looking around him, trying hard not to think about his own comfortless apartment.

Candi looked as if she was expecting his question. "I make films," she said.

Miki did his best to remain cool. "Oh," was all he said. He'd already told her he was an actor, without mentioning that his only professional appearance to date had been in a bunny costume.

Candi seemed to know what he was thinking. "I'm sorry," she said, her fingers brushing his sleeve. Miki liked that gesture. He would have preferred it if she'd ripped off her nice white blouse and thrown herself across the table, but he truly liked that gesture.

"I didn't want to tell you until we got to know each better ," Candi was saying. "I had to know you only wanted me for myself."

Miki was confused. What was she talking about? With a pair of boobs like that, who wouldn't want her? Something else was puzzling him. "What was that about computers?" he asked.

"My films are made to be shown on computer. Over the internet."

"What sort of films?"

Candi laughed. "Adult movies, of course. What other sort of films *are* there on the Net?"

Jesus Christ, Miki said to himself. He wondered if perhaps he'd died and gone to heaven. Rich and beautiful and a porn producer - he wanted to marry this chick! He couldn't hold it back any longer. "I'm in the same game," he said, modestly. "As a stud, I mean."

Candi clapped her hands delightedly. "I knew it!" she cried. "I have an instinct for these things. With that face and that bod, I just knew you were one of us. I have to admit the name Miki Thrust was also something of a clue."

Even though Miki had the feeling she was ribbing him, he was too happy to care. It was like he'd won the lottery without knowing he had a ticket. This chick, Candi, was going to help him realise his dream, he just knew it.

"Would you like to see my studio?" she asked, leading him into the next room.

"It's very simple," she said, as they surveyed an array of equipment that might have given Spielberg an inferiority complex. There were spotlights on the ceiling and several cameras on tripods around the room, angled for a variety of shots.

She went over to a bank of computer monitors that could have found its way onto the flight deck of the Starship Enterprise without anyone noticing. "Everything's controlled from this operating console," she said. "I press the one switch and we have lights, camera and ... action."

She stared at him from under her eyelashes. "Care to give it a try, lover?"

She showed him into a sparsely-furnished room leading off the studio, where he removed his clothes and carefully rinsed his more intimate areas in a small washbasin; he didn't want to blow this chance on the grounds of personal hygiene.

When he got back, Candi was reclining on the big bed that was the centrepiece of the studio. She was naked and smiling. As he went towards her in a state of - he hoped - controlled excitement, Miki stubbed his toe against a piece of equipment.

"Jesus Christ," he said.

LA WOMAN

Candi took charge from the start. Although it was a blow to his ego, he went along with her intructions, knowing that his future depended on her goodwill. The overhead lights burned into his eyes when Candi rolled him onto his back and straddled him with a triumphant look on her face. He struggled to get from under her, but she was too strong for him. Must be out of practice, he thought. He hadn't realised she was such a big girl - and she seemed to be getting bigger all the time.

"Welcome to my world," she said.

He came to in a room that was furnished with a bed and little else. Some form of concealed lighting reflected off the bare white walls. It was very warm and he took off all his clothes to feel more comfortable, then doused himself with cold water from the washbasin in a corner of the room.

Memories of how he'd got there were returning to him. He stood up and tried the door. It was locked. I'm a prisoner of love, he thought, feeling very lightheaded. The last thing he remembered was being pinned down by Candi. The sex had certainly been different, he decided, but not great. There were muffled sounds coming from all around him; and every so often a bell would ring and a door would open and close.

He had the creepy but comforting feeling he wasn't the only one locked in there.

What if the the chick was a collector? He imagined her cruising the supermarkets and malls of LA on the lookout for fresh meat. In spite of the situation, he couldn't help but feel proud that she'd chosen him over all the other great-looking studs around.

He remembered something Ramon had told him about the porn business. The johns - the guys who bought the films - very often liked to imagine it was themselves flapping their straps there on the screen. It helped if the stud happened to be the same colour at least.

He pictured Candi with a stable of different types. A black dude, of course, a Chicano, an older guy with the makings of a gut, perhaps a goofy-looking college type with glasses and a long thin dick. Miki thought, I'd be the clean-cut kid next door, the all-American boy.

Then he brightened. Variety, that was the key. Now if she was really selling her stuff over the internet, she'd need chicks as well, right? Candi was great-looking, but the johns wouldn't want to catch her every time. After all, what would the average guy do if given the choice between a bowl filled with apples - even those juicy big red ones - and another containing a whole load of different fruits?

LA WOMAN

Exotic pineapples and curvy bananas and smooth-skinned peaches: he was starting to feel horny just thinking about it.

The bell rang once more, right outside his room this time, and the door opened.

Wow, what *had* she put in his drink last night? It felt as though he'd been pumped full of laughing gas, he was positively floating along this corridor, couldn't run away if he tried. He found himself walking towards the big bed in the centre of the studio, where Candi was reclining and smiling at him. It looked like a one-girl show, after all.

He overcame his disappointment by thinking he could anyway put some new moves on her, no more of that sitting-on-top-of-him shit. He'd show her what a real man could do.

At that moment, he stubbed his toe against the same piece of equipment. Miki cursed. Candi clambered aboard again.

When it happened a third and fourth and fifth time, Miki realised he was in some weird kind of loop and there was no way out.

"Jesus Christ," he said.

RIDERS ON THE STORM

The *New York Times* ran a story the other day accusing my boss of helping to suck America dry. Something to do with the draining of moral fibre, the leeching of emotional equipoise, blah blah.

The piece was written by the usual intellectual stick insect, out to impress his friends and neighbours in the borough of Manhattan. Yet even while his pals were tut-tutting in agreement with the guy's bleeding heart sentiments, most of the rest of the country was tuned in to *The Reggie Sadler Show*.

Christ, I get respect just working for the Man. A regular table at my favourite restaurant. The favours of young women who think they can obtain a ticket to tomorrow's show that way. It would be easier to gain an instantaneous audience with the Queen of England, of course, but I don't let on until afterwards.

Word is that a rival show sends out sachets of fake red stuff with their invites. It's the kind of thing that gives our business a bad name. With *The Reggie Sadler Show*, the viewing public understand that they're getting genuinely dysfunctional people kicking genuine lumps out of each other. That's why they love it. The sponsors, too.

The last time one of our guests was carted off to hospital, some do-gooding Congressman proposed that we should be taken off the air. There's more chance of the Pope canonising a TV evangelist.

My job is to keep up the flow of crazies; and that day I was heading home through the desert after visiting a community of born-again Hell's Angels calling themselves White Bikers for Christ, who'd written in asking to appear on the show. They came on like the Ku Klux Klan on wheels and we planned to put them up against the Fellowship of African-American Gays, a bunch of vicious mothers with a tendency to beat up anyone who upset them (I understand they made a start with the guy who invented their name).

It's one of the reasons for the success of the *The Reggie Sadler Show*, the mix of guests.

But the White Bikers were a letdown, turning out to be several old guys in cracked leathers, their ravaged, bloodshot appearance hinting that, in spite of the new affiliation, their connection with Hell would be the more permanent one. The Bikers may have been willing, but the Fellowship would have murdered them.

To add to my frustration, the car developed an interesting lurch just outside a hick town only a short way from the safety of the metropolitan boundary. While it was being looked at, I trudged a couple of hundred yards through the blazing heat to a nearby diner. There I saw Gram and Magenta for the first time.

RIDERS ON THE STORM

Funnily enough, they were the only normal-looking people in the place. Everyone else could have been an extra in a cheap horror movie, from the squint-eyed truck-driver slurping down what was probably his third or fourth helping of heart-attack food that day to the bad-smelling waitress, whose incessant yawns revealed an impressive set of yellowing fangs.

I asked if I could join them; safety in numbers, I thought, as the truckie gave me a mean if divergent stare (I wondered vaguely how he kept his eyes on the road).

We got talking - that's my job, communicating with people, coaxing any paranoia out of them - and I soon realised that I'd hit the mother lode. These were authentically strange people, the real deal, with the added uncommon twist that they hadn't the faintest idea of how absolutely fucking weird they actually were.

The upshot was that I wangled myself an invite back to their parents' place a few miles off the main road and back into the desert. They waited patiently while my car was fixed, then drove on ahead, their battered pickup loaded with animal feed, through a landscape that quickly became like the backside of the moon, bleached cattle skulls and the corpses of more recently deceased creatures to our left and right.

Jesus, no wonder all the crazies chose to live out there!

Talk about wanting to be on your own. If these people had any neighbours, they must have been living in holes in the ground. But the parents were as charming, and staring mad, as their offspring.

Before we'd been chatting for half an hour, I was on the phone to our producer. He trusts my instincts and booked them into the slot that had been reserved for the White Bikers versus Fellowship match-up. That wouldn't be for several weeks, but it gave me time to do some more research on these people.

I especially wanted to research the luscious Magenta, plump and succulent as a prize-winning heifer, her blonde hair shining in the moonlight as the whole family waved me off. Even knowing what she got up to only gave an extra boost to my fantasies.

It felt so good thinking about her that, when I hit one of the short-lived thunderstorms sent to tease the parched earth in those parts, I was tempted to offer a lift to a lone hitchhiker standing drenched by the side of the road in the middle of nowhere. Then I decided he could only be another - and probably dangerous - crazy. Instead I pressed on the pedal.

The rest is history. When the Candlewick family appeared on *The Reggie Sadler Show*, it was the first-ever case of medically-authenticated vampirism to be shown on national television.

"It isn't usually our own blood," old man Candlewick explained. "We only drink that on special occasions, Thanksgiving and the like."

He smiled at his own modest joke and the audience took it as a cue to laugh nervously. No, their libations were most often taken from the veins of their animals, apparently calf's blood was the sweetest, goat's blood the richest. People were wriggling uncertainly in their seats by that time, but couldn't take their eyes off him. I knew then we had a hit.

In fact, they were a sensation - and that despite the program not containing a single fight, not even a curse word. When, right at the end, the family sipped delicately from a bowl of fresh blood in turn, everyone in the place got to their feet and cheered thunderously.

I understood the public's morbid facination. Hadn't I felt it myself when I'd seen them pass around the same bowl in their spartan sitting room that first evening? These people thought drinking blood was healthy and good, enjoyed the taste of it, for Christ's sake! Even the Man seemed a little overawed by the family, their quiet dignity, the refulgent good looks of the two children, their understated yet evident insanity. For once, he passed up on the usual sly digs at his guests.

Now I'd been there when the strategy of treating the subject sympathetically had been decided, had even loaned a hand with the script that Reggie was mouthing with such conviction, but he almost had me as fooled as the rest. It was a great performance.

When a TV critic in one of the more scurrilous supermarket tabloids floated the rumour that the program was being put up for an Emmy award in a serious documentary category, Reggie decided there had to be a follow-up show.

By that time, I'd talked the Candlewicks into moving to LA. The young ones didn't need much convincing and I could tell even the once-pretty Ma Candlewick wasn't reluctant to leave behind their harsh and lonely existence. The problem was old man Candlewick, dignified and stupid as one of the rams he kept coralled for his blood-letting pleasure.

But even he was persuaded after a visit to Disneyland and a meeting with Mickey Mouse. I thought I caught him licking his lips once or twice as he eyed the plump figure of the make-believe rodent. Perhaps he was estimating how many pints of blood it held. I told you he was stupid.

It concerned me that, at first, the family's health seemed to suffer. Inside weeks, the glow of their desert tans had faded, replaced by a sallowness that betrayed depression and even sickness. Just when I thought they might be on the point of returning to their old life - even the beauteous Magenta, who thought Rodeo Drive led straight to Heaven - things took a turn for the better.

Old man Candlewick told me that he'd come across someone in the wholesale meat trade who could provide blood from just-slaughtered animals - sheep, goats, even cattle.

Although he didn't mentioned money - none of them ever did, it was the other thing that marked them out from the rest of mankind - I said *The Reggie Sadler Show* would foot any bills. With Reggie believing he was in with the chance of an Emmy, we would have bought the family a herd of buffalo if they'd asked.

They looked better within days. What it proved, though, was that the family had to have blood. So it wasn't just an affectation, or something they enjoyed doing, they *needed* blood to survive.

They really were vampires.

Things weren't the same with Magenta after that. I knew then we would never sleep together. It was just the thought of lying next to her in the dark, asleep, my throat unprotected ... crazy I know, given that, apart from the one thing, these were probably the most normal people in the whole of California, almost certainly the least dysfunctional family ever to appear on *The Reggie Sadler Show*.

I remained friends with them, though, especially blond young Gram, who seemed to look upon me as a role model. *Me* a role model - I couldn't help liking these people, even while I wondered what made them the way they were. I mean they weren't your typical vampires. But they wouldn't talk about it, even to me, except to joke that they didn't have any relatives in Transylvania.

There was no attempt at serious analysis when they appeared on the show for a second time. Our house psychiatrist did a spot, but only came out with the usual stuff about bats and strings of garlic and cloaked figures. I could see the family shift with embarrassment as they listened to him.

It all started to go wrong midway through the show. The audience began to lose interest, one or two even yawning, and then Reggie reverted to type, trying to pick a fight with old man Candlewick over some trivial point.

His guest refused to be drawn, which usually triggers one of the Man's temper attacks, until the other person is driven from the stage or to tears. But for some reason he went easy on old man Candlewick. I wondered if he was going soft-centred.

Even the blood-drinking at the climax raised no more than a lukewarm round of applause. As the audience trooped out afterwards, you could read the disappointment in their eyes. Not a single punch thrown, just that same old vampire shit. The only novelty about Americans is that they only love novelty.

I knew then that the Candlewicks would never again appear on television, except perhaps in some cable show introduced by a man in a set of plastic fangs.

Reggie took it well that he'd lost out on an Emmy. And when old man Candlewick was charged with murder not long afterwards, he offered to fund the defence. I wondered even more about that.

The old man didn't stand a chance.

The body of a young girl had been found close to the Disneyland complex in Anaheim, her throat ripped apart. The LAPD, with its reputation to uphold, failed to notice the corpse was strangely pale, as if drained of blood. But, a reporter friend later told me, they retrieved the situation with a brilliant piece of detection. When a visiting European forensic scientist commented on the unusual condition of the body, apparently twenty or thirty detectives shouted out together, "Reggie Sadler!"

The whole Candlewick family was taken into custody from their modest apartment, also in Anaheim, but only the father stood trial. He was a forlorn figure on the stand, as white as if his own blood had been drained, muttering the same phrase at every opportunity, "We should never have come."

His only plea seemed to be that he'd suffered a bout of temporary insanity - like he'd been normal before! - seeing the beautiful young victim, who lived in the same apartment block, day after day, dreaming about what she would taste like. Even his own attorney flinched when he came out with that one.

Asked by the DA why his equally young and attractive daughter had been spared, old man Candlewick replied simply, "Because I'm not a monster." That broke the whole court up, even the trial judge failing to suppress a smirk, the spectators at the back whooping and hollering. We could have been on *The Reggie Sadler Show*.

The old man was right. Out there, removed from temptation, he'd just been your average maniac, his worst impulses under control, quaffing his legitimately-earned draughts of blood while he quietly contemplated the big desert moon. As with so many others, the city had corrupted him.

Chalk up another one to the American dream.

Reggie and Magenta got married a few weeks after her father was sent down for life; I'd worked it out by then and wasn't surprised. Naturally our viewing figures are higher than ever, people probably hoping to see the Man turn into a werewolf in the middle of a show.

RIDERS ON THE STORM

We don't give a shit about what they think, though, him and me and the rest of the production team. We're the ones in the tube, after all, happily surf-riding in Hell, with the dreams breaking all around us and the lives crashing down.

They seem very happy, Reggie and Magenta, although she's still receiving treatment for her problem.

They have a young son, Reggie Jr. He seems like a sweet kid, blonder even than his mother and uncle, but I can't help wondering about things like inherited genes and, OK, the blood that runs in his veins. It could turn out to be very interesting when he gets older.

Imagine it, a Reggie Sadler who literally sucks blood. Now *that* would be a story.

SUNSHINE OF YOUR LOVE

We first met in the swamps of Glastonbury, in 1968, and I last saw Jeannie for sure at another gathering of the tribes a couple of summers later. In between times, we had some fun and we made love and then she broke my heart. But even now, more than thirty years later, I can picture her arching like a cat in a long diaphanous dress in the warm glow of an August morning.

She worshipped the summer.

I'm an unreformed hippy, I suppose, one of the few middle-aged men left on earth who still thinks bellbottom jeans look good. Nowadays, though, drugs come in bottles with child-proof caps and the only place where I'm allowed to listen to loud music is in the car, the opening riffs of Smoke on the Water crashing out as the kids cover their ears and shriek at me to turn down the volume. My wife likes string quartets.

Jeannie went in for sunshine and dope and deafening bands, in that order. Our first encounter wasn't a great success, as rain cascaded on the festival site for days, turning the ever-present mud into an evil-smelling porridge that seemed to reach to the centre of the earth.

Her boyfriend was an acquaintance of mine, a fellow veteran of long nights in the jazz and blues clubs of Soho, and introduced her to me as his chick. She gave me a wan smile and began coaxing him to return to town. They left shortly afterwards, but I couldn't stop thinking about her.

We met again a few weeks later at a party in someone's flat, the Stones booming out on the record player, a marijuana fug in the kitchen. She came up to me and claimed that her ex-boyfriend was a bastard and how she hated all men. Yet she was looking me directly in the eyes when she said it. We ended up in the host's bed and got thrown out for our cheek, laughing the whole three miles back to her place in Victoria.

I stayed away from the hard stuff even then, less into amphetamines than alcohol, but soon learned that Jeannie popped pills like she was treating a serious medical condition, just to get her through the day.

Although I wanted a serious relationship, she soon made it plain that I was a full-time friend but only an occasional sleeping partner. More than once, she abandoned me in a club to go off with a total stranger. I let it all pass. Simply being around her, even when she was in one of her foul winter moods, was sufficient for me. Yet I couldn't help worrying about her, wondered sometimes how she kept going, her fragile mind and frail body under continuous chemical assault.

That January and February were the worst, her intake of acid increasing dramatically, anything to get through the dampness and gloom. For a period, she seemed to give up eating altogether, pushing to one side the food I brought from the curry shop on the corner, laughing off my claims that I could see her shoulder blades through her clothes.

It was the appearance of the first shoots of spring that saved Jeannie, her whole being uplifted by the promise of fine weather. I persuaded her to spend a long weekend with my sister and her family in Hampshire.

We went for strolls in the unseasonable sunshine, stopping off for meals of bread and cheese and pickle in old-fashioned pubs, and she began to look less like an escapee from a death camp. Even though I could see it was hurting her badly, she stayed away from dope the whole time we were there. I was proud of her, began to dream of a future together.

When we got back to London, however, she reverted to her customary wild behaviour, borrowing money to score grass almost before we stepped off the train. My sights instantly lowered, I slotted back into the role of loyal support and protector. My feelings for her, though, remained unaffected. I still lived in hope, you see.

My faith proved justified, too, as Jeannie's spirits rose with the barometer and her search for drugs and casual sex grew less frantic. She even started to put on weight. By the time the first major rock festival of the summer came around, she wasn't seeing anyone else and we were doing things almost like a normal couple - going to the cinema, watching TV, shopping. She could last the day on a single tab of acid by then.

But we needed only the odd joint of marijuana to get us through the festival on a high, the sun dappling the roof of the tent as we made love to the thunderous chords of Hendrix and the Who. The weekend passed by in a magical blur of sight and sound and touch, a memory I will carry to the grave.

We were happy all that summer, but already the warning signs were there. Jeannie often looked withdrawn in the wet or cold, refusing to share her thoughts with me.

One day, walking in our favourite park, I could feel her shiver violently as she watched the leaves falling from the trees. Although we had made plans to move in together, she informed me towards the end of September that she'd changed her mind.

Her spaced-out look told of increased drug-taking; and I soon learned that she'd graduated to heroin. It wasn't long before she started to go with other men behind my back. Still I said nothing, afraid of alienating her, pathetically grateful for a smile or the occasional show of tenderness. As autumn edged into winter, her mood swings became more aggressive and unpredictable. When I discovered her in bed with one of my friends, she accused me of being a peeping tom and attacked me with her fists.

It made no difference. I always found reasons to forgive her.

She went home, up North, for Christmas and I stayed in London, miserable and lonely, picturing the terrible things she was doing to herself. To my intense relief, she turned up at my flat on New Year's Eve and we spent the night together, watching the celebrations on TV and drinking cheap red wine. She burst into tears after we made love, but wouldn't say why. The next day, she refused to let me touch her.

Not long after, when I called around to see how she was, her landlord said she'd gone away, owing him rent. I couldn't find her anywhere.

It felt as if I'd been hit very hard in the stomach, punched again and again. I went around in a daze for months, thinking too much, drinking too much. My friends worried that I might do something stupid, but suicide was never an option. Foolishly optimistic, Jeannie used to call me. And slowly the pain wore off, the wounds began to heal.

There were rumours about Jeannie, that she was going out of her skull on smack. In April or May, someone met her in Dover on her way to the ferry, making for North Africa in the company of a notorious pothead, someone with a history of ill-treating his women. Although the news hurt like hell for a while - remembering my own promise to take her to a land of perpetual sunshine - it also destroyed the last of my hopes.

I decided to get on with my life. And yet, absurdly, it still felt like an act of betrayal when my flatmates persuaded me to attend an outdoor festival in July.

I half-hoped it would rain the whole weekend, knowing she would have been miserable and bitchy. But instead the sun shone from a cloudless sky, and I wished endlessly she was with me. As I wandered the festival site, the memories kept returning, filtered through a marijuana buzz, until every blonde girl in brightly-coloured clothes began to look like her.

Closely examining each pretty face that went by, I almost missed the figure going through its feline poses in the distance.

As my heart turned a loop, something else inside me said the clever thing would be to turn and walk away. Then she looked in my direction and gave one of her summer smiles. The dissenting voice was swamped by an adrenaline rush of feelings. Love and happiness and enormous relief, wanting to be close to her, to smell the scent off her biscuit-brown flesh.

SUNSHINE OF YOUR LOVE

The band finished its set just then and a crowd of people drifted away from the stage, coming between me and Jeannie. When I fought my way through the mob, almost swapping blows with one guy in a stars and stripes tank top, she'd disappeared from sight. I spent the next two days there looking for her and the week after that sitting in my flat, afraid to go out in case she tried to get in touch.

I had just about resigned myself to another abandonment - no longer rushing madly to the phone or the door - when word came that she was gone for good, killed in a traffic accident in Marrakesh.

Even through my shock and grief I was puzzled, especially when an acquaintance, newly returned from Morocco, told me that she'd been living there right up to the time of her death. My friends felt sorry for me, of course, but I could see they thought I was losing touch with reality, had been hallucinating, seeing things.

Yet I knew it had been Jeannie. How could I have failed to recognise her, the face and body that had been my life?

I saw her twice more that summer, in fact, both times on glorious days in the open air, listening to the music she loved. I wasn't afraid at all, only comforted to see her again for those fleeting moments, to know that she could still take pleasure in the sunshine.

In the autumn, posted abroad in a new job, I started on the long, hard road to maturity and happiness. Eventually I found a lady to share my existence, after many years of searching for someone who looked like Jeannie. My wife doesn't know any of this. I don't think she'd understand.

I've never been back to a rock festival, convinced the experience would be too depressing in too many ways. But this afternoon I stumbled across a live gig on the box. It was coming from Hyde Park, always one of our favourite places.

I was about to switch off the set, feeling like a different species to the hordes of youthful celebrants, when I glimpsed a familiar smiling face in the crowd.

I'm almost certain of it. The music was loud. Significant, too, that it's been a scorcher of an August day.

She always came to life in the summer, that girl.

BOUNTY

Almost at her destination when the rental car broke down on the lonely highway, she cursed and wished she was back home, facing a blazing fire instead of the coming trudge through the refrigerator cold of an autumn evening in Kansas.

Remembering that she'd seen just one other vehicle in the previous hour, she swore again. Her quarry - she still had to identify him or her for sure - was guilty simply for living in such a place.

She walked for what seemed like miles, freezing in spite of the thickly-padded coat, before she saw the sign displaying NO VACANCIES. The sky was turning purple, its one enormous eye growing brighter, as she approached the long, low building along a dirt road leading off the highway. Although there were several vehicles parked around, only the end cabin showed any lights.

This turned out to be a reception area. It was deserted, but she could hear the murmur of voices from beyond a glass door partially draped with a net curtain. She peered inside and saw half dozen people sitting close together in a small inner sanctum.

They were so engrossed in their conversation - all except for one bored-looking blonde young woman - that she had time to take in the details of the poky room: faded wallpaper clashing with rickety velour armchairs, black and white family portraits on every wall, an array of stuffed birds.

When the girl noticed her, they all turned to stare, as if seeing a ghost. She pushed open the door and said, "Excuse me, but I need some assistance."

"Hey, lady," one of the men said, "can't you read?"

An older man, grey-haired and self-important, hushed him into silence. "Pardon my friend's manners, ma'am," he said, "but it's true what he says. The motel is fully booked."

When she explained her problem, they discussed it among themselves without showing the least inclination to offer any practical help. She was struggling to contain herself, afraid of losing her cool, when another young woman entered the room.

"What is it?" the newcomer asked.

Obliging and business-like, the young woman had things organised in no time, despatching one of the group to check out the rental car and someone else to fetch coffee. It was done very discreetly, the orders channelled through the grey-haired man in the guise of polite requests. Then the woman turned and held out her hand. "By the way, I'm Melanie. I own this place."

"Hi, I'm Diana."

BOUNTY

They exchanged smiles. The others - all men now the blonde girl was on coffee duty - huddled together in a corner. On being handed the Styrofoam cup, she swallowed the scalding liquid without a pause, ignoring the blonde girl's look of astonishment. It would keep her warm for a few seconds at least. She noticed the grey-haired man, who had been introduced as Norm, draw Melanie to one side and whisper urgently to her.

The man sent to inspect the rental car returned and said that it must have blown a gasket; he couldn't do anything about it at night, without any parts.

"It looks as if you'll have to stop here," the motel owner said. Norm suddenly seemed angry, but Melanie turned to him and said in a soothing voice, "It's OK, she can stay with me in the house."

She was led to the back of the motel, where a two-storey building stood on a slight rise about thirty yards away. "My house," Melanie announced.

She stood basking in front of the log fire in the cosy living room while her hostess explained the situation. "Now you might think they're a pretty unfriendly bunch, but they have their reasons. And it's true what they said - they've booked the whole motel for the weekend."

"But there's only six of them," she said, "and you must have at least a dozen cabins."

The motel owner smiled. "They like their privacy."

"People have strange passions, don't they?" Melanie continued. "I know I did. Money, that was my passion." The woman's voice had taken on a wistful quality, but then she shook her head energetically. "No more, though, people are more important. Even that crew down there."

"And what's their particular form of strangeness?"

"They're the Kansas City Chapter of the Norman Bates Appreciation Society. All six of them. Well, five to be exact, the girl has only come along to play the victim. You know, Marion Crane."

Melanie went on, "You see, they like to spend time in places like this, small, old-fashioned motels, anywhere that looks similar to the one in the film. Made of wood with a pitched roof and a stoop running the length of the building, a big house nearby. There aren't many such places left, even in the backwoods. That's why they keep coming back here for their conventions." Stressing the incongruity of the last word, but with a gentle smile.

"To be truthful, they keep me going during the winter months." Seeing her bemusement, the woman chuckled dryly. "Would you believe they spend the whole weekend talking about the film or Hitchcock, you know, things they get off the internet or from newspapers?

"Oh, and they always re-enact the murder in the shower at least once. That's why they have to have a blonde woman. Curt seems to me like a nasty piece of work ..." - she had already made a note of the rude young man - "... but he brings along a different girl every time."

Still blissful at the hearth, she became conscious of Melanie's enquiring stare. "My, you certainly feel the cold, don't you? It looks as if you'd like to climb in among those flames. I'll bet you're from California or somewhere nice and warm."

When she nodded, nostalgia returned to Melanie's voice. "A long way from home."

"A long way," she echoed dolefully, recalling the interminable walk along the exposed highway. Then, to break the mood, she asked, "So you haven't always lived in Kansas?"

Melanie gave a pained smile. "Oh, I was a stranger here once myself. New York City, that was my home. I loved it. The energy, the people, even the noise."

As the wind picked up around the house, causing a loose tile to rattle on the roof, they seemed to be sharing the same mournful thought. She felt more homesick than ever for the roaring fires.

"I was a commodity dealer on Wall Street," Melanie continued. "Twenty-six years old and earning big bucks. The same old story, too much too soon. Drugs and sex and rock'n'roll. Especially the drugs. To tell the truth, I was a nasty bitch, greedy and ambitious. And then I had an accident ... but you don't want to hear this."

"No, please go on. If it helps," she said, smoothly.

Melanie seemed doubtful, but then spoke up. "I haven't talked about this to anyone in over two years."

Guessing all at once that the young woman had chosen to isolate herself in this dreadful place, in hiding from the world, she made her voice soft. "What happened?"

Melanie looked as if she was about to plunge into ice-cold water. "I killed the two people closest to me, you see. My mother and my fiance, who just happened to be in the car I was driving. I was high as a kite, of course." The pretty face had an agonised expression.

"I was in intensive care for several weeks. They told me afterwards I technically died on at least two occasions, but somehow they always managed to bring me back. They were brilliant, the medical staff in that place. But when I

BOUNTY

finally got out of hospital, I couldn't face anything about New York. I had to get as far away as possible, somewhere as different as possible. So I bought this motel with the money I had left. Call it a penance, if you like."

Melanie forced herself into the present with a visible effort, asking, "So what are you doing in these parts?"

Her search over, relaxed at last, she sat down. "I'm a bounty hunter," she said.

"Oh," Melanie said.

She laughed. "Mentioning my job is always something of a show-stopper. Must come from the same reflex that makes people look away when a policeman passes by in the street. The sense of original sin."

She could tell that her new acquaintance was curious, her mind taken off her own problems. "A bounty hunter," the motel owner exclaimed. "Are you after someone now? Is that where you were headed when your car broke down?"

She remained expressionless, revving up the other woman's interest. "It's someone here, isn't it? It's got to be Curt. He never talks about himself and all those girls, he has to be some sort of pimp. I'm certain he beats up on them, too. Is he on the run from the law?"

Melanie had another thought. "You're not telling me it's Norm? Those are his birds in the glass cases, by the way. He always seems to have a lot of cash. He says he's a banker, you know, there must be plenty of opportunities for a crook in his line of work. He lived near San Diego a few years back. Don't tell me you've tracked him down from California?"

"Well, we do lose people," she admitted, laughing. "They get away and lie low and it takes a while to catch up with them. It doesn't help that our records aren't all they should be. Don't worry, if Curt or Norm are doing wrong, we'll certainly get them in the end."

Melanie looked puzzled, but the phone rang before either of them could speak again. "Yes, Norm," the motel owner said into the speaker, "I'll be down in a minute."

When they crossed the strip of ground to the motel, the Midwest Chapter of the Norman Bates Appreciation Society was waiting for them outside the building. There was no sign of Curt or the blonde girl. Norm had a worried frown. "He went a little too far this time, Mel," he explained. "Broke her nose, I think, when she asked for money, you know, to do it ..."

He lapsed into an embarrassed silence and was shocked and relieved in equal parts when Melanie said, "It's OK, Norm, she knows. Where's Curt now?"

BOUNTY

"Driving her to hospital, or so he says. I thought you'd best know about it, just in case the police call by later on."

The bounty hunter fought to keep her temper in check, her mood darkening in the cold air, but still sent the men shuffling back when she snarled, "If Curt's threats and your money can't persuade her to stay silent, you mean?"

While Melanie was ringing the hospital, she followed the ranks of the Society into the inside room, where plates of sandwiches and glasses of milk were set out on a table. "I'm sorry about that," she said to the chastened Norm.

"That's OK," he muttered. "All our nerves are a little shot just now."

"I suppose it means you won't be staying on here?" she asked, casually.

"We've never gone home without doing the shower scene, it's our most sacred tradition." The man looked as if he was about to burst into tears, until one of the others leaned forward and whispered something. They argued backwards and forwards in an undertone, before Norm turned to her and said, "I don't suppose you'd do it?"

Speaking in a stage whisper, he pointed to the dark head bent over the phone in the next room. "We can't use Mel, you see, the wrong hair colour."

They led her to the cabin next to the office, the one always used for the re-enactment, and turned discreetly away while she changed into the swimming costume that Norm chose from several that he carried around in a suitcase. From the same case he brought out a grey wig, a large fake knife and a smock-like dress. He put on the dress and wig.

She went into the bathroom and switched on the shower, drawing the plastic curtain after her. The room was under-heated and perhaps that triggered her over-reaction when Norm suddenly pulled back the curtain and stood there in his ridiculous costume, brandishing the knife above his head.

Maybe she was just pissed at having to deal with an amateur playing at being a bad guy, pissed enough to teach him a lesson he'd never forget. Above all, she wanted to return home to the roaring fires and had to get rid of Norm and his friends before that could happen. It was one of the rules that no-one must see the quarry being bagged.

And so, turning to face him, she revealed her true nature for a fraction of a second.

That was more than long enough. He dropped the knife, terrified, and then she heard the whole bunch scrambling madly for the cabin door. The frenzied roar of car engines came to her from outside while she dried herself and got dressed. When she walked to the next cabin, Melanie was standing in the doorway with a puzzled look on her face. "What's with those guys? They looked like they'd seen a ghost."

"Where are your car keys?" she demanded.

The other woman's bewilderment increased. "What's going on?"

"You're coming with me on a journey, that's all."

Melanie was quick on the uptake, she had to give her that. "I'm the one you're after, you mean?"

"Yes, you are. Now let's go."

"But there must be some mistake. What have I done?"

"You survived, sweetie, you simply survived. It should never have happened."

Shivering, the bounty hunter pulled the heavy coat more tightly around her body. "If it hadn't been for those fucking quacks, I wouldn't be in this fucking place," she muttered to herself. "I'm going to make sure I don't get assigned to anywhere but the tropics in future."

"But who sent you after me?" Melanie whimpered, all resistance destroyed by a single glimpse of her face.

"Didn't I mention it? There's only the one bail bondsman where we're going, and he doesn't like anyone running out on him. You're guaranteed a warm reception, honey." She smiled with pleasurable anticipation at the thought of seeing the conflagration again, hearing the tortured screams.

"If it wasn't for all the paperwork waiting on me, I'd be the happiest succubus in Hell tonight ... let's go!"

The smell of scorched rubber. A scream of pleasure, dying away: "I CLAIM MY REWARD!"

The desolate howl of the wind.

ANGER

Big Dave raised himself from the chair and broke wind loudly, wishing that Blackthorne was in the room. With any luck, though, the smell would linger until the other man came off his security round.

The trouble was he just didn't get on with Blackthorne. The bloke was a total liability on the night shift, no way he'd enjoy a laugh and a bit of fun like Georgie and the rest of the lads. And now staff shortages and the summer schedules were throwing them together too often for Dave's liking. He suspected the Chief's warped sense of humour was also playing its part.

Blackthorne was much younger than Dave and the others, and looked like shit with his shaven head and pinched features. He was a weird one alright, hardly ever spoke and spent his break periods reading books and magazines about black magic and the occult.

In spite of appearances, Blackthorne was a good worker. He was back in the control room now, entering details into the log with silent concentration. That was half the problem. The man did everything quietly and efficiently, with the minimum of fuss.

Dave was the opposite. Loud and brash and impetuous, whistling continuously on his rounds, clumping across the marble foyer of the large office block they guarded. He slammed doors to shut them. He liked to talk, he liked to moan.

For all his bluster, he wasn't totally insensitive. He knew the cage-rattling was mutual. He could see the younger man wince sometimes when he was being particularly noisy. To be honest, it was about the only pleasure he got from working with the guy.

It annoyed Dave that people seemed to regard him as nothing more than a big-bellied loudmouth. He could be hurt as easily as the next man.

Take this business with Carole, for example. OK, so he wasn't the best husband and father in the world, but was that any reason for her to walk out on him? Not as if he hit her or anything, although he'd been pretty close that last time. She was really beginning to piss him off.

He could feel himself trembling at the thought of his wife's treachery. He'd slip out in a minute for a swig from his hip flask; drinking on duty was a red card offence, but he needed something to calm him down.

At that moment, one of the surveillance screens caught his eye. The picture was coming from the camera trained on their non-executive car park, a couple of hundred yards from the main building. The pedestrian approach to the car park was via a chain-link bridge that crossed one of the many canal basins in the old docks, rapidly being transformed into a waterfront business park.

They'd been having problems with a gang of kids from the nearby council flats - petty vandalism and the odd theft from parked cars. However, this was a solitary figure, standing very still. A fog had swept in from the bay - a rare occurrence for the time of year - and made the monochrome image even less reliable than usual.

The picture was blurred and distorted at the best of times, but now the street lights filtering through the mist gave it an almost nightmarish quality. The impression of watching a silent horror film was reinforced by the figure on the bridge. Why would anyone be there, alone, at two o'clock in the morning?

Blackthorne glanced across at the same screen, but then carried on with his paperwork. Puzzled, Dave was about to pass a comment when the mist suddenly thickened, shrouding the motionless silhouette. Visibility improved within seconds to reveal a deserted bridge. Dave relaxed, probably just some insomniac from the flats, gone home before the weather got any worse. Even though his anger against Carole had abated, he went into the lavatory for a drink anyway.

Weeks passed before he saw the figure again.

His wife and kids had meantime returned home and then done another runner. And hadn't he swallowed a bucketload of pride to ask her back in the first place!

Carole had been demanding, while her cow of a mother had gloated herself stupid, even though she was glad to be rid of the kids so she could go back to watching her soaps undisturbed. He'd forced himself to put up with all their crap, though. Anything was preferable to living on his own. Getting home from work or the pub and staring at the walls.

Although things had been OK at first - Carole allowing him to touch her for the first time in months - they were soon back to their old ways, quarrelling over money, his drinking, the kids. They'd both put up with the situation for a while, on the basis that even a bad marriage was better than nothing. But their conversations grew shorter and more bad-tempered, until even Dave felt there was little else to say.

Carole had been the first to crack - and off she went to test her mother's patience once again. It was his only consolation at the time, the thought of the old cow's face when she saw them back on her doorstep.

Dave's goodwill had extended even to Blackthorne for a time, during the short-lived reconciliation with his wife. He'd been moved to chaff his co-worker good-naturedly once or twice, although he wasn't always sure the younger man saw the joke. In spite of hating God-botherers, even the rumour that Blackthorne belonged to some strange religious cult had aroused only his amused contempt.

However, all his charity vanished when Carole walked out the second time. Suddenly the digs were intended to cut and wound, every ounce of his bitterness and malice turned against his workmate. Blackthorne endured the taunts in sullen silence.

Now it was half past three in the morning, and Dave yawned as he sat tired and depressed in front of the bank of screens. With any of their colleagues there would have been a sensible arrangement, allowing one man to sleep while the other stood guard. But he felt unable to lower his dignity by suggesting this to Blackthorne. Instead he'd added it to the many grievances festering in his mind.

Another visit to the lavatory soon for a quick slurp from his hip flask; there was no other way he could get through the night.

He'd have to be careful, though, he was starting to have minor accidents at work, dropping keys, mislaying paperwork, that sort of thing. Sometimes he slurred his words. He'd caught Blackthorne looking hard at him more than once. If word got back to the Chief, that bastard would descend on him like a ton of shit. No job on top of everything else; resentment mouldered in his gut like an undigested meal.

A flush crossed his face when he thought about that afternoon, sitting in the car outside the old cow's house, debating whether to drag Carole into the street by her hair. He'd thought better of it in the end, knowing he would never stop once he started on her. I'm not ready for murder, he thought.

Not yet anyhow.

In that same instant, he saw the stationary figure standing next to the car spaces reserved for senior management, much nearer to the main building now. It was still no more than a dark outline.

Cursing the poor quality of their cameras, he wondered how he knew it was the same person. He just knew it was. He shouted to Blackthorne, but the other man only gave him a curious stare. Without stopping to explain and sufficiently drunk to be brave, Dave lumbered towards the main door and clattered down the broad sweep of steps at the front entrance. There was no-one in sight.

Blackthorne joined him outside, typically efficient with his torch and mobile phone at the ready, and they made a sweep of the perimeter of the building. Dave knew they were wasting their time.

ANGER

He often thought it was only his hate that kept him going, loathing of Carole and his mother-in-law and Blackthorne. Sometimes he wondered about his colleague being on that list, but never for long. Everything about the man infuriated him, from his bug-eyed concentration at the computer keyboard to the books and magazines he constantly read.

The word was going around that Blackthorne and his cronies - apparently all the weirdos met up in the same pub in town - were not so much Christian as on the opposite side of the fence. And indeed the man had started to wear a signet ring inscribed with the motif "666". Georgie said the number was connected with devil worship. It was just another irritant to Dave.

And yet, strangely, he now preferred being on shift with Blackthorne to any of the others. Their continual idle chatter got on his nerves. His heart wasn't in the horseplay any more, the feeble-minded practical jokes, farting contests, lewd banter about being a free agent.

Better the company of Blackthorne, watching his creepy workmate out of the corner of his eye, laboriously putting together a theory during their non-convivial silences. Although he couldn't resist the odd rude comment when he saw Blackthorne reading one of his magazines, he kept his thoughts to himself for the most part. Learning to play the other man at his own game.

His spare time was spent parked outside the old cow's house, waiting for something to happen. A signal to act.

It was the same at work, almost as if Blackthorne had become a surrogate for his wife. One night, the younger man spilled some hot coffee over himself and said, "Jesus Christ." Then he frowned guiltily. Dave had never heard him him swear before; and wondered if his new tactics were beginning to work.

It was when Carole first mentioned divorce that he seriously began to think about killing her. He had the urge to grab her by the throat, but they were meeting in a pub and her two large brothers were standing watchfully by the bar. He went into work afterwards, because the only alternative was to drink himself into unconsciousness. The last thing he needed was a heavy-duty hangover to add to all his other problems.

He was still at boiling point when he crossed the foyer at the start of his early morning round, a wind from the sea hurling torrents of rain against the glass roof of the atrium high above his head. He'd hardly seen Blackthorne all evening, probably wisely keeping out of his way.

He was about to enter the lift when some instinct alerted him to a shadow outside the main door. Thoughts of Carole were driven out of his head and he turned quickly to see the same figure - he was sure of it - slouching away into the darkness through a deluge of rainwater and sea-spray. He had the impression of something misshapen and barely human. But that only served to strengthen his theory. Draining the last of his whisky, he decided to confront Blackthorne.

Blackthorne was watching television in their restroom, his weasel features expressionless. Dave noticed a ring attached to the other man's right nipple, clearly visible under the regulation blue shirt.

His growing disgust was betrayed only by the slightest of tics in his temple, however, and he marvelled at his self-control. In the past, he would have started off by shouting and blustering. Now, casually, he said, "Your friend must be getting wet out there." Blackthorne stared at him dead-eyed, but said nothing.

Dave stayed calm. "I've got you sussed, my old son, so why don't you just come clean." Still no reply. Dave knew he was losing the battle when his voice started to rise. "Go on, admit it." Then he lost it completely. "Go on, before I beat the shit out of you."

Blackthorne finally spoke. "Admit what?" He was some actor; it sounded like genuine puzzlement in his voice.

Dave took a step forward, his tic now pulsing wildly, and the smaller man raised his hands in self-defence. They pawed ineffectually at each other for a few seconds, until Dave felt his breath and aggression draining away.

He motioned for the fight to stop. "Let's call it quits, shall we?" he wheedled. "You admit you've been playing a trick on me and I won't say no more about it. How does that sound, Chris, eh?"

Blackthorne was obviously unimpressed by the use of his first name. "And what exactly was this trick, Dave?" Making the last word sound like a term of abuse.

Dave continued to be placatory. "You know, getting your mate to hang around outside to put the frighteners on me. And you pretending not to see him."

He forced a laugh. "And just now, you know, when he wore that gorilla costume or whatever it was. It's lucky I was in on the joke by then or else it would have given me a nasty turn."

Blackthorne's face had a knowing look. "My *mate*, as you call him, is a very special person. Can you guess who he is?" He tapped one finger against his nose.

Starting to feel uncomfortable, Dave shook his head. The other man persisted. "Go on have a guess!" Clearly enjoying himself, and at the same time, paying off old scores. In spite of everything, Dave couldn't help thinking it was probably the longest conversation they'd ever had.

ANGER

"He's the Devil," Blackthorne said, in a matter-of-fact way.

Dave didn't understand at first, then gave a frightened little moan and turned quickly, as if expecting to see a threatening figure in the doorway. The younger man sat down and resumed watching television. When he glanced back over his shoulder, his look seemed to say: you really are pitiful, too much booze has rotted your brain, that's the trouble. What he actually said was, "No wonder your old woman left you."

The change in Dave was immediate. Not even fucking Satan could get away with saying that to him! "I was a good husband," he said, standing over Blackthorne. "I WAS A GOOD HUSBAND!" Screaming now, he was pleased to see the other man grow uneasy.

"OK, man, no need to lose your cool."

Blackthorne was suddenly terrified and Dave knew the reason almost at once. The figure was in the room with them.

It's funny, he thought, I know it's here, but I can't see anything. Blackthorne, on the other hand, could clearly make out a presence that was frightening him to death. He was emitting curious bleating noises now, pleading for his life, as Dave reached forward to put him out of his misery. The big man felt strangely at peace with himself.

Then everything went black.

Emerging into what felt like the worst hangover of his life, he groaned out loud at the sight of Blackthorne slumped in a corner of the room. A crimson mark on the man's neck indicated how he had died. Dave staggered to his feet and looked around fearfully. But he was alone with the body.

When he heard the howl of sirens, approaching fast, he guessed that someone must have pressed the alarm button during their ferocious struggle. The horror of it suddenly flashed back to him. The bulging eyes, the noise of the man's death rattle. As he stared in wonderment at his large but flabby hands, he recalled too his dreadful insight in those final seconds, shocking enough to cause him to pass out.

He looked mournfully at the body of his dead workmate. The creature wasn't one of Blackthorne's mates, he'd realised too late. He hadn't seen a figure in a gorilla suit, and certainly not the Devil.

There'd been nothing out there at all, in fact.

Except his anger.

FOOTBALL

The signs were bad from the kick-off. Henry was in a foul mood, Vicky having just dumped him, telling him over the phone that she wouldn't take his crap any longer. Wise girl, she'd gone into hiding shortly afterwards. His brother didn't take kindly to rejection.

He'd been forced to go along with them by his long-suffering mother, afraid that Henry might do something even more desperate than usual. "You're the only one he listens to, Danny," she'd pleaded. "He'll be more careful if you're around." Poor old mum, wrong as always. With Henry, it was actually everyone else who had to be careful. Very careful.

As they sank the first of many pints, Danny miserably pondered the afternoon and evening that stretched ahead. He didn't even like football, would have preferred to be studying quietly in his room. Not that he was going to share that particular thought with any of his companions.

They were toasting each other just then, the usual bellowed chant, making their presence known to everyone else in the pub. "ONE FOR ALL AND ALL FOR ONE!" Tattooed fingers clutching beer glasses like the weapons they all too often became before the night's end. The other fans in the place - including some who were more than old enough to know better - were cheering them on.

A voice shouted to him over the din, "Having a good time, my son?"

Danny smiled grimly back at the flushed and bespectacled face. Shake was the only football hooligan he knew who wore glasses. He was also weedy and caught a lot of colds. The others, who would have walked into a hundred metal doors, a thousand, rather than admit to being less than physically perfect, treated him with merciless derision. But most of them enjoyed having him around.

There was a Shake attached to every gang, Danny had noticed, the village idiot guaranteed to make his associates look and feel good. On the occasions he tagged along with his brother's crew, almost always under pressure from mum, Shake immediately turned into his best buddy and technical adviser. He liked to scoff at Danny for his lack of insider knowledge, jeering at his failure to grasp the nuances of thuggish etiquette.

"Cor, didn't you even know *that*!"

Sometimes brother Henry grew irritated, looked as if he wanted to smash Shake's head against the nearest brick wall, but Danny always managed to steer his hapless companion out of earshot before the explosion came.

Now, after several more rounds of drinks, the noise and aggression levels ratcheting ever upwards, the mob had spilled out onto the street.

FOOTBALL

Henry bellowed everyone into silence, re-asserting himself as their leader. Subdued, they began to stalk like some dangerous and multi-headed organism through the lunchtime crowds. Danny prayed that no isolated visiting fan would wander into their path. The luckless idiot would have bad memories - if he had any memory at all - for the rest of his unhappy life. He thought about slipping away, telling mum that they'd already left when he got to the pub, but could feel Shake's myopic gaze fastened on him.

A thin arm nudged him in the ribs. "This is what Henry calls Search and Destroy," Shake explained, unnecessarily. "Just like we're in the SAS, geddit?" There was a dribble of something horrible from one side of his mouth.

"Shut up, you!" Henry ordered. He gazed with contempt at Shake. "Tell me if he's bothering you, Dan," he said, turning to his brother. "You OK?"

Say it, Danny urged himself. No, I'm not OK, I'm scared shitless actually and want to go home. It's not as if I'm part of your gang and I don't even like football. It has long been accepted by the whole family, aunts and uncles and cousins twice removed, that I have the brains and you are the headcase street fighter. You get on with what you do best, broth, and I'll go back to my books.

Instead, imagining how his brother would react to a show of family disloyalty at that moment, remembering his stupid promise to mum, he muttered, "I'm fine."

"Good," Henry said. "Let's go!" They set off again, ominously quiet, every face but his straining to be about their business.

To Danny's relief, the police were out in force in the city centre, the visiting supporters encircled and almost outnumbered by blue uniforms as they made their yelling, handclapping way to the ground. The opportunities for mayhem proved to be strictly limited, the odd skirmish or two, but nowhere near the total warfare required to satisfy Henry and his followers. As a result, Danny could tell, his brother was still riding on a high, black cloud when they settled in for the night in their favourite boozer.

He's going to crash-land on someone before long, he thought apprehensively. The whole crew was angry and frustrated; and there were several short-lived but bloody scuffles - screams and sounds of shattering glass - as the pub's squad of bouncers struggled to maintain an uneasy peace.

Bolder now, with what seemed like gallons of beer sloshing inside him, he stayed close to his brother. At one point, he pushed Henry away from a confrontation. "Cor, did you see that?" Shake's voice was almost falsetto with shock and everyone else suddenly froze.

FOOTBALL

For one bowel-melting second, he thought Henry was going to hit him, but then his brother gave a chip-toothed grin. "Nice one, Dan," he said. "I'll be sure to tell mum you're watching out for me."

While the others roared with laughter, Henry punched him playfully in the stomach. Almost doubled over with pain and trying not to puke, Danny went along with the joke. Things quietened down after that, as if everyone was taking their cue from their leader's sudden good humour. They even began to laugh about the day's missed opportunities; and cheerfully boasted of what they would do to the next bunch of wankers they came across. Danny, through an alcoholic fog, vowed to be miles away when that happened.

Shake was looking especially pleased with himself. Danny had seen him get in several sly punches during the fighting and now the skinny one was talking him though the complexities of gang life with added assurance.

"No, stupid, you have to drink it in one go, like this."

Danny was grateful the general hubbub kept Shake's words from reaching Henry.

When Henry started on the whiskies and grew maudlin, he told himself his job was almost done. This was an occasional ritual on match days, his brother bemoaning the loss of his latest girlfriend. Forgetting his earlier threats to decapitate the bitch. Informing the whole pub about how much he loved his Mand or Shannon or Vicky.

Almost before Shake opened his mouth, Danny felt sure that something terrible was about to happen. He had the urge to move away, very quickly. "Never mind, Henry," Shake giggled, "plenty more slags where she came from."

Silence, but for the sound of a beer tap dripping into a sink. If his brother uttered one word against Shake at that moment, he knew, the poor fool would end up as another sort of puddle, splattered over the dirty wooden floor. But Henry smiled and said, "Nice one, Shake."

There was some disappointed-sounding laughter, several of the gang obviously hoping for a last ruck to end the day. Shake, his glasses waggling violently, cackled louder than anyone, perhaps appreciating his lucky escape. Danny somehow didn't think so.

When the pub closed, Henry and several of the others said they were going off to get chips. Danny, feeling ill with drink, made his excuses. Mum would be waiting up anxiously for his news. As he glanced back to the little group staggering off, he saw that Henry had one powerful arm around Shake's skinny shoulders. It looked almost like a brotherly gesture.

FOOTBALL

Shake was never seen again. Except by him.

Not long after the first sighting, having guessed the truth, already persuaded he was going mad, Danny brought up the subject of the murder in a loud voice in the pub. Alarmed, his brother pulled him to one side and warned him to keep his trap shut. Danny could see him glaring around at the others, trying to work out which of them had leaked the secret.

"Did him over good and proper," someone confided to him later, too drunk to care about the leader's wrath. "Henry was shouting, 'Kick his head in. Kick his head in.'" Looking into Danny's eyes with an uneasy smirk. "He couldn't stop laughing."

Danny learned that they'd buried Shake in a field somewhere. Since the murdered youth had no family or friends outside the crew, no-one at all to miss him, there'd been nothing about it in the papers or on TV. That would explain, perhaps, why he was continuing to pester Danny. His only pal in life and death.

They, the crew, had done the wicked deed, but he was suffering the consequences. It couldn't have been less fair. He wasn't a hooligan. He didn't even like football.

He stopped studying at home - there didn't seem much point. Instead he began to hang around with Henry and his gang, for the company and in the hope that, one day, someone else would display the same symptoms, apprehension and sweaty agitation, and prove it wasn't just him. Going round the bend.

The apparition or spectre or whatever its proper title - anyway, Shake - wasn't with him all the time, but that almost made things worse. The awful anticipation of waiting for it to appear, in college or on the street, suddenly leering at him from the worktop in their small kitchen. One time, when he was riding on a bus, the thing kept pace with them for more than a mile, bounding past unsuspecting pedestrians as he prayed for it to go away.

He finally had to accept that Shake was his own private horror on a routine evening in the pub. Big brother, sure at last that they'd got away with murder, was reminiscing good-naturedly about the failings of his dead follower. "What a wanker!"

The thing was less than six inches from Henry's left elbow at the time. To Danny's consternation, it appeared to be smiling, joining in with the fun. He himself felt closer to tears.

He tried reasoning with the thing. *Henry is the one you should be haunting, he's to blame for all your problems.* When it continued to watch him, sneering in the old familiar way, he grew angry. *Look, Shake, I never really liked you. In fact, I hated your guts. BUGGER OFF!* It didn't work. Shake continued to pop up without warning, as irritating in death as he'd always been in life.

Danny was tempted, in his more drunken moments, to lash out and kick at the thing, thinking the typical hooligan response would perhaps break the spell. Never able to summon up the courage, he usually opted to dash off with his oppressor in close pursuit.

Sometimes he would shut his eyes, pretend to sleep, until it faded from sight. Henry and the others were amused but not surprised by his antics. Just another nutter in the crew. Mum was already convinced that he'd gone the way of his brother.

Danny considered taking the running away option to extremes. I'll borrow money off mum and catch a plane to the other side of the world, he thought. Then he wondered how he would feel, waking up in a hotel room in Sydney or Auckland to see Shake grinning at him from the top of the TV or springing around his bed. Better not to know for certain - that escape was impossible.

There were the occasional periods of delirious relief, days and even whole weeks, when the phantom failed to appear; and he would wander around in a fever of hope then, almost daring it to show itself.

Once or twice he even started to believe that Shake - or at least the only part of him that counted now - had finally vanished into the ether. Pictures in his mind of the thing making its way back to the secret burial ground and re-attaching itself for good to the remainder of the corpse.

Shake, however, retained the ability to turn up where he wasn't wanted. And Danny would curse his luck again, saying to himself, but I don't even like football, as the thing rushed towards him.

Bounce. Bounce. Bounce.

Always looking as if it was about to put him right on some point of hooligan protocol. Just the head, complete with glasses and know-all smirk.

FUTURE GHOSTS

Somehow, for some reason, he had been persecuted almost all his life by visions of imminent death. A string of encounters with things that were about to go bump in the night. They were his fate, those premonitions.

Future ghosts, he called them.

He was seven years old the first time he could remember, on a shopping trip with his mum. They passed an old lady, a family friend, in the street, but mum ignored her. He wondered if it was because the lady had something wrong with her face. But when he tugged at mum's arm to explain about her friend, she said it was only his imagination.

That evening, however, he overheard her tell dad that someone had died after falling down some stairs.

He was always daydreaming in class, doodling his way through lessons. Although art was his favourite subject, his drawings often showed smudged figures in bizarre colours. They were indecipherable even to him. His teacher said he showed talent, but needed to discipline his fantasies. Most of his classmates simply believed he was strange. He began to think the same.

As soon as he could, he left school and then home, desperate to get away from that place, the small town where scary things kept happening to him. The sight of a friend in the distance, shrouded in a kind of fog, shortly before the boy drowned in the local canal. A glimpse of hazy apparitions at the roadside, just prior to a fatal traffic accident.

He never told mum and dad about his experiences, knowing they wouldn't understand and frightened they would consider him a freak. He hoped that life would be different in the big city. Instead, on his first night in his new home, the faceless shape of a girl walked towards him out of the wall of the tiny bedroom. He left in a terrified rush, convinced he was suffering from a hideous curse, and only wondered afterwards who took the room and what had happened to her.

One city followed another as he endeavoured to shake off his affliction. But there were visitations everywhere. He lost touch with mum and dad, too ashamed to return home.

On one occasion, walking past a high-rise hotel, he saw an indistinct figure tumbling from the sky and ducked, only to straighten up with a foolish sideways glance when he realised it was just another haunting. More figures were plunging from the hotel windows as he rushed off.

For once, he dragged his thoughts away from his own misery and telephoned the hotel people and the fire service to warn them of what was going to happen. When they just about laughed in his face, he went to the local police station and stuttered and stumbled through a cock-and-bull story about a dream he'd had. The duty sergeant began to eye him thoughtfully. Fearful of being detained as a potential arsonist, he escaped into the night.

No-one believed him. Thinking about it, he could understand why.

The building burned down not long afterwards, and several people threw themselves from top-floor windows to escape the blaze. In spite of his efforts to avert the tragedy, he couldn't help feeling he was to blame. Unnerved, suicidal in the next few days, he finally accepted that he had to speak to someone about what was happening to him. He needed professional help.

Afraid of being confined in an institution if he approached the authorities, he went to a private psychiatrist. The man concluded that he was suffering from an hallucinatory condition, a string of long words he didn't understand. He was practically accused of being on drugs. Obviously not believing his denials, the psychiatrist said he had no choice but to soldier on.

The message seemed plain. They were his destiny, future ghosts. There was no escape, no-one to help him.

After that, he drank too much, blurring the distinction between reality and illusion still further. At least the booze softened the repeated blows of seeing the about-to-be-dead. But it also made him feel even worse about himself, prompted him into taking out his fear and anger on other people. He began to get into fights in bars; and would have ended up locked away for sure, in prison or something worse, if it hadn't been for a vision of a very different kind.

Katie was her name.

They met in a pub - she had some friends with her and he was on his own, as usual - and got to talking as they stood together at the bar. When her friends went on somewhere else, she stayed behind. She told him she was a student and had a boyfriend; he told her he was a wanderer, pretending it was a matter of choice. But he could tell she felt sorry for him. She joked that she could never resist strays.

They arranged to meet again in the same pub. Katie told him that she wanted them to be friends and nothing else - she loved her boyfriend who was working away. But it still felt like a date to him when they met up the following week. As they continued to see each other, he couldn't help thinking of her as his girlfriend. His first girlfriend. Even more astonishing, she was caring and sensitive and beautiful.

Katie seemed to sense from the first that something was wrong with him. One time, as they walked past a future ghost and he shivered, she asked him what was the matter. He had to bite his lip to prevent himself from blurting out the truth.

FUTURE GHOSTS

Her gentle proddings slowly broke down his reserve and habitual mistrust, however. Over several weeks, in spurts, he unravelled his story. When he'd told her everything, she just stared at him. Even though he had left out all the worst details of his hauntings, the horrendous images, he expected her to flinch away and leave him to his grisly fate at that point. Instead she became instantly practical, said that he had to escape from the city. She seemed determined to save him.

She took him to her parents' farm in the country and talked her father into letting him help around the place. He stayed on when Katie returned to college, but she promised to telephone and visit at the weekends. Hating their separation, missing her every second of every day, he knew there was no choice. It could be his last chance.

Although it was a temporary arrangement at first, he tried hard to be a good worker and got on well with the rest of her family. The days grew into months, until a year went by.

His mind was apparently on the mend in the quiet of the country, the threat of the curse gradually receding. He even began to drop in at the village pub, although never for more than a couple of pints. Always hurrying back to his little cottage before dark, afraid that something might go wrong, ill at ease except in his own company.

He only came alive at the weekends, when Katie accompanied him on long walks through the countryside. It was as if an electric shock ran through him every time she linked her arm with his. On the occasions she couldn't make it, her boyfriend Darren back in town, he felt almost physically ill.

He had never met Darren - it was as if Katie wanted to keep the various parts of her life separate - but he already hated the man. For the first time, he actively dreamed about someone becoming a future ghost.

There were two bad experiences at the farm.

The first occurred when he was feeding the pigs one day. He looked up to see a figure coming along the lane that ran past their farmyard. The man was shaded into a silhouette by the sun, but he could tell from the slouching walk that it was one of the labourers from the place next door. His shouted greeting was ignored, however, and he flinched as the smeared face strode out of the brightness and silently by.

Dreading the wait for news of the man's death, in the next few hours or days, he rushed back to the cottage and started to pack frantically. Katie's dad, worried about him, telephoned his daughter and then stopped him from leaving, until she arrived at the farm after a headlong drive from the city.

FUTURE GHOSTS

They went for many walks in the week that followed - the man was dead by then, an accident with his tractor - and she eventually persuaded him that running away was the wrong option. Where would he go? After calming down, he accepted everything she said.

She was his only point of reference, after all, the one mitigating factor in his strange and lonely existence. He felt as if he couldn't go on without her any longer, almost blurting out his true feelings before she left for the city.

Still, the tears in her eyes as she said goodbye seemed to promise hope for the future. Wasn't pity close to love, after all?

Then the second bad thing happened.

It came when Katie telephoned to say that she had to go away; Darren had asked her to marry him and she would be moving to a distant part of the country. They both began to cry over the phone. Katie said she'd come to see him soon and swore that she would never lose touch. He knew she didn't really understand the situation. It was their fate to be together.

And so he was on his way to the city in a stolen car, the keys taken from her dad's pocket while the family watched television. He couldn't wait for her to come to him. He had to make her see sense. It was his turn to be persuasive. He wasn't much of a driver, had never passed his test, and the car was a heavy monster, a farmer's vehicle, not easy to control. It was fast getting dark and starting to rain. He struggled just to switch on the headlights.

But he had to see her, to convince her she had no choice. They were destined for each other. It had become deadly urgent all of a sudden, because something else had happened. Another bad experience. The worst. He glanced sideways at the glint of the kitchen knife on the seat beside him. He had brought it along to deal with Darren if the man attempted to stop Katie from going with him. He sighed heavily. Now he required it for another purpose.

I'm scared, Katie, he thought. I need you with me. Come what may.

Because he had just glanced into the rear-view mirror and thought at first it was the dazzle from other vehicles affecting his eyes. The awful truth then as he stared into blankness, a face without any features.

There was no time to lose, he wouldn't be a future ghost for long.

The rain was worsening and there were flashing blue lights behind him. But he had to get to Katie. He stepped hard on the accelerator ...

MAMA

Mama never liked any of the girls he brought home.

She ranted and yelled until he felt embarrassed for the poor creatures and was forced to remove them from her presence. They didn't enjoy being removed, kicking and squealing for the most part, but it was what mama wanted.

It was new to him, going around with girls.

Always just him and mama before then, snug together in their little house. They hadn't needed anyone else. But, he had to admit, the old lady wasn't such good company any more.

The idea came to him suddenly, invite someone else to share in their life. He was nervous at first, worried about mama's reaction; after all, there'd been only the two of them for more years than he cared to remember. Yet he had to think of his future. So he'd gone ahead, to test the water.

But she never liked any of the girls.

All things considered, it was a shame. He went to so much trouble each time, and talking to strange women didn't come easily to him. Luckily, there were places where they congregated at night, certain bars in certain districts of the city. Rough places for the most part, which was why he always carried around his protector.

The girls were often noisy and brash, a boldness in their eyes that could still shock him, but he was growing used to their ways. He was even beginning to enjoy himself. The selection process was almost the best part, moving around the bar in his quiet manner, catching someone's eye and then engaging her in conversation. Studying her face and body. Listening to her voice as she made all sorts of promises, named her price.

If there was something about the girl he particularly didn't like, the tilt of her nose, perhaps, or the size of her earlobes, he would move on. He had his standards.

He rarely talked to the loud and strident ones, bulging out of their clothes, makeup plastered over their insolent faces. Mama would never stand for anyone like that. He himself preferred modest young women, the shy beginners, had become expert at spotting them in a crowd. It often seemed that they were glad to see him, too, as if recognising a kindred spirit in the mass of screaming, jostling strangers.

Then he would adjudicate, as they sipped his drinks, responded to his stumbling attempts at small talk. When he finally made his choice - the good points outweighing the bad, he had to struggle sometimes to overcome his fastidiousness - he would at once feel very strong, the most powerful man in the room, the whole city.

He always tried to hurry the girl away as soon as possible after that, out into the dark. Taking her home to meet mama.

They were usually only to glad to go with him after seeing his bankroll, the nice-looking car parked a safe distance away. Sometimes they created difficulties, said they wanted to get it over with in their own nearby apartment, or even in the car. One or two of them seemed anxious about how masterful he had become.

His protector soon put an end to every argument. It was another good feeling, to see a girl come to her senses in the same room as mama.

And now he was on the prowl again, another self-effacing stalk on the wild side. Months since he'd last taken a friend back to the house. A sweet little thing, he'd forgotten her name. Not good enough for mama, of course, so she'd had to go with all the others.

He went into a dive where he'd struck gold in the past, struggling to make his way through the melee. The place was like a magnet to females of every kind, but had a bad reputation, the scene of almost nightly brawls between drunken customers. Only the previous week one of its regulars had been shot dead in his apartment not long after leaving the bar.

Because at least three other middle-aged men had been murdered in similar circumstances in less than a month, the local newspapers and TV stations were talking up a plague of serial killers at work in the city's red light district.

There were some terrible people in the world, he said to himself, looking at the coarse and ugly male faces all around him. He felt glad his protector was in its customary place in an inside coat pocket.

He marked out his target within minutes. She was standing on her own in a corner of the room, sufferance approaching disgust on her youthful face. Since it matched his own feelings, he was instantly drawn to her. "May I buy you a drink?" he offered. She looked him over and broke into a warm smile.

"Thank you," she said in a demure voice. He liked her right away.

She told him her name was Monique and that she had only recently taken up her line of work. He was surprised to find himself talking easily, his awkwardness forgotten for once. It was the girl who took the lead, raising a pencilled eyebrow when he offered to buy another round of drinks.

"Ah, yes," he said, confused, and then: "Can we go somewhere?" It wasn't his usual routine, the initiative taken away from him, the moment of transformation weakened. This one, however, seemed worth the sacrifice.

"You go on ahead," the girl prompted, "and I'll join you outside."

MAMA

Her sense of discretion pleased him; it was something else they shared. She got into the car without any fuss, no need for his protector, and his excitement steadily built as they approached the house.

He ushered the young woman into the sitting room. Most of his visitors were nervy by this time, on edge, as if finally sensing the change that had come over him. Monique looked around coolly and said, "Nice place."

She was the the best girlfriend he'd ever had, he thought with admiration. A pity she was going to be removed. He looked at mama then and knew at once that something was horribly wrong. The old lady silent, her shrieks of disapproval not ringing in his head.

He staggered with the shock, grabbing at an armchair to steady himself. As he looked down in wonderment at his large and suddenly useless hands, he had no idea what to do next. But one thing was certain.

Mama liked this one.

Monique was meantime examining the many photographs hanging on the walls. "It's always just the two people. A man and a woman. She's older than him. Oh, isn't that you? She must be your mother then."

He nodded, too confused to speak.

"You're obviously very fond of each other," she said. "All these pictures."

Slumping into the chair, he gestured towards a small casket on the mantelpiece and found his voice at last, a rasping sound from deep inside him. "That's mama over there." They were usually the last words his guests ever heard, but now he offered them only in explanation.

"You must miss her," the girl said.

He struggled to think who she meant, so many dead people in this small house. Then he remembered - his mama. It felt funny talking about her as if she was gone. "I loved her a lot, but sometimes she could be strict." Realising it sounded like a criticism, he hurried to redeem himself. "Not that it did me any harm, you understand."

The girl's smile reminded him of the old lady, the way she looked before chastising him for some piece of misbehaviour or other, the wire coat hanger on his arms and legs. "I always had it coming," he said, certain the girl would understand.

He'd known all along that this one was different. Not like the others, silly little things who deserved to die, but a real lady. The same as mama. He had the urge to explain things, about the troubled times he'd been through, in the hope she would want to comfort him. He wondered how it would feel to embrace living, breathing flesh again. Faint memories of the soft voice after the beatings, the soothing lips on his salty face.

He was conscious of Monique scrutinising him sternly, resembling mama more than ever. They had so much in common, the three of them. It would be the happy family of his dreams.

He regarded her fondly when she spoke. "It's a funny thing. You loved your *mama* ..." - he stiffened at the mess she made of the last word - "... and I hated my father. The reason I picked you out, because you're the image of him."

The young woman laughed spitefully in his face. "Yes, it was all planned. Same as the others."

Unable to make sense of her words and yet knowing she was somehow annoyed with him, he started to rise from the chair. Perhaps if he threw himself on his knees, she would forgive him.

"Sit down," Monique commanded. He sat back down.

She went on. "He was a terrible brute, you see, truly evil. He broke my mother's heart and tried to break me in every way possible. I still carry the scars.

"I dreamed of killing him from the time I was a small girl. Got up the courage to do it, too, even bought myself a gun. But then he robbed me, the old bastard, by dying of his own accord. Peacefully in a hospital bed, would you believe."

She seemed to be lecturing him now, the voice rising in a familiar way. "It was like he'd escaped scot-free, never been brought to justice. I couldn't believe my luck, even thought about killing myself for a time. One way of escaping my misery. But then I thought of a much more attractive alternative."

He recognised the look in her eyes, all the bad things in her life showing there. Didn't he see the same in his shaving mirror every morning? He tried to tell her he understood, that they were made for each other, but she wasn't listening.

"After all, there are lots of others like him out there, preying on little girls. Evil men, middle-aged perverts. Why not revenge myself on them? They are not my father, but they're the next best thing. It works, too. I feel a whole lot more positive about myself these days."

The girl looked about her and wrinkled her nose.

"You really are a case, do you know that? Living in this smelly little house, thinking your smelly old thoughts."

She appeared to be very angry with him. "And now I'm going to punish you for my father's sins. Do you understand?" She pulled a gun out of her shiny handbag with one practiced swoop and levelled it at his heart.

MAMA

They were so alike, he thought, hopelessly in love. "Yes, mama," he replied.

ANOTHER COUNTRY (JAPAN)

For a time, after her breakdown, Laura felt as if she was being watched. It was nothing tangible, simply the suspicion of being spied on every time she stepped out of doors. But the feeling wore off as her therapy progressed, until it became no more than a small spot in the back of her mind.

Dr Gartbaum asked her to to keep a diary as part of her treatment, a record of her fears and feelings; pleased with the results, he often complimented her on her literary style. When he finally pronounced her fit to face the world again, she finished with the diary but wanted to keep on writing.

With no job to occupy her, medically retired, she was soon spending much of her time in libraries and bookshops and working through *How To ...* manuals. But when she did a course with a writing college, the result was some pseudo-journalism and a clutch of lifeless short stories. Although her tutors said she could turn a phrase, praised her use of metaphor, they and she knew it wasn't enough. A spark was needed.

She considered jazzing up her diary as fiction, but sensed it wouldn't be a wise move.

Yet she could think of nothing fresh to say. Story plots came limping forward and were rejected as unfit, condemned as sickly memories of books she'd read. Every line of dialogue she wrote seemed to be dying on its feet.

She tried telling herself there was no such thing as an original idea - after all, wasn't the computer simply an advanced abacus? - but began to wonder if everything in her mind was second-rate as well as second-hand.

It nagged at her that the dreams of authorship would be replaced by less welcome visitors, another breakdown. She had to fight against looking around nervously in the street. At that point, as she was about to call Dr Gartbaum, a mail arrived from Japan.

Gail had been her best friend in college and afterwards. They'd shared a flat while moving up their respective career ladders, bemoaning their bad luck with men, joking that they would grow old together.

They were almost into their forties, confirmed spinsters it had seemed, when Gail met Shiggy, seconded from Tokyo to the City bank where she worked as a senior accounts manager. He had something mysterious in his eyes and smelled of exotic body oils; and the two women had exchanged tearful farewells at the end of his spell in London.

Since then, for five years, Gail had been inviting her to visit. This time, Laura accepted. After phoning her friend, fixing up dates, she read everything she could find about Japan. It was certainly different, a place where doors opened outwards and taps turned in the opposite direction, where people appeared to laugh and cry at the wrong times.

She prayed that all the strangeness would light the fire, send her imagination off in new directions.

There was no-one to meet her at Narita. As she stood tired and confused in the arrivals concourse, Laura had the feeling of being watched. She glanced quickly across, but saw only some giggling schoolgirls and a man engrossed in his newspaper. Her friends arrived shortly afterwards, full of apologies, complaining about the Tokyo traffic, and she was reassured by their welcoming smiles.

Although she'd revealed little about her illness to Gail, she could tell her friend knew something was wrong. After the frenzied sightseeing of the first few days - from the futuristic electrical fantasies of night-time Ginza to the awesome immutability of the Yasakuni Shrine - things settled down when Shiggy returned to work and Yumi, four years old and full of life, resumed his place in nursery school.

They talked then about their collective past and plans for the future. In a lull in the conversation, Gail suddenly said, "You've changed." There was concern on her face.

Laura attempted to laugh it off. "Haven't we all?" she replied, gesturing towards the other's greying hair.

Gail looked annoyed. "You know that's not what I mean," she said.

Seeing her friend's worried frown, Laura tried to explain, but knew that no-one, however sympathetic, could ever really understand.

She made no mention of her sense of being watched, didn't want Gail to think she was completely loopy, with a small child in the house. When she spoke of Dr Baumgarts' therapy, her writing, told her friend about the diary - she carried it everywhere - Gail smiled for the first time. They embraced without another word.

As the weeks went by, Laura believed her mind was under repair in Japan, in the happy chaos of the Watanabe family.

The country itself intrigued her, the evidence of unaccustomed thought processes at work, people who seemed to be at ease with the past and unafraid of the future. Did not fear the inevitability of their end.

The scene in a temple courtyard, for example: a group of middle-aged and elderly men chattering animatedly, grinning beatifically, as they lit joss sticks to the dead. The same tribute awaited them in the afterlife, she knew, and they looked as if they could hardly wait. Meantime, and somehow typically Japanese, the most wizened of their number was filming the small ceremony, expertly wielding a camcorder that looked like a gadget from outer space.

She had read about Shintoism, the belief of many Japanese that their ancestors continued to exist all around them, that their own spirits would live on for ever.

Some Western commentators held the view that its tenets were drilled into the soul of the nation. Thus they placidly accepted the regimentation of their lives, the small wooden houses and often wooden ambitions. The present-day counting for far less than in many other cultures.

She was taken to see a performance of the ancient drama form of Kabuki and wrote down her amazement at its other-worldly sights and sounds.

She began to record in detail what she saw and did each day and Gail offered encouragement by claiming her writing was becoming clearer and more cogent. Laura grew anxious when Shiggy read her handiwork with pursed lips, but then he said in his near-perfect English, "Many of your conclusions show insight." Flattered, she dared to hope there was something in her brain after all.

She seemed to be getting stronger in other ways, too, and occasionally even forgot about the small spot in the back of her mind. They had planned to visit Kyoto on the bullet train in the last week of her stay. When Shiggy and Yumi went down with a virus, Gail talked apologetically about cancelling the trip.

Laura surprised herself by insisting that she would go on her own. It seemed a kind of test. She was calmer than her friend at the railway station, assuring Gail she would be alright. Didn't she have her tourist phrase book?

Across the aisle, as they rocketed almost silently through the dreary Tokyo suburbs, an old lady in a kimono, smiling peacefully, worked a string of beads through her fingers. Laura watched her for a few moments, then began to scribble in her notepad.

Still writing as the train approached Kyoto, she suddenly grew conscious of being under scrutiny. She gasped with relief to meet the curious stare of a small boy in a sailor suit.

The hotel in Kyoto was ultra-modern and obviously a popular stop-over for business people, with the internet available in every bedroom. She wasn't surprised to learn that it also had a Buddhist chapel in the basement.

She went for a walk before dinner. At first, as she gawped around a series of elaborate temples, her new-found confidence enabled her to withstand the searching looks of other strollers. Normal for Japan, she told herself, the close examination of *gaijin*, foreigners. When dusk fell, however, she had the feeling of being watched from the shadows and hurried back to the safety of her room. She spent most of the night and all of the next day writing.

She left the hotel once in the next forty-eight hours. If the staff wondered about her behaviour, their reputation for inscrutability held up well. One young male receptionist, who spoke reasonable English, arranged for notepads to be delivered to her room. Gail rang several times and sounded anxious. "When are you coming back? You haven't forgotten you're going home on Saturday?"

As if she needed reminding there was a deadline!

She felt guilty about her friend - and remembered her time with the Watanabes fondly, even if it had been a cruel deception.

Her short excursion from the hotel had confirmed that things were getting worse. Much worse, the watchers gathering. The spot in her mind hurtling forward like a cannonball.

She finished writing with an exhausted flourish. Her one and only novel. The story of a beautiful heroine and her pursuit by demons to a fantastical country, a region that hardly existed except in memory and imagination. She found peace there at last.

Laura wondered what Dr Baumgart would make of her work. He seemed very far away, much more distant than the span of half the world. They had both lied, of course, the good doctor and Gail, but only to help her. Her fault for believing them. No more dreams, the writing not even second-rate.

But it would do as a testament.

She hadn't slept for two days, for fear the watchers might be in wait behind her eyelids. But they were almost certainly congregating in the street below, willing her to appear outside the drawn blind. They would get their wish soon enough, although she wasn't planning a long journey. She would leave when she was ready.

She placed the manuscript on the bedside table, then took the diary out of her overnight bag and laid it next to the notepads. Her past and future, side by side. She speculated what would become of them; they might attract attention out of novelty value, if for no other reason.

She giggled at the absurd possibility of being a published author.

She also gave thanks for coming to Japan and learning that her current existence was a tiny link in a many-stranded chain, connecting everything, running through time. The dead multitudes behind, infinity beyond.

She felt at home in a place where it was everyday life that often seemed unimportant, the present that might have been another country. She would come to terms with her fears here. It was the perfect stage for her happy ending.

The room felt so warm and comfortable that she was almost reluctant to rise from the bed. She raised the blind and pushed open the door to the small balcony. Yes, as she'd suspected, they were thick on the ground down there, several stories below, squinting from behind every pillar, staring balefully from around every corner.

She thought at that moment of the last lines of her novel.

The beautiful girl stepped out into the sunlight of a new day, sailing far away from the eyes of her enemies, towards the bright future.

She stepped out.

SPIDERWOMAN

The town had always smelled to him of sex and money and violence. Terrible, random violence. But now it also reeked of defeat, stank with foreboding.

As the car bombs went off, a paralysing fear ran through its streets, like junk in the veins. The remaining few American troops were demoralised and often drugged-up, a danger mainly to themselves. The Cong were at hand and thirsting for a bloody revenge. There were unconfirmed reports of cannibalism in the provinces and of babies being born wrapped around with snakes.

A drinking companion of his swore that a zombie had been seen prowling in the red-light district. Nothing seemed too far-fetched in those interesting times, in what had become an ante-room to Hell.

Saigon before its fall, 1975.

His usual bar, the Crazy New Yorker, was a fragment of the exploding world, hurtling towards oblivion with its cargo of frightened Vietnamese and bewildered-looking GIs. Everyone clinging on for their lives, desperate for anything that resembled love.

A hundred bargains struck every night, hard cash for soft bodies, while all the boys pretended to be men and the dollar-faced women shrieked like schoolgirls. When the male voices reached a frenzy of excitement, he always knew that Spiderwoman had arrived for her evening's work. Only ever dressed in black, whether cheongsam or skimpy western dress, she was invariably the centre of attention, one man after another lured to join her on the tiny dance floor.

Her real name was something unpronounceable, although she called herself Annie. But she was only ever Spiderwoman to him, after a stoned Aussie pressman had joked that no man's flies were safe from her. He'd decided the name fitted for all kinds of reasons.

Since he hated creepie-crawlies, it was one misfortune among many to be sent to a country where cockroaches could be as aggressive as guard dogs and beetles were armoured like minature tanks. Loathing spiders more than anything, he still remembered a book from his childhood, filled with drawings of fearsome-looking arachnids. The caption below one menacing picture in particular ... *Come into my parlour, said the spider to the fly.*

He couldn't help thinking of it, with amusement, every time he looked at Spiderwoman. In turn, apparently recognising that he was secretly laughing at her, she treated him with a disdain she reserved for no-one else. It didn't bother him - he was used to being the poor relation, his accent constantly mimicked, the token Brit, drafted from London to the Saigon Embassy to help with the mass evacuation they all understood was coming. He was content enough to sit in the corner with his beer, go home with the occasional girl, take his pleasures quietly.

The sober and sweltering light of day always made him feel most vulnerable. Sundays were especially bad, no work to hold back the apprehension. Going around in a sort of daze, expecting the worst to happen at any moment, that car over there packed with explosives, or perhaps that one.

The strangeness of the shops. Curious smells and surreal shapes in the street markets. Even the big westernised food stores weren't immune, lumpy parcels labelled "Python" and "Crocodile" among the meats in their freezer cabinets.

A popular fable told at dinner and cocktail parties was the one about the restaurants that sold monkey brains. Only the monkey was still alive, the top of its skull placed through a hole in the centre of the table and then sliced off, the anaesthetised body strapped below, the squirming grey matter picked at by rich Chinese businessmen seeking to perk up their love lives.

"There's nothing these people wouldn't eat to get a hard-on," he'd heard a diplomatic colleague say, "bull penises, bits of people, too, I wouldn't be surprised ..."

The story was circulated among expats to reinforce their feelings of superiority, but made him think about the craziness of life in general. In a funny way it made him feel better about being there, knowing that he'd probably only be somewhere else just as bizarre. With his church-mad parents, for instance. That thought always made Saigon appear more acceptable, its lunacies at a level he understood.

He was shocked nonetheless to see Spiderwoman out of doors for the first time; somehow it seemed against the natural order of things. Still dressed in black but with less extravagant makeup, she was going into an open-fronted shop in a squalid back alley. As he stood watching, she handed over a package to the fat and scruffy owner.

The gesture had a furtive quality and he wondered about it afterwards. The town was full of fifth columnists, Cong sympathizers, conspiring to hasten the final victory. Could she be even more spider-like than he'd imagined, spinning something other than the customary bargirl fantasies?

The Crazy New Yorker was close to the US Embassy and always had its quota of spooks - CIA agents - and other sundry espionage types. They were easily recognisable for all their attempts to appear as casual as their fellow Americans, not so sunburned, aways looking as if they'd be more comfortable in suits and ties.

SPIDERWOMAN

No doubt, like so many drunken men, they'd be only too eager to boast about their exploits. And she would be skilled at extracting the information from them. Sucking out their secrets.

He watched closely that evening as she vamped her way around the room, talking into a dozen lecherous faces, grinding herself against sweaty crotches. Avoiding him as usual.

Previously the ritual had seemed to him no more than casual promiscuity, a sexual version of pass the parcel. But now it began to look more like a selection process on her part. And yet she went home with a common grunt, whose military knowledge probably just about covered holding his rifle the right way up. He felt relieved, but also a little disappointed.

All his doubts returned the next night, however, when he saw her leave with an obvious spook. She wasn't stupid after all, attracting suspicion by only ever going with intelligence officers. He decided to follow when they got into a taxi, feeling a little like a secret agent himself.

An hour of standing outside her darkened apartment quickly removed any romance from the situation. Feeling foolish, he decided that he was being pulled into her web along with the rest of them - if for a very different reason - and vowed to keep his misgivings in check.

All the same, and in spite of knowing that people disappeared all the time, shipped back to the States or blown to pieces or in a hundred other ways, it still nagged at him that he never saw the spook again. So, a couple of weeks later, he gave it one more try when she left the bar with another US Embassy official. There was an added incentive now, one of the other girls having revealed that Spiderwoman hated his guts. That made him uneasy. Given his suspicions about the people she knew, perhaps he had no choice but to strike before she did.

He decided to go for broke, huddled with a packet of Rothmans until the morning and the first stirrings of life in her apartment, still not certain what he expected to see. In the event, it was more a case of what he failed to see. Any sign of her overnight guest.

At 10 am, just as he was about to give up, almost dead from exhaustion and nicotine, he saw her leave the building. She was alone and carrying something wrapped in waxed paper. Debating whether to go after her or break into the apartment, he took the coward's option. God only knew what might be waiting for him in there, perhaps even some of her friends from out of town. *Come into my parlour* ... shuddering at the thought, he cautiously followed her through the crowds.

SPIDERWOMAN

He wasn't surprised when she entered the same shop and handed over the package. Something was passed to her in turn, and he felt sure it was cash. He doubted if she'd ever done anything for love; even her patriotism would carry a price.

After she'd gone, he studied the place in more detail, its shelves filled with nameless things floating in bottles. The store was a backstreet pharmacy, one of hundreds in the city, selling home-made medicines of all kinds. Cures for everything from toothache to tertiary syphilis. The only customers were middle-aged or elderly men; and it crossed his mind that some of them might be ordering monkey brains for dinner.

The shit hit the fan almost immediately afterwards.

As the Cong made their final push towards the capital, he was too busy to give any more thought to Spiderwoman, working fifteen, sixteen hours a day to get everyone out in time. The gulping of helicopter rotors became an incessant background noise. They sounded to him like a nation dying.

He paid a flying visit to the Crazy New Yorker on his last afternoon, expecting to see the place boarded up, perhaps already looted. To his surprise, it was still open, although the only people in the huge room were a couple of the bar staff. Recognising him, one brought out a bottle of Chivas Regal and they drank a silent toast together.

He enquired about some of the girls who'd worked there. The older of the two men sighed. "They all go away."

"And Annie?" he asked, thinking that she must already be an officer in the approaching army.

The other pointed upwards without a word. It was not the answer he'd anticipated. "How did she die?" he asked.

The Vietnamese gave a throaty chuckle. "Not dead," he chided. "She go in American helicopter. To States."

On the plane home, he thought about the doomed city and Spiderwoman, and concluded they had a lot in common. Sex-mad and materialistic, full of nasty surprises. And yet the woman hadn't been an enemy spy, so what had she done with her guests? An explanation had crossed his mind, but was almost too horrific to contemplate. He would never know for sure. Still, the story would be fun to tell around dinner tables in the years to come.

Whatever the truth of the matter, he felt glad about one thing. That Spiderwoman had hated him.

THE AGENCY

Milland was fractious and tired, could even feel sweat between his toes, when he finally made it into the agency.

Although anticipating at least one serious interruption to his morning journey, he hadn't counted on it being such a long one. More than an hour standing in the stuffy hell of a train, marooned in the suburbs by the latest city-wide power cut.

On his trudge from the railway terminus in blazing sunshine, the streets in chaos, bus schedules in a mess following the outage, he had passed several people who appeared to be close to breaking point. Zombie-eyed or complaining to themselves in loud voices. They were in for a busy day at work, he thought.

In contrast to the mayhem outside, the agency was as calm and ordered as ever, computers humming, the telephone system already going into overload. Thanks to the provision of an emergency generator, located in the basement of the building, they had long been spared the suffering of most others in the city. It was just one of the pointers to the importance the government placed on their efforts.

"Afternoon," Denney greeted him pointedly.

He was Milland's supervisor and a dogmatic stickler for the rules. Someone to whom work seemed more important than friends and hobbies and, especially, family. He was always the first one in; and Milland sometimes suspected that he merely carried on when the night shift took over at seven o'clock, catching a little shuteye in the early hours, too dedicated to go home.

Feeling a little less like death as the air-conditioning swept over him, thinking about the agonies of his commute, he was inclined to believe the man had a point. No-one would miss him that much anyway, he thought with a spasm of self-pity. The kids growing up to be as cold and self-obsessed as their mother.

That was the trouble, no-one cared about other people any more, he mused, powering up his computer. More and more youngsters adrift on the streets, drowning in a sea of drugs and hopelessness. Old people abandoned by their families to a wretched and isolated last fifteen or twenty years. Hospitals in a state of collapse. The welfare system unable to cope with the ever-growing number of non-productive mouths.

He'd wondered aloud if what they were doing amounted to much more than a pinprick.

"Every little helps," his boss, ever the zealot, had countered.

The man was standing next to him now as he got his first coffee of that day. "The third time in less than a fortnight," Denney said, his face twisted into a smile.

THE AGENCY

"Any more of it and I'll be forced to put you on a formal warning. I have to repeat to you, Bob, that it's the slippery slope."

An unmistakable threat prickled behind the fake concern; and Millan felt a shiver that owed nothing to the air-conditioning.

No-one was safe, he knew.

He stepped around a beggar every morning on his way to work. The man was typical of the army of vagrants that haunted the city, apart from the collar and tie he always wore. His accent, as he begged for money, was politely patrician. Milland sometimes wondered what had laid him so low. An overdose of stress in his life, or the worsening economic conditions, or just plain bad luck.

The crumpled figure looked more desolate every time he passed by. Not long before the inevitable phone call, Millan had decided, their number plastered over every third billboard in some parts of the city.

He escaped from Denney and went back into the large central room. As he tentatively awaited his first call of the morning, his nerves still twanging, Flitcraft looked over the partition between their desks and offered an encouraging grin.

"The slippery slope speech again, Bob?"

"Yeah. Mind you, could have been worse. He was almost smirking when he said it. He looked as if he hated me the other times."

Flitcraft chuckled. "Oh, haven't you heard? We're back in the lead."

It was purely unofficial, the race between sections to chalk up the highest hit rate each month. Denney's moods fluctuated in accordance with the ratings. When, as now, they headed the table, he could almost convince the uninitiated that he was more than just a soulless automaton.

The man's arid personality seemed ill-suited to their line of work, its life and death nature, but in fact his success to disappointment ratio was remarkably high.

They all had their bad moments, though. When the caller failed to respond, the occasions when the phone at the other end was slammed down in mid-conversation. In spite of the agency's best efforts, it wasn't an exact science what they did.

The bleakness of their daily grind took its toll, too, and Milland had been told that not many people lasted beyond five or six years. That was if the annual testing didn't catch them out first. He had the uneasy feeling he'd only just scraped through the last time.

Denney, on the other hand, had been with the agency from its inception, ever since the change in government policy that had led to it taking over the counselling of the desperate and suicidal from a clutch of voluntary organisations. He was akin,

Milland supposed, to the sort of nurse who never allowed emotions to get in the way of doing a good job. It helped, mind you, if there were no feelings to begin with.

Those among them of a less Calvinistic temperament, without ice water in their veins, sought refuge in black and often childish jokes, finding something to laugh about even in the grimmest moments.

Flitcraft, after sitting down, asked innocently if he wanted the number of the employment exchange. Milland threw a large paper clip over the barrier.

As they sometimes did, unexpectedly, mercifully, the phones had fallen silent.

Milland heard the rustle of a newspaper on the other side of the partition. Flitcraft's voice, sounding disgusted, his good humour gone. "It says here that some pipsqueak of a politician thinks the best way to clear the homeless off the streets is to put them all in a camp somewhere. Fucker!"

As if in counterpoint to his words, the wail of a siren came from outside. It was a common enough sound in the city, but this was loud enough to penetrate even into their hermetically sealed environment. Lucy Murrow, Milland's neighbour on the other side, got up from her desk and went over to the window. "There's been an accident," she called out.

The two men joined her. In the sun-drenched street below, a throng of onlookers had surrounded a parked ambulance. Two perspiring paramedics were loading a figure on a stretcher into their vehicle. The man was unshaven and scruffily dressed and appeared to be very dead.

The car that had presumably knocked him down was resting at an angle across the road. Milland took in the nearby telephone box. It was one of the special ones that could be found all over the city, providing free calls to the agency at any time of the day or night.

"Do you think he was on his way to phone us?" he asked.

Motherly-looking Lucy laughed. "That was a piece of bad luck then," she said.

They all laughed, Flitcraft loudest of all, and for the first time Milland observed signs of strain on the other's face. He wondered if, like him, Flitcraft was already thinking about the imminent annual review.

Returning to his desk in a reflective frame of mind, he sighed when the phones started up again.

THE AGENCY

His first call of the morning was one of the bad ones, the young man at the other end mumbling away to himself, not listening to a word he said. Milland suspected it was a hoax. They got them occasionally, from very drunk or very stupid people. In spite of the cameras inside the phone boxes, the draconian penalties levied on anyone found guilty of abusing the system. After a few minutes, the caller rang off with a shouted obscenity.

He slammed the phone down with an oath of his own - and all at once became aware that Denney was standing over him.

"Now, now, Bob. Don't you know the customer is always right?" With the rictus of a smile at his own joke, before pursing his lips. From experience, Milland knew it was the prelude to a lecture.

"He was playing the fool," he muttered in self-defence.

"That is beside the point, Bob. We live in a free society. Unfortunately there will always be those who regard that as a mark of weakness, who will seek to play games with the democratic process. It's one of the penalties of allowing people to exercise choice."

Then he brightened, his voice lowering to a purr. "And that is exactly why we train you so well, so that you can influence the decisions our customers make. Help them to help themselves, so to speak."

In spite of his dislike of the man, Milland found himself nodding in agreement. Perhaps it was the secret of the other's success, he thought, struck by the almost messianic gleam in the deep-set grey eyes.

"So remember," Denney continued, "there is no excuse for us to lose our tempers. Dignity at all times. It's the least we owe them."

He saw there was a young woman standing behind his boss. Denney motioned her forward. "This is Miss Laverick, Rebecca. She's just joined us."

The girl was pretty, in a brightly-coloured dress, and several men around the room were staring at her with interest. Flitcraft was practically hanging over the partition. Milland was put in mind of a fresh bloom in a bowl of wilting flowers. The girl only had eyes for Denney.

In spite of the rigorous psychological profiling and preparation they all went through beforehand, it was always a shock to the trainees, the harsh reality of it all.

And yet, in spite of her air of faint unease, the young woman looked resolute, eager to prove herself to her new master. Other females in the office invariably wore the same expression, as if determined to appear tougher and more durable than the men.

THE AGENCY

"Oh, by the way," Denney went on, "the boffins have come up with a revised methodology for getting through to our customers. It's an improvement on the current thought reform process. There's talk of a team in this branch being used to pilot the project. I understand we are in pole position."

He'll wet himself with pleasure in a minute, Milland thought.

But Denney was already lumbering towards his next witticism. "Anyway, we'll discuss performing the reform, or is that reforming the way we perform? Ha-ha, in more depth tomorrow. And now, my dear, I'm all yours for the next couple of hours."

As he steered Rebecca towards his cellular office, Flitcraft called out in an undertone after them, "And this, my dear, is where your brainwashing begins."

He disappeared from sight and Milland could hear him flicking through his newspaper again. Then his friend whistled. "It says here that the second biggest electronics firm in the country is about to go under. And someone on the box this morning was predicting another cut in welfare payments. Say what you like about this place, Bob, but we'll never be out of work."

He suddenly sounded anxious. "Don't you think?"

If only it was that simple, Milland told himself. He wondered what Mary would say, the kids, if he came home and told them he'd been sacked. Mary would probably throw him out on the street.

He felt a surge of fury and revulsion and fear. Please God, he didn't want to become one of *them.*

He jumped when his phone shrilled out. Wanting to take out his anger on someone, anyone, he felt grateful when a gaunt and weather-beaten face appeared on the tiny video screen.

Even though the subliminal message embedded in the agency's advertising was designed to attract only the incorrigibly indigent, the irreparably unhinged, they quite often received calls from people who were just going through a bad patch. Office workers who had had a particularly lousy day. Young girls complaining about their abusive boyfriends. Widows seeking solace.

But that wasn't their job.

Selection, in fact, was the one area in which they had relative freedom, no hard and fast rules to follow. It was left to the judgment of the individual operative to decide whether or not to proceed. Milland himself stuck to the principle that anyone in a decent suit could safely be turned away. Luckily, with tact, most of the unwanted callers could be persuaded to go elsewhere for assistance or comfort.

THE AGENCY

By contrast, the regulations with regard to consent were unyielding.

Every call was monitored and the slightest contravention on the part of the operative meant instant dismissal. The customer had to assent to the proposition put to him or her on three separate occasions during the conversation.

As Denney was so fond of saying, it was the price of living in a democracy. The right to a choice. The government and its supporters, the general public, wanted it no other way. And so, reassured by the shabby and abject figure in front of him, Milland went into his well-practiced routine, the sincerity drilled into his voice.

He knew he was winning the battle when the man at last said in defeated tones, "Do you really think so?"

"Yes, I do," Milland responded, feeling as if he really meant it for once, still fuelled by resentment of Denney, of almost everything in his life.

After putting down the phone, he went over to the window and pressed his forehead against the glass. When the almost indiscernible wail of a siren came to him, he wondered if it was one of theirs, and pictured the vehicle howling through the congested streets, the medic with a full syringe at the ready. The automatic door of the phone box clicking open. The submissive or bewildered occupant hustled into the cool of the special ambulance. The plunger striking down.

Denney had re-appeared from his inner sanctum, having been asked to assist one of the operatives with a tricky call. He was visibly annoyed about the interruption. Rebecca remained in his office, a large notepad on her lap. Her eyes were still fixed on their boss.

Milland was declaiming, "Haven't you grasped yet that they're like children? You have to be firm with them ..."

Flitcraft's voice from across the partition, talking to a customer. "There's no reason to go on living, Harry. You do know that, don't you?"

BLACK MAGIC WOMAN

Following the divorce, he was struck by how shrunken everything had become: his hovel of a house, the rust-bucket that was the only car he could now afford, his bank balance.

Even his ambitions had shrivelled, pulverised by the knowledge that Norma was putting the screws on the kids, turning them against him. When the girls first showed signs of not wanting to see him any more, his world for a time was reduced to the one insane notion involving retribution and death.

It was another idea that saved him.

He would find a woman, preferably young *and* beautiful, and make sure Norma saw them together. It would drive her wild, the jealous old cow. If it provoked her into doing something stupid, enough for him to sue for custody of the kids, so much the better. How to go about it, though?

The work colleague he'd been sleeping with - adultery the reason for the divorce - was now reconciled with her husband. And wasn't Norma pleased about that! She'd actually phoned in the middle of the night to spew out her poison. "How does it feel to be on your own? You *bastard!*" Shrieking out the words.

He wasn't getting any younger, starting to lose his hair, his whole life seemed to be a case of diminishing returns. What chance of attracting his dream woman, his means of revenge? He'd tried - how he had tried! - using the personal columns of the local and national press, even a dating agency. None of it had worked.

The problem was the old, old one. The women he liked were exactly the ones who never wanted to see him again after the first fact-finding date. Only the frumps showed any interest, but a middle-aged female with curves in all the wrong places wasn't going to upset Norma; she would just be someone his ex-wife could identify with, perhaps feel sorry for. Norma might even be pleased, believing he couldn't find anyone better. That didn't bear thinking about.

Then he read a newspaper article about a man who'd found a wife in the Far East via the internet. The virtue of doing it that way, so the story alleged, was that it saved on expensive air fares, gave the chance to get to know the other person via e-mail, assess her personality, judge her standard of English. There was a wedding picture of the happy couple. The man was even balder than him; more importantly, the woman was young and slim and extremely attractive.

His home computer was one of the few possessions left to him - mainly because Norma hadn't wanted it - and he was soon gazing at a website which consisted of a series of colour images of olive-skinned young women, feeling like an adolescent thumbing through a lingerie catalogue. Some of the girls were more nubile than anyone he had ever met.

When he spotted a particularly beautiful face, framed by a mane of lustrous black hair and captioned *Elena*, he sent off an e-mail expressing his interest. He received a reply saying the girl would be happy to correspond with him and asking for an up-front charge of one hundred pounds.

That made him uneasy.

Although the website blurb said the introduction agency was owned by one Trevor Campdown, an expatriate Englishman based in Manila in the Philippines, he knew that anyone could claim to be anything in cyberspace. He felt he had no choice, however, but to send off the scrapings of his bank account.

He had reservations, too, about the first e-mail he received from the young woman, giving some details of her background. He wondered if the whole thing wasn't simply a trick - girlish messages across the world really the handiwork of an international fraudster seeking to relieve the gullible and vulnerable of their cash.

It seemed too well-crafted for one thing, syntax and even spelling almost perfect. He carefully worded his response, complimenting her on her English while implying that she must have employed a ghost writer.

Her reply threw him. *Why do you think I cannot use your language*, it ran, *I was ten years at convent school, I am college educated. I am not a liar.*

He was hooked from that moment. No more doubts. Especially when subsequent e-mails were shot through with passionate honesty, full of expressions of longing for a new life, accompanied by further pictures of Elena in various innocent poses, showing off her slim figure and luminous smile. He decided he had to go to Manila to meet her.

The journey was necessary anyway, to clear the paperwork required to bring her back home as his wife. His wife. He pictured the look on Norma's face when they ran into her in town, accidently on purpose. When they kept on running into her.

She would obviously work hard on the girls after that, but would overstep the mark with any luck. The children weren't stupid or blind. Realising how happy their father was in his new relationship, the girls would be happy for him. Want to share in his happiness.

The money for the trip was raised by cashing in his one remaining insurance policy, his sole triumph in the divorce keeping it a secret from Norma and her lawyer. Having no more reserves of cash should have made his horizons seem even narrower. But somehow it had the opposite effect when he stepped from the plane into the sweltering and colourful bedlam of a Manila afternoon.

The journey to the hotel, accompanied by Campdown, with brightly-painted jeepneys threatening collision with their taxi every few yards, the experience like a giant fairground ride, left him feeling exhausted but exhilarated. He wondered if Elena would be as exciting. But when they met the next morning she proved to be the opposite of her e-mail persona, reserved and polite and cool.

For a moment, he believed his original suspicions had been correct. She soon won him over, however, with her prettily-accented but almost fluent English. And when she finally rewarded one of his fatuous remarks with a dazzling smile, he knew he was already close to falling in love.

He wondered, though, if there was a catch and mentioned as much to Campdown afterwards in the hotel bar.

"She *does* seem too good to be true," agreed the other man, looking hot and sweaty in spite of his white linen suit, "but what you see is what you get with these people. She's only recently come on our books and you happen to be the first one to meet her. You're a very fortunate man, that's all."

Accustomed to his luck being all bad, he felt like embracing Campdown. Instead he handed over the various monies needed to carry through the arrangement, including the hefty agency fee.

In the days that followed, as he saw more and more of Elena, he started to believe that things really had changed for the better. It was only at odd moments, lying on his hotel bed after an evening spent in her company in the open-air bars and restaurants of the teeming city, almost dizzy with alcohol and emotion, that the thought crossed his mind. Too good to be true.

One reason for Elena wanting to leave the Philippines was that she had no relatives left there. None at all, she said, almost unheard of in a country where the bedrock of society was the extended family. Where every taxi driver seemed to have uncles or cousins in the vehicles he was attempting to drive off the road.

She explained that she came from a village in the north of the country and was the sole survivor of a mudslide that had engulfed her community. A rich aunt in the capital and taken her in and paid for her schooling, but she too had just died. The beautiful young girl was completely on her own.

He couldn't help thinking her bad luck had turned out to be his own good fortune. It had to be destiny.

Before he left Manila, she showed him her apartment in a modest part of the city. It was spacious and well-furnished - if a little old-fashioned to his taste - but

Elena evinced no great affection for her home. When they were greeted with curious and even hostile stares on leaving the building, he wondered if her neighbours were a cause of her unhappiness. Elena explained that the people there weren't used to seeing foreigners, but he felt he now understood why she wanted to get away.

They parted reluctantly at the airport, but she would be joining him in a few weeks, as soon as the immigration formalities were completed. He was tempted to ring Norma, preferably at two in the morning, to tell her he was getting married. Perhaps even invite her to the wedding. No, he decided, best to make it a complete surprise, meet up in the street, turn it into a public humiliation. But somehow it never happened.

When Elena eventually joined him, he was so happy, taking her around, showing her the sights, that he had no time or inclination for further plotting against his ex-wife. He had explained his circumstances to Elena, that he didn't have much money. It seemed to make no difference to her, as if she wanted him for himself.

His world already seemed much bigger.

Then his daughters told him that Norma was seeing someone else. He was surprised at how mellow she sounded when he rang her, minus the snarl she usually reserved for their conversations. "Yes, it's true," she admitted. "We're thinking of getting married."

Her reaction to his own news increased his astonishment. "Congratulations," she said, without any trace of sarcasm.

He thought his happiness was complete when he married Elena in the registry office, with his two daughters as unofficial bridesmaids, permission granted by their mother. Elena had settled into her strange new lifestyle with astounding assurance; he sometimes found it hard to believe that she herself was still almost a child.

Then Norma became unwell.

It seemed trivial at first, just tiredness and headaches, but soon developed into something more serious. She was rushed into hospital and put on a drip while the doctors argued over what was wrong with her. None of them really seemed to know.

Although he'd hated her once, wanted her dead, he was sorry for his ex-wife now, even visiting the hospital to assure her that the children were coping well. By that time they'd moved in with him and, luckily, Elena was proving to be a tactful and caring foster mum.

BLACK MAGIC WOMAN

Norma died after a week in intensive care, her sickness still undiagnosed. In the weeks of upheaval that followed, after the funeral, the arrangement with the girls became a permanent one. He told himself, I never wanted it this way, but couldn't suppress guilty thoughts that somehow he had won the jackpot. The children were distressed at first, of course, but slowly came to terms with their loss. Elena's calming presence, he was sure, had much to do with their recovery. He wondered if anything was beyond her.

Returning early from work one day, he found her accessing the internet on his computer, ordering medicines from an online pharmacy in the Far East.

"They are required to make me healthy and beautiful," she said, with one of her smiles. If she'd been purchasing several dozen rhino horns, he would have been unable to refuse her.

After the arrival of a parcel covered with exotic stamps, she spent several hours in the locked spare bedroom, refusing even to eat. Various strange smells reached him from under the door. "No-one must see while I work," she explained afterwards, "otherwise I might make mistake. And then I will not look so beautiful."

The only blight on his life was at work, where he'd lost out on promotion to a colleague after their immediate line manager retired early. He suspected nepotism was to blame; the successful candidate had an uncle in Human Resources. Worse still, his new boss was proving to be an unreasonable bully.

Elena noticed the worry on his face and her velvety interrogation soon drew the whole story out of him, all his frustrations and suspicions. "No problems, my darling," she said in a soothing voice. "Everything will be OK, you will see."

Litman, his boss, fell ill not long afterwards and was rushed to hospital. He was dead within three days, the doctors still debating how to treat him. The shock felt throughout the office was tremendous. No-one was more shocked than him.

The post mortem revealed that the man had an undiagnosed heart problem, which was given out as the probable cause of death. Luckily, no-one else seemed to share his suspicions. Two people who had crossed him, two unexplained illnesses, two corpses. Telling Elena of his promotion, he wondered at the note of triumph in her congratulations.

His unease grew.

When another parcel arrived from the Far East, she again hid herself away in the spare bedroom. Making her own cosmetics - or so she said. There was some connection between all these events, he was sure, but what could he say to Elena? To anyone? Above all, he was afraid of losing her.

BLACK MAGIC WOMAN

Although Elena's behaviour was unchanged, as she moved serenely between childcare and domestic chores, he was continually watching her now, covertly studying the almost perfect face. He had no idea what he expected to see there.

Among the many mysteries about Elena was a large sandalwood box that she had brought with her from the Philippines and kept, always locked, in her wardrobe. He was certain she used it to store the "medicines" received by post. Perhaps it held other secrets, something that would reveal the truth about his wife. She carried the key to the box everywhere with her. Except when she was in the shower.

Waiting for the sound of water on honeyed limbs, he went into the bedroom and quickly found the key under the pile of neatly folded clothes on her vanity stool. As with everything Elena did, the contents of the box were systematically arranged, a stone mortar and pestle and different-sized metal bowls and cups to one side, her ingredients to the other. There were many tubes of paste labelled in a foreign script and packages of vividly-coloured powder. Scarlet and orange and deep purple.

The three dolls were in the middle of the box.

The two smaller ones, no more than six inches high, were obviously meant to be a man and a woman, the latter with wisps of golden thread to represent hair. Norma's dyed-blonde hair. Their bodies were a tangled mess, arms and legs and torsos fused together as if they'd been squeezed in a vice.

He pictured tiny internal organs damaged beyond repair.

The third doll was much larger, with brown cloth for a face and topped with a small forest of black thread. In contrast to the others, this one was plump and luxuriant-looking with all its limbs in perfect symmetry. Every part of it was covered with some mixture that had hardened to a translucent sheen; there looked to be many layers under the shiny top coat.

Unable to put any shape to his thoughts, he quickly put away the box when he heard the shower being switched off.

After the children had gone to bed that evening, he sat unseeing in front of the television until Elena came into the living room. To his horror, she was carrying the sandalwood box. She spoke quietly. "You have seen inside this?" He could only nod. Her next remark stunned him. "Good. I think it is time you know about me." Then she asked, "Do you love me?"

He wanted to throw himself at her feet, but attempted to match her calmness. "You know I do." She seemed satisfied with his answer.

BLACK MAGIC WOMAN

"I am not what I seem," she said. "But first you want to know about these, I think?" She opened the box and took out the two smaller dolls. He didn't dare to speak.

"They had to die and so I killed them." The words were awful, terrifying, but spoken with such coolness that they eemed to delineate the natural order of things. "I did it for you, my darling," she went on. "Those people make you so unhappy. I was very sad for you."

He realised then that she was crazy about him. As well as being just crazy. The phrase had never seemed more appropriate. I don't know whether to laugh or cry. Voodoo - but wasn't that peculiar to the Caribbean? Although there were so many questions he wanted to ask Elena, to express them would be to participate in her lunacy, to admit to his own madness. And yet it had happened. Two dolls, two dead people, no arguing with that.

She was holding the larger doll. "This is me," she said. As if he hadn't realised! Her black eyes bored into him, holding him like an animal in a bright light. "I am older than I look."

"How much older?" He whispered the words, anticipating what she was about to say, the premonition compressing his chest.

"Much older. I am eighty-two years."

The grip tightening, he blacked out.

He was on the couch when he regained conciousness, Elena kneeling beside him with a concerned look on her face. He wanted to shrink away from her and at the same time to kiss the worry from her eyes.

He had heard her use the same gentle tones with the girls, when they were having nightmares after Norma's death. "My father was a great *bomoh*, a medicine man. He taught me many things. Things not known by any other people in this world. He taught me how to be a young girl for all time."

He also taught you how to kill, he felt like saying, but was compelled to return her shy smile when she murmured the words, "A beautiful girl."

He had recovered some of his composure, was able to frame a question. "But why did you want to leave the Philippines?"

"It is true that all of my close family are dead, but I still have many relatives there. Some of them know of my condition." She could have been talking about suffering from a cold.

"One of those people had moved into my district and was telling others about me, I think. I have long wanted to get away, to find a new life in another country. It was a sign for me to do it."

She looked at him fondly. "Then I met you and it was another sign." When they kissed, he knew there was no way back, realised the world was bigger than he had ever imagined. Accept everything, it was all he could do.

So he smiled, if warily, when she took another doll from the box. He knew at once who it was. The manikin looked half-finished, still without legs, but had white cloth for the face and the semblance of a business suit forming the top half of its body.

"This is you," Elena said, unnecessarily. "When it is ready, I will treat it in the same way as my own spirit figure."

Her words only gradually made sense. "You mean ..." He gaped at her, too nervous to say any more, scared he had misinterpreted her meaning, more afraid that he understood perfectly.

"We will both live for ever." She giggled the bedtime phrase. "Happy ever after."

He held back at first, thinking of her alternative use for his doll, but finally committed himself to her embrace. Accept everything, he repeated to himself. He was even able to joke, pointing at the few threads on the head of his doll and then to his own balding pate. "Do you think you could put some more, you know, up there?" Her melodious laughter swept away the last of his reservations.

How proud he would be at the forthcoming company dinner dance! Introducing her to his colleagues. His new boss. Elena caught his eye at that moment. It was almost as if she could read his thoughts. "I can always make another little man, my darling," she whispered.

He shivered. His world now had no end.

HARD DAY'S NIGHT

There were several unfamiliar faces around the cavernous room when he got in just before midnight. It was Christmas, always their busiest time of year, and he remembered an appeal had gone out for volunteers to staff the graveyard shift.

He felt tired and depressed about the torments that lay ahead. Rees, the outgoing supervisor, handed over with obvious relief. "Rushed off our feet," he said. And the man's departing "Goodbye and good luck" contained more than a trace of cheery sadism.

While getting his first coffee of the night from the rest room, he prayed for a moratorium on bad news, a respite from cries for help, but knew there was more chance of the earth reversing on its axis.

As the inevitable calls came in, a dozen in the first hour, he was forced out of his mood of introspection. Going from booth to booth, he tried to encourage the younger ones especially, their shells still soft, who took things more personally than the old cynics like himself.

Not that his carapace was doing him much good these days, he mused. So many phone calls, so much anguish.

His most recent bad memory was the woman who'd rung twice to tell of a lifetime of family problems and self-loathing. He had been so close the second time!

She had seemed to be calming down, taking in his advice, even telling him of her love for flowers, especially roses, when suddenly he'd lost her. He had realised at once - the result of long experience - that she was determined to finish it. When the phone clicked at the other end, he had known he would never hear from her again.

But his sense of waste this time was mixed in with something different, something new, and he'd begun to wonder if, deep down, he didn't actually despise the caller for throwing away her life.

Compassion fatigue - it was a death sentence in their job. He had seen it happen to others over the years; and they were all working elsewhere now. For an organisation built on good works, it could be merciless with its own. He was already viewed with suspicion following his divorce.

They liked their people to come from supportive backgrounds, the stable to deal with the unstable. It crossed his mind that perhaps he was moving over to the other side. When he rang with his life story, he hoped the helper would be professional enough not to recognise his voice.

Black humour normally saved them, but this time it was too close to home; feeling more despondent than ever, he went for another coffee.

HARD DAY'S NIGHT

Even if he managed to cover his tracks, the stay of execution would be a short one, with his annual assessment coming up. The psychological testing would soon find him out. Time to look at Situations Vacant, he decided wearily, pouring hot water into the battered old mug with LOVE HURTS printed in red on its sides.

"Hullo."

The voice was friendly, buoyant even, unusual for the time and place, and he felt prepared to dislike its owner at once.

When he turned round, she was smiling at him with a look that said, remember me? He stared blankly and then recalled that he'd helped out one of the newcomers earlier on, when the girl had been having difficulties with an awkward caller.

"Hullo," she repeated, quizzically. And then: "Are you alright?"

He felt like breaking the habit of fifteen years, snarling at her, of course I'm not, you silly bitch, can't you tell? Instead he leaned against the sink, his forehead throbbing, wondering if he would be able to complete that shift even.

"Sit down over here," she said, ushering him to the table used for their rushed meals. They were the only ones in the small room. He could hear the others outside, talking in the soothing tones they were taught to use as the means of getting through to frightened and desperate people.

"Tell me what's the matter."

The young woman was trying the same technique on him, but with almost comical ineptitude. She must have come straight out of training onto one of their busiest shifts, he decided, a baptism of fire indeed. He knew they were short of people - too many out there wanting, too few wanting to give - but this was ridiculous.

"You haven't been with us long," he said, not intending it as a question.

"No time at all," she admitted, still smiling.

He'd seen it many times before, of course, the beginners who put on a show of bravado, breezily defiant in the face of all that relentless misery.

It was soon knocked out of them as a rule - one or two especially harrowing cases generally did the trick - after which they adopted the corporate persona, a sort of all-purpose gloom. Realising the world to be a far worse place than ever they'd imagined. The ones who stayed with them, that is.

Somehow this young woman seemed different. Her jauntiness was hiding something alright, but not just the usual nerves. Instinct told him the problems were in her own past. A troubled mind, though, was not much use to other troubled minds. He should know. He wondered what she was doing there, how she had got past their vetting procedures.

Did they have vetting procedures any more? He was too tired to care.

She was thanking him now, but he couldn't take it in, struggling to focus through the headache. "That's OK," he muttered. "It's just a matter of experience, that's all."

He thought about saying more, but didn't want to hurt her, debated whether he should send her home out of kindness. Then he saw the admiration on her face - my hero - and decided it was time for a few hard truths. Someone else, another stranger to him, came into the rest room just then and looked at them curiously. When he saw they were returning his stare, the man hurriedly helped himself to coffee and left.

He spoke urgently now, feeling guilty about being away from his desk, trying hard to sound less angry than he felt. "You know we're both in the wrong job, don't you?"

"No," the girl said, "you're really good at what you do."

"And what *is* it exactly that I do?" Funnily enough, it was the question he'd been asking himself all night.

"You save people," she said, simply.

"And what about the failures?" he asked.

"There are no failures."

She still had the determined grin on her face, almost as if it wasn't her normal expression but something assumed for the occasion.

It was beginning to get on his nerves, and he snapped at her in his best supervisor tones, "Well, I happen to know better." Recalling his most recent disappointment. The click of the phone going down.

"There are no failures," she repeated. He was surprised by her doggedness, looking as if she wanted to grab his shoulders and shake him.

He spoke very deliberately. "There's a saying, pissing in the wind. Sometimes I think that's all we're doing here."

Again she stood up to him; he gave her full marks for perseverance if nothing else. "My mother also had a saying. The road to hell is paved with good intentions." The catch in her voice told him everything he needed to know. Mums and dads, he thought. The old bugger Larkin hadn't been too far wrong on that one.

"But I don't believe it," she went on passionately. "Good intentions are just that, they're *good*. They're never wasted, believe me." She fell silent then, her outburst spent, looking pale and exhausted.

HARD DAY'S NIGHT

He glanced at his watch. Half past three in the morning. It was the period of the graveyard shift he always dreaded, his senses at their lowest ebb, half-expecting the next caller to be the devil himself playing a practical joke. "I'd better get back," he said. "You stay and have another coffee. Then I suggest you go home and have a long sleep."

Her smile seemed more natural now. "I was going to do that," she said.

He was halfway through the door when she spoke again. "I just wanted to thank you for your help. I'm extremely grateful. We all are." Her voice was very soft, as if it barely had the strength to reach him.

Wondering how she could presume to speak on behalf of her colleagues, some of whom she had probably never even met before that night, he returned to the main room and saw that most people were hunched over their tables, bedraggled and sleepy-eyed. The phones were silent; and he offered up thanks for that.

Sitting in his spartan cubicle, he considered the young woman and their brief conversation. He would have to recommend that they get rid of her, of course, what else could he do? No room for sentiment in the caring game. And yet, even if she seemed blatantly unsuited to the work, he couldn't help thinking she was right about some things.

Which meant, he told himself, that he had no choice but to soldier on. In spite of his misgivings and doubts.

Hearing the phones start up again, he decided it was time for another of his rounds. Strange, but suddenly he felt a lot better. Even his headache had disappeared.

The girl was nowhere in sight in the main area and he felt vaguely disappointed that she'd left without even wishing him goodbye. Then he thought of the rest room, perhaps she was still finishing her coffee.

The place was empty when he pushed open the door. But on the table lay a single white rose. The dew still glistened at its heart.

LONG TRAIN RUNNING

She made the last train with nothing to spare and collapsed into the nearest seat, waiting for her heartbeat to subside.

The pain behind her eyes, the weight in the pit of her stomach, were noxious compounds of drink and anxiety and fatigue. She felt elated in spite of everything, in the knowledge that she'd soon be seeing John, her husband of six years, father of her two beloved children. One difference to this homecoming. He would be dead.

She'd allowed plenty of time, leaving it until Stephanie was in the loo before calling on her mobile. He had sounded unnaturally calm. "It's done."

To celebrate, she had ordered another bottle of wine, with the result that it was almost midnight when they left the bar. They'd parted at the corner with promises to do it again soon, and then had come the race to get to the station on time. The final mad dash across the rain-slippery street, car horns blasting, the hot breath of a bus.

Still gulping down the fetid underground air, she looked around with prim distaste as they slid into the first of many tunnels. It was a long time since she'd been out this late in the big city - always played the homebody before meeting Gerry - but nothing much had changed.

The middle-aged drunk slumped in one corner, a battery of aggressive-looking teenagers, the obvious loony with his staring eyes, probably been passing out leaflets about the end of the world all evening. The anticipated cast of misfits and losers. She was only surprised by how few people were on board the train, no more than half a dozen passengers in her carriage, but concluded it was probably always the same in the middle of the week, especially given the fog and wet outside.

She thought again of her husband - no, smiling to herself, her *late* husband - a hypochondriac and general fusspot. She'd scarcely been able to stand his touch towards the end, struggling not to flinch when he insisted on holding hands in public.

John was a perennial victim of bad weather. At the onset of every winter, right on cue, a severe bout of the sniffles guaranteed to drive him to his sick bed, his refrain for the next few days that he was dying.

Well, it had certainly killed him in the end.

His eyes had been turning red, the sure sign of a looming damp spell, when Stephanie phoned for a chat and complained that it was too long since they'd last met. The idea had come to her all at once. After arranging a night out with her friend, she had phoned Gerry. Discreetly, of course, everything they did was discreet. No-one suspected, least of all John, that she was having easily the most passionate love affair of her life. The other man, Gerry, a meek and mild schoolteacher like herself.

Gerry had been all for her idea; and she knew then that they were true soul-mates, destined to be together. There was no other way, they'd both agreed. John would never give up the kids without a bitter fight. She couldn't have endured going through the courts, the risk of her affair coming to light. She would never have been able to face them in the staff room again.

Her headache was getting worse, turning into a boozy sort of migraine; she could barely make out the other end of the carriage, one or two figures sprawled there like corpses.

Again she thought of John. She knew exactly what would confront her when she opened the front door, the body at the bottom of the stairs. An accident they would call it, a sick man going to the kitchen for some warm milk - as was his habit, she would inform the inquest - and stumbling in his heavily-dosed condition, an addict to paracetemol.

"Don't worry, I know exactly what to do," Gerry had assured her.

There had been a look on his face that she knew of old, a sort of suppressed excitement. She'd first noticed it when he talked about his impending visit to an abattoir, part of the preparation for his environmental health course; again when he made plans to see a bullfight during a senior school trip to Seville. Sometimes, thinking about that look, she wondered if he was nearly as inoffensive as he seemed.

It made no difference to her feelings about him. There was anyway the consideration that a mouse wouldn't have been of any use to her, she'd needed someone who could be daring and ruthless. Gerry was certainly strong enough for the task, she had known from his love-making, a keep-fit fanatic who spent long hours in the gym.

She had insisted on not knowing the gory details while they discussed their strategy, rehearsed her alibi, fine-tuned his means of entry to the house. Telling Gerry to shut up when he began to talk about choke holds and how to apply them without leaving any marks. He had given her a hurt look and fallen silent. She'd felt powerful then, as if in control of a sleeping tiger.

Now, with darkness sliding around the train, she dreamed of the time, after a discreet few months, when she would bring together all the ingredients to guarantee a long and happy family life. Her two children and Gerry. Their special secret. She had already made a start on her wedding plans.

LONG TRAIN RUNNING

That reminded her, she must remember to remove the heavy gold ring from John's finger before he was placed in the coffin. Pity to waste it.

The little ones hadn't been in the house, of course. Staying the night with her mother, John in no fit state to look after them. She was a good and thoughtful parent, she knew, unlike whoever had created the raggedy young couple sitting across the aisle from her. Druggies from their appearance, deathly-white, a rash of needle marks on the girl's upper arm. In the milky incandescence that was beginning to hurt her eyes, they looked menacing and scared at the same time.

The overhead lights flickered twice just then, almost like a signal, and the pair got up and blundered towards the carriage door. The train came to a halt. Lost in her reverie, she hadn't been following its progress, didn't know where they were. The moisture streaming down the windows meant she was unable to decipher the station name. She gave up trying, too exhausted to care.

As they staggered onto the dimly-lit platform, the girl looked back at her; it could have been terror on the pinched face. Her boyfriend appeared to half-drag her away. They disappeared into the gloom. It was none of her business - probably only her imagination, her brain under siege by the events of that long day. Anyway, she had more than enough troubles of her own, struggling to remember her cover story through the thickening headache. As they started to move again, she tried to shut out the sickness creeping towards her lungs and chest.

A change in the rhythm of the wheels jolted her back into an awareness of her surroundings. The train was out in the open, passing along one of the overground stretches of the route, and she squinted through the glass in the hope of making out a familiar landmark. But all she could see clearly was her own face, pale and drawn, pouched under bleary eyes. Too many restless nights in the past week, worrying about whether it would all go without a hitch.

She was on the last lap now, but there were still things to do. The phone call for help, her fake hysteria. And then a long, long sleep. She had the feeling Gerry was already in bed, all his dreams sweet ones.

Suddenly a glow appeared out of the darkness, became an irregular red border along the far horizon. She supposed that it came from the city centre - but how could that be? For a split second, she thought she saw tongues of flame leaping in the blurred distance, wondered if whole districts weren't on fire, before they hurtled once more into the blackness. She really shouldn't have had that last glass of wine, she decided queasily, and closed her eyes again.

Still wandering in an uneasy sleep when the train jerked to a halt, she somehow knew that, seconds before, the overhead lights had blinked twice. The drunk was already standing by the door, hanging onto the handrail as if he wanted it to anchor him to the spot. He looked terminally confused, so comical that she almost laughed out loud in spite of her own discomfort. The man could barely stay upright, and she wasn't surprised to see a patch of blood on his expensive overcoat, probably fallen over or bumped into something.

With a look over his shoulder, he lurched onto the deserted platform and dragged himself away; until his erratic footsteps were swallowed by a deep silence.

She was losing the fight to concentrate, but roused herself enough to peer around the carriage.

The madman was staring straight at her.

Quickly turning away, she had an almost uncontrollable urge to cry out, then thought of the sleepers at the far end. Yes, there was still someone there, indistinct but evidently awake now, his head moving. She relaxed a little, but still wanted to rush from the train and phone her husband to collect her from wherever it was. Then she remembered, giggling weakly. No more husband. Anyway too late, they were already on the move.

The lunatic scrutiny continued for what seemed like an age, an eternity, and all the while she could feel the nausea building in her throat, her mind growing weaker.

When the lights went off and on, off and on, she almost blubbered with relief. It was his stop, she knew. As he disembarked from the carriage, she could see that he was unsound in other ways, trailing one leg awkwardly behind him, his right arm at an impossible angle. Maybe he had stared at the wrong person that night. One last glare at her - desolation mixed with derangement - and he was gone.

She gathered up her things as they started off once more. Her turn next. She wondered what she was doing on the train. Something to do with her husband, an accident. There was another man, too, quiet-looking but dangerous. Couldn't remember his name, impossible to think straight any longer.

Nothing in her mind except some fast-disappearing pictures: bowls of cut flowers in a bright living room somewhere, small bodies happily splashing, a ring of faces animated by candlelight. She wept when they were finally consumed by holocaust images, bleak visions of an encircling inferno. Whimpering, she yearned to curl up like a baby.

Something stirred in the semi-darkness along the carriage. The figure stood up in a spasmodic way. It was a man, the last of the sleepers down there, rotating his head in an effort to remove the stiffness from his neck and shoulders. The absurdly normal gesture made her want to clap her hands. Hysterical woman, she told herself, what would he think of her? She would go up to him, adopt her little girl lost look, and explain that she was having problems with her memory. Temporary amnesia. He would surely get help.

The man had noticed her presence, the head jerking in her direction.

As she was about to call to him, the sickness reached her mouth, spurt after spurt. She was horrified, looking down, to see gouts of red on her new raincoat. Then the agony struck, from the crushed ribs pressing against her heart. When the lights flickered, she rose unsteadily.

There was a furnace smell in the carriage.

The man came shuffling down the aisle and she saw that he had something wrong with his neck, the head flopping from side to side as if only loosely connected to the rest of him. And yet he was smiling at her.

Even through her fear and pain, she wondered if she knew him.

But it wasn't until he fumbled for her hand, the harsh fluorescence exploding off the heavy gold ring, that she began to scream again and again ...

LIGHT MY FIRE

During the whole of my marriage I don't remember giving a single thought to my mortality. Too busy, I guess, with the everyday hassles of family life, scraping to get by. But after the kids flew the coop, the divorce, there often seemed to be little else in my head.

Truth is, I was scared of growing old and ugly.

I was musing on the ageing process that Friday night. I was on my own, peering into the big mirror behind the bar, wondering mournfully if my hairline had receded even further. I hadn't had a date in months, not since the last one gave me the brush-off, after accusing me of being a moody fuck.

My looks were going fast, I knew. It had to be the reason why women were in short supply. And the bitch had wondered why I was down! I needed another stiff drink, just thinking about my life.

A guy came into the place and sat next to me. Now if I scrubbed up like *that*, I thought, glancing sideways, I would be one happy dude. There was a stir around the room, among its female population. One young chick was practically coming out of her halter top trying to get a better view of him. He was a babe magnet on rollerblades and it didn't make me feel a whole lot better.

Funny, but he appeared not to appreciate his good luck. In fact, he seemed downright miserable.

The chick in the halter top put some money in the juke box and began to shake her rump to an old Doobies number, her smile a wide-open invitation. My neighbour looked even more pissed off. I couldn't hold myself back any longer, curiosity and envy and self-pity all chewing away at me.

"That's hot," I said, with a jerk of my head towards the chick. Not a flicker of response.

I thought, he must have one hell of a problem. Suddenly I didn't feel so bad about myself. Calling for a celebration drink, I included the bringer of this unexpected light. "And whatever my friend wants."

The stranger made as if to refuse, but finally said, "OK, the same again."

"She likes you," I said, unnecessarily.

He continued the silent treatment, his face set to depressed. He reminded me of my Uncle Joe, after being told he had a week to live. Only this guy looked like he'd romp home first in a wholesome living contest. He was beginning to interest me.

I was working on a theory that he'd lost his shirt on the stock market when he pulled out a billfold that contained enough green ones to paper a fair-sized room. He asked the barman to set them up again. Putting my jaw back in place, I said, "Thanks. I'm Kevin, by the way."

"I'm Ritchie."

We shook hands; his clasp was disgustingly firm. We talked some. He still wasn't the life and soul of the party, but had obviously decided to make an effort. We exchanged smirks when the chick gave up and, looking foolish, stamped back to her giggling friends. That seemed to relax him. He told me he was just passing through. I asked where he was headed.

"Nowhere in particular," he replied with a wry smile, running a hand through his thick head of hair. I wondered how old he was. About my age, I reckoned, only *much* better preserved. I reviewed my thinning locks in the mirror once more.

"Life is a bitch," I sighed. My companion muttered his agreement.

To my astonishment, Halter Top continued to give him the glad eye; she was slim and attractive and probably had a number of years on my daughter. I thought about my crappy job as a car salesman, about being stuck for the rest of my days in Dearborn, Michigan.

I would have gladly swapped places with the stranger, for all sorts of reasons.

In my line of work, however, you learned to deodorize your true emotions, especially the basic ones like resentment and jealousy. "A travelling man with a wad of cash and pursued by panting babes. Sure is a hard life," I joshed.

The guy wasn't fooled, though, must have caught a whiff of rancour. He came alive at last, snarling at me, "You don't know diddly squat about it!"

His firm jawline fluttered out a warning, but my jowls wobbled their defiance, the unfairness of it all suddenly hitting me, overcoming my slimeball instincts. "One thing for sure, dude. If I was you, I wouldn't be sitting in this dump, feeling sorry for myself. If I was you ..."

At that moment, he seemed to take me in for the first time. He held up his hands in truce. My voice still trembling, I accepted his offer of a drink.

As I sulked over my Scotch, I could sense him watching me. His question came out of left-field. "Do you think I'm handsome?"

I twitched uneasily, thinking about his rejection of the chick, but he gave a reassuring smile. "Just interested to know, that's all."

Vowing to kick his balls and run if he attempted any sort of move, I stuttered, "I - I guess you are."

LIGHT MY FIRE

He shook his head. "My nose is too big," he said. "And my ears stick out."

You know something? He was right, too. But it didn't make any difference. The guy looked so healthy, it was positively fucking sick - like he was giving off a kind of aura, the whites of his eyes almost luminous in the subdued lighting of the bar. The fact is, he was just *bursting* with life. You couldn't blame the chicks.

"It's a side-effect, you see," he continued, half to himself, "and so's the itchy feet."

Even though he was almost chummy by now, his words didn't make any sense. Reading my face, he pulled himself together. "Know how old I am?" he asked. It was my own question turned on me, but I had a flash we were going somewhere very weird.

He didn't wait for an answer. "Put it like this, I was in senior high school when the Japs bombed Pearl Harbour."

I did a quick calculation and said, "Yeah, right."

He gave an understanding nod. "You don't believe me."

"Hell, what makes you think that?" I exclaimed. "People come up to me all the time and say they're thirty, forty years older than they look."

"I don't blame you," he said. "It was the same with me. I got talking to a stranger ..."

"He must have been one bitching plastic surgeon," I interrupted, laughing in his face. He fell silent and I sensed my gibes were driving him back into his shell. I wondered about that. If he was running a scam, the guy would have had me gawking at a fake birth certificate by then. Instead he just appeared embarrassed.

To retrieve the situation, I went with one of my favourite sales techniques, the straightforward wheedle. "Hey, man, I believe you. Don't go cold on me just as it's getting interesting." Ritchie didn't buy it for a second, I could tell, but then he looked me over and that seemed to make up his mind.

He took out a phial, a quarter full of some muddy liquid. His voice dropped to a respectful undertone. "It wasn't the knife, but this."

I have to admit I felt disappointed. "Shouldn't that stuff be sparkly, like in the movies?" But, again, it was kind of reassuring. A professional con artist he wasn't, passing off a couple of inches of sludge as a magic potion!

For someone who knew zilch about marketing his product, he managed to press all the right buttons. "It was in a place like this. I was on my own. Drowning my sorrows." While I squirmed, he was staring straight into my eyes. It seemed, for a moment, as if he could see inside my head.

LIGHT MY FIRE

"I'd always been a ladies' man, but knew I was losing it fast. I was scared half to death, worrying myself into an early grave. The stranger said he could offer a remission from growing old. One sip of this, he told me."

As he waved the phial under my nose, I considered walking out of there before he claimed to be the son of Jesus Christ. And yet a vague hope kept me rooted to the stool. That he wasn't lying or on the run from an asylum.

Now he'd captured my attention, Ritchie came out with the punch line. "One sip and I could live for ever."

I watched him for even the embryo of a snigger. Nothing. The guy meant every word of it. More to gain thinking time than anything else, I asked, "You mentioned side-effects?"

He said, "You always feel as if you've just come out of fitness class." He didn't sound over the moon about it, but I thought, hey, everyone is entitled to a bad day.

"More than that, things get put back." He pointed to his mane, then switched the digit to the chick, still smouldering in her corner. "You become extremely attractive to other people. I've figured it's something to do with the blood pumping extra fast, as if I'm giving off some sort of magnetic glow. An overpowering life force."

He pulled out a crumpled photo. The image was definitely him, but different, the eyes looking dull and the brown hair making a rapid exit. He must have been at least forty pounds overweight.

"Me back in 1970," he explained. "I carry it around to remind me of myself."

My voice had dropped to a whisper. "And I'd stay looking good forever?"

"With any luck," he replied.

A smidgen of suspicion remained. "Why are you telling me this?"

"Because I see me in you, a long time ago."

His eyes had a take it or leave it look. When he made as if to put the phial back in his pocket, I wanted to snatch it from his hand. My opinion of the guy had gone into reverse - he was brilliant. Sold, one shot of his shit-colored elixir.

Turned out it was for free - and that *really* clinched the deal - my new buddy going coy at the mention of cash. "Just passing on the torch," he said.

I was about to tilt my head back when something struck me. "What the fuck do you mean, with any luck?"

Ritchie made like he was a quack giving me a clean bill of health for all eternity. "Think of it as the best medicine ever. It gets you in unbelievable shape.

After that, every organ but one will remain in perfect working order. What it won't do is turn you into Superman. If a plane falls out out of the sky, you're not going to emerge smiling from the wreckage."

I thought, I can live with that, but then came some more catch-up. "You said every organ but one. Fuck, I just knew it," I whined, glancing towards the chick in the halter top.

He was the closest I'd seen him to amused. "It's your brain that'll be the exception. Nothing there will change. You won't get any wiser or more intelligent. It'll chug along in the same old way."

"Whew," I said. A final check in the mirror before lifting the phial to my lips.

Almost as soon as I swallowed carefully - it tasted OK, like apple juice laced with tequila - I noticed he was back in sorrowful mode. That made me nervous, suddenly conscious of not having a get-out clause.

"If the stuff is so good, what's with the long face?"

All my questions were operating on delay. "And how do you know that, about not being Superman?"

Ritchie turned teacher, quizzing me silently, waiting for his star pupil to come up with the answer. The penny finally dropped. "The stranger," I asked. "What became of him?"

"Oh, he jumped off a high building. Must have died of happiness."

Boom, boom, boom. I prayed the supercharged version of my heart was already in place. "Don't look so worried. Could be you're the one this stuff was meant for, still going strong a hundred years from now. I can tell you're a single-minded sort of fellow." Although the words sounded fine, I wasn't enthused by his twisted smile.

But then he raised his glass in a salute. "Here's to the new you." I soon came out of shock as he plugged my future prospects, felt even better when a gorgeous blonde along the bar began to eye me like a rabbit trapped in a set of headlights.

"It works fast," Ritchie said. He shifted on his stool, acted dead beat all of a sudden. "And now I'll be on my way."

I wasn't giving him my complete attention, the blonde by this time practically dragging her tongue along her chin. Across the room, Halter Top was obviously having difficulty making up her mind between the two of us.

"Got a date, uh," I murmured.

He said, "Couldn't have put it better myself." I caught him watching himself in the mirror. The guy looked great to me, but he didn't seem so impressed, scowling at his reflection. I thought, he don't like himself so much. Still, that was his problem. I had troubles of my own, wondering which of the ladies to take home that night.

"You'll be moving on soon, too," he was saying. "Wanderlust is another of the symptoms."

"Can't wait," I replied. But, first, I was going to ensure that Dearborn had the *fullest* benefit of my presence. Another chick caught my eye, then another.

When I looked around, he'd gone. The phial was on the bar counter, by my elbow. I pocketed it with a shrug and turned back to my adoring fans.

Everything he said came true.

Within weeks, I was the fittest-looking guy in town. People kept asking where the hair transplant had come from. I had already cut a swathe through the female populace - even my ex, who'd loathed me from about year four of our marriage, wanting a piece of the action - when I started to crave a much bigger stage.

There seemed only one place for someone like me, larger than life and on the make. Los Angeles, California.

I haven't returned home once, lost touch even with my kids. There must be grandchildren, great-grandchildren, I've never seen.

It's the price you have to pay.

Hollywood rolled over and begged me to tickle its belly. I did the rounds, went with superstars and society women. Husbands weren't a problem, seemed to regard it as an honour that I'd picked out their old ladies.

When I wanted a change, I simply parked my butt in the lobby of a grand hotel, in Bel Air or Beverly Hills, and waited for the offers to roll in. I always chose the next one for her looks and the size of her jewels.

I got taken around the world many times, a middle-aged toy boy, at my ease in every Caribbean hideaway and Mediterranean flesh pot. I loved the sensation of always being on the move - geographically, sexually, emotionally.

A half dozen Presidents have come and gone, and in all those decades, I only stayed with one person for longer than a few months. That was Helene, a French countess I met in Biarritz on one of my subsidised beanos. We made a home in Paris and I struggled to remain faithful to her, fighting against my every instinct. I even thought to share my secret with her. One sip and we'll be together for infinity. My good intentions didn't last, of course, and I ran off with her best friend.

When Helene killed herself not long after, I felt, for a time, very alone.

LIGHT MY FIRE

It's the price you have to pay.

There were lots of others after Helene. But as the years went by, I realised I was changing, slowly growing out of synch with myself. Everything remained A1 except where it really counted, in my head. It got so bad I decided to escape from the bright lights for a while. I climbed in my car and drove. Several thousands of miles later, I'm still on the road.

Money is no object. I live frugally, in cheap motel rooms, and there are at least two offshore accounts I haven't even gone near. Women are no longer a problem. I make it clear to them that I'm behind glass, only for show, look but don't touch.

I catch my reflection and see myself through their eyes. The effect is like a trick mirror, an illusion, simply my body ignoring the feeble signals from up top. Truth is, I'm turning into a zombie, a dead man walking. My wanderings have become a search, but I'm not looking for Ritchie. He committed suicide a long time ago, I know, proving to himself he wasn't Superman.

No, I'm on the hunt for another me. Prompted by my tired and faltering brain to find someone who's desperate for a stab at immortality. Then I'll say to him, just passing on the torch.

MEMORIES

I loved her once, I think to myself, looking on from the shadows as she slowly undresses in front of the large mirror in what used to be our bedroom.

Perhaps I still do, in spite of everything.

She goes into the bathroom and switches on the shower, giggling as the water strikes her supple body. If she saw me watching her, the laughter would soon turn to screams.

But perhaps she never really noticed me, even from the first. I always accepted that she was shallow and self-centred, fascinated by her own good looks. That was half the attraction, perhaps, to get her to register my presence. I was full of confidence in those days. It helped, too, that I was wealthy and successful in my job. She expected no less.

The warning was there from the start, I suppose, the vindictiveness she showed in her divorce case. Yet all I could see were the dark eyes filled with tears, the perfect mouth that spoke of ill-treatment and neglect. The poor wretch, her husband, didn't stand a chance, even the judge surreptitiously admiring her tragic beauty in the courtroom.

She made her gratitude plain when we went for a drink to celebrate victory. Hoping it was more than sympathy on her face as I spoke of my own divorce, I received only a peck on the cheek at the door of her luxury flat, the home I'd enabled her to keep. But there seemed to be a promise in her eyes.

I pursued her ferociously after that, with costly flowers and astronomically expensive meals. She accepted my generosity with thanks and a dazzling smile, but obviously felt no obligation to return any favours. I still couldn't get past her front door. She told me she was seeing someone else.

Although I had no reason to think she was lying - my own eyes revealed her attractiveness to other men - it made me redouble my efforts. The breakthrough came when I invited her to Paris for the weekend. I could see her pleasure at my offer, the realisation on her face that perhaps I was turning into a good long-term bet.

As we were shown into one of the best suites in the Ritz, I sensed she was even more impressed. That same afternoon, under silk sheets, we made love for the first time. She wasn't especially passionate, but I felt privileged just to be so close to her, to feel the softness of her lips and smell the fragrance off her skin.

In the evening, over dinner, we talked seriously for almost the first time. I was curious about the reasons for her bitterness towards her ex-husband, knowing the stories about mental and physical cruelty were half-truths at best. This woman wouldn't take easily to any kind of bullying, not for a moment.

MEMORIES

She was frank with me. There had been blazing rows about the marriage still being childless after three years. "There was no way I could have a family with him," she said simply, looking me in the face. "I didn't love him enough for that."

I think it's pathetic now, her fear of growing old and losing her looks, the true motives for her decision against pregnancy. Not wanting to disfigure her body, or having children around to mark off the years. At the time, however, it seemed to take the challenge to a still higher level.

I had to make her love me enough.

Watching from the dark as she re-enters the bedroom, a towel concealing her slenderness, I think back to those days and would like to weep with bitterness and regret.

I was so absurdly sure of myself. Success and riches can have that effect, creating monsters of hubris, spoilt brats, dead souls. Extreme beauty has a similar potential. We were on a collision course from the first, I realise that now.

After we got back from Paris, I felt sure that I had the upper hand at last. She accepted it meekly when I said she had to stop seeing the other man. I still remember my satisfaction on first being introduced as her boyfriend. The people she knew were, like her, much younger than me, but I got on well with them all. She told me, laughing, that everyone considered I was a good catch.

There were several hundred people at our engagement party. Even my ex-wife came, looking tired and older than her years, and I thought I could read wonder in her eyes as she gazed on her radiant successor. She was probably debating my sanity. How right she was.

We'd been married for less than twelve months when my new partner complained of being bored, said she was tired of shopping and lunching with her girlfriends.

She decided to invest the money from the sale of her flat in a shop, in one of the more expensive parts of Chelsea. Selling the kind of jewellery she loved to buy. She indicated that we might start a family once the business was up and running. And somehow, with a promise here and a melting smile there, she persuaded me to put money into the venture, more than I would have liked. But I was happy to see her happy.

Then the spending began for real. She proved to be a hopeless businesswoman, more interested in show and glitz than hard economics. The shop was massively overstocked and she sold almost none of it; I sometimes thought the whole operation was only an excuse to enable her to wear all the fancy and over-priced bits and pieces of her choice at any time she wanted.

MEMORIES

I realised the extent of the problem when she asked for more cash to keep the concern afloat. We had our first quarrel then and she sulked for days afterwards. Until I gave in when she talked about leaving me.

From that moment on, I always felt one step behind her. Neither of us raised the subject of children again.

Now I watch as she sits in front of the mirror and starts to apply mascara to those glorious eyes. Pulling a pretty face, she laughs to herself, still in love with her own loveliness. I feel sick with frustration.

I had to bail her out when the shop went bankrupt, although she acted as if the disaster was entirely my fault. To console herself, she went on a clothes-buying spree. When I saw the bills, I shouted at her again. She looked hurt and, feeling guilty, I said I was sorry. It grew into a familiar pattern.

As she became ever more spendthrift, our quarrels turned public. My wedding gift to her had been a brand-new Mercedes. When she told me in a restaurant that she'd sold it to pay off some debts, my angry response made her cry - artfully staged tears, I'm sure - and I was almost punched by a chivalrous fellow diner.

She proved adept at making me out to be the aggressor, goading me in an undertone at parties, flirting with other men until I exploded with jealous rage. She would at once play the innocent, a shocked look on her face. People would invariably take her side.

I had the feeling she was even turning my work colleagues against me, phoning them to complain about my unreasonable behaviour. I was fully aware that more than one of my friends would have willingly taken her off my hands. With or without my consent.

Then she began to drop hints that I would go the way of her first husband, stripped of my dignity and assets in a court of law. She was threatening me, a top divorce lawyer!

I couldn't believe her cheek, but had the uneasy feeling her confidence was justified. I had made a fool of myself with her in front of too many people to be sure of anything any more. My self-belief was draining away, along with my money and my feelings for her.

Certain of her power over me, she began to spend more and more time away from home. I grew convinced that she was cheating on me and saw it as my chance to strike back and safeguard my interests. Even the most besotted judge would be unable to take her side if presented with evidence of her infidelity. I hired a private detective to follow her.

MEMORIES

She seemed to accept defeat gracefully when I showed her the photographs. As she apologised for hurting me, I told myself it wasn't genuine sorrow in her dark eyes. But I couldn't be sure.

While I considered my options, we moved into separate bedrooms. Although still reluctant to take the final step - stupidly hesitant to let go of our short-lived marriage - I made preparations to write her out of my will. Unknown to me, she was dreaming up a plan of her own.

She's putting on a frilly negligee now, dabbing expensive perfume on her neck and shoulders. All paid for with my money, subsidised by my overconfidence and fatal pride.

The belief that I'd won, her words of remorse, causing me to dither about changing my will. Arrogance back in its usual place, working the assumption that I could still get her to love me. And all the time she was plotting her surprise.

Someone is coming to spend the night with her to judge from the careful preparation, the smirk of anticipation on that exquisite face.

At least it won't be her partner in crime. I've scared that bastard away for good, fixing him with a baleful stare whenever he visited the house. Until he sensed that something was badly wrong and broke off the relationship. It hasn't taken her long to replace him, though.

She has never felt me watching from the dark.

It's the last and most wretched of all my misfortunes. I long to drive her, screaming, from the room at this moment, but know that I will never be able to hate her enough, even the worst memories adulterated by her smell and touch.

The irony is that I was probably always just a shadow to her, in common with the rest of mankind. It's the secret of her success, I suppose, coldness and infinite self-regard wrapped in the most alluring of packages. There's nothing in the world that can touch her.

Nothing out of it either, I now know.

When they found my body in the street, apparently the victim of a hit-and-run driver, she must have fallen under suspicion although she was on holiday in Jamaica at the time. Everyone knew we were on the point of divorce, had quarreled massively over several months.

I guess, as usual, she talked and cried her way out of trouble, flashing her eyes at policemen and court officials and anyone else who could get her off the hook. I know for a fact that she slept with one of the investigating officers - probably the most senior - in this very bedroom, in our bed. I was already peering from my darkness by then.

MEMORIES

The case against her must have fallen through for lack of evidence, the photographs in my study safe long since burned, the private detective no doubt bought - or scared - off.

The man is middle-aged and greying and impeccably dressed. He reminds me of myself. He's a new one to me, but she treats him warmly when they come into the bedroom, as if they know each other well. I try to lip-read as they chat, curious to know whether he's already taken her to Paris.

They are lying together on the bed now and she undoes his shirt at the neck. They will make love soon, I know, and remember our first time. The Ritz Hotel.

I wonder how I can remember.

I wonder what I've done to deserve this. Watching from the dark. With my memories.

THE ONLOOKERS

James Brandon was on his way back from Bristol when he first saw them watching by the roadside.

He'd been up since five that morning, and it was now foggy early evening, with rain pulsing into his headlights. He thought about his girlfriend Julia waiting for him at home, having been warned over his mobile to be ready. They were going out for a Chinese meal to celebrate six months together.

It was a record for him, but about time he began to settle down, fast approaching his thirties.

He glanced at the dashboard. Damn, the clock was showing half past six. Although already moving at speed in the outside lane, he decided it was time for some extra wellie. At that moment, the traffic ahead began to slow and he cursed as he put his foot to the brake; given the weather, it was bound to be a pile-up of some kind.

In his job, system software consultant for a major computer firm, he did more than his fair share of driving, sixty or seventy thousand miles a year up and down the motorways of England and Wales. He was used to seeing the outcome of high-impact collisions. Mangled cars, even a few mangled bodies.

There were blue lights ahead and they had slowed to a crawl by now. All around him, drivers were straining to peer through the gloom. Ghouls, he thought, knowing he was doing the same. No getting away from it, people loved to see the results of a good accident. Some people more than others, he recalled ...

They'd been slowly passing the remains of a white Ford Escort on the side of a dual carriageway just outside Bracknell. Looking across, he'd seen a smear of blood down one stoved-in door and noticed the driver in the next lane taking in the same thing. He was young, about James' age, and driving a similar high-performance vehicle. When they exchanged glances before accelerating away from the scene, the other driver had smiled and given a thumbs-up.

James, in spite of some shock at the man's reaction, had believed he understood the message. It seemed to be, that will never happen to the likes of us.

It was true he considered himself an excellent driver, certainly superior to the vast majority of road users. He enjoyed travelling at speed and couldn't understand those people who didn't. Alright, he despised them, actually got a kick out of tailgating some idiot doing sixty in the middle lane and blasting with his horn until the other driver veered away like a scared rabbit.

A former girlfriend had broken up with him over his driving, after accusing him of being a bully. She hadn't understood it was part of his job to get from A to B as quickly as possible. So what if it had become a habit, bombing around even at the weekends? He had a powerful car and knew how to use it - surely that wasn't a crime? Luckily, Julia didn't seem to mind, although she sometimes looked nervous when he performed a particularly hairy manouvre.

Now, coming alongside the crash, he saw that it was a bad one, a lorry having jack-knifed and taken out a couple of family saloons. Police cars and ambulances were everywhere, even a fire engine.

He was approaching an outstretched figure, a woman in a white dress, surrounded by paramedics.

That was odd.

Only two of the people were ambulancemen, kneeling down to attend to the woman. They paid no attention to the other figures standing silently around, who all appeared to be civilians. But surely the police wouldn't allow onlookers this close? And where had they come from? He felt certain they weren't victims of the pile-up, no-one had walked away from that carnage.

Although it was getting darker by the minute, he could just make out stains on the clothing of several of the watchers. Blood. That was it - they had to be from vehicles not directly involved in the crash, other drivers and passengers who had stopped to assist the injured.

The accident scene was receding in his rear-view mirror.

Just then one of the onlookers turned around from surveying the stricken woman; and James suddenly had the feeling they were staring into each other's eyes through the mist and murk and drizzling rain.

He remembered that moment later on, lying in bed next to Julia, but within minutes was fast asleep.

He became busier than ever, travelling on three successive days to the same client in Derby. Though he could have stayed at a hotel in the area, all expenses paid, he would have missed the driving.

He would also have missed seeing Julia. They were getting closer all the time, and he told himself that this relationship was for keeps. He was driving faster now, literally racing to get home at night. He took risks that worried even him at times, but always managed to win his duels with everything on the road, the most powerful BMWs and Porsches. Radar traps and police patrol cars held no fears for him.

He was in love, he decided happily one morning on his way to Swindon. Doubly contented, having just blasted three dawdlers out of his way in quick succession, he was about to put his foot down to celebrate when he spotted the familiar flashing lights ahead.

THE ONLOOKERS

It was the usual routine, traffic being funnelled into a single lane by strategically-placed police vehicles, and he was soon dawdling alongside the crash scene. It looked as if a motorbike had tangled with a transit van and come off worse. The biker was lying several yards from his machine, paramedics gently cradling the helmeted head. A policeman gesticulated at the passing cars to keep moving.

James took in none of this. His attention - his whole being - was focussed on a group of people standing close by. Although they were further from the body this time, as if the daylight had made them cautious, he could plainly see that their clothes were dirty and tattered, randomly patterned with streaks of red.

Yet their faces were blurred and indistinct, only the eyes registering on his dazed consciousness.

He realised the car had come to a standstill when the policeman appeared at his window and motioned violently with a gloved hand. If he pointed out the onlookers, James sensed, the other man would laugh in his face. Struggling to hold back a spasm of nausea, he pressed down on the accelerator as if it was the most fragile thing in the world.

He looked in the rear-view mirror as he moved slowly away and saw one of the group - it could have been a young woman - staring back at him.

He knew her gaze was scornful, even accusing. She suddenly raised one hand and pointed towards him; and then he accelerated hard, his own eyes blinking with shock and fear. Glancing back, he saw the figure return to contemplation of the accident victim along with her companions. He noticed a tattered white dress among the muddy browns and greys.

He didn't mention it to anyone in the days that followed. What could he say - I've seen a bunch of phantoms on the hard shoulder of the M4? Brilliant. Even Julia would think he was nuts.

Was he going mad? If so, it was happening in a very rational way. He could still hold normal conversations, still took an interest in the world and its affairs. Immediately after the motorbike incident, he'd driven straight to the client in Swindon and put in a full day's work, only occasionally having to force his banter with the people around him. He felt proud of that, it showed there was nothing wrong with his nerves.

But if he couldn't plead insanity, what then was happening to him?

Too many hours alone on the road, perhaps? Or was it the consequence of ambition and fatigue and overwork, the fallout from all the early starts and late finishes of his week? He had no idea if hallucinations were a symptom of stress,

THE ONLOOKERS

but understood that the human brain could take some weird twists and turns.

And yet, apart from the one problem, his life had never been so sweet.

The relationship with Julia was definitely an item; they'd even discussed getting married, for Christ's sake! He was doing well at work, too, his manager dropping broad hints about imminent promotion, a new job at headquarters. It would involve much less travelling, but James wasn't bothered by that. He felt he was growing up at last.

A few days after the motorbike incident, he asked for some time off. His manager looked surprised by the request - the problem had always been to get James to take his full quota of annual leave - but obviously felt unable to refuse even at short notice. They both understood that workers as valuable as James had to be indulged sometimes.

He spent his holiday with Julia and had never been so relaxed. They talked about marriage more and more often. One day, when they were driving to a local shopping centre to look at furniture, he noticed Julia glance across at him as he slowed down to allow an old couple to cross the road.

"A first time for everything," he joked.

Thinking it wouldn't worry him if he never saw another motorway, he told himself it had nothing to do with his recent scare, and made no attempt to analyse his feeling of relief when the anticipated promotion came through. The new job would start in a fortnight.

Meantime, he still had some business to finish off with a client in Nottingham. He astonished his manager once again, this time by asking him to authorise a hotel booking in the area, but the man was only too pleased to comply. James felt that he had radically changed in only a few short weeks, had become much less brash, a nicer person in lots of ways. Other people seemed to like him better now.

Julia didn't look surprised by his decision to stay in a hotel. She was obviously getting used to her new boyfriend.

"It's only for a few days," she reassured him.

And so James was on his way to Nottingham at the start of the last week in what he already thought of as his old job. He didn't care that the dashboard clock showed 8:15 and he was not yet halfway to his destination. It was a cold, bright morning in December and he was thinking, it would be hard to get much happier.

Over the weekend, Julia had casually dropped it into the conversation that she was expecting. He hadn't believed her at first, then jumped to his feet punching the air with both fists.

THE ONLOOKERS

"Of course," he'd said, when he was finally able to speak, "this means our wedding will have to come forward."

Julia had nodded mutely, stunned by his reaction.

When the car behind began to flash, he recognised the message at once and pulled over into the inside lane, watching a little enviously as the Mercedes E200 raced away. Then he shrugged and smiled. Expectant fathers shouldn't be travelling at that speed. He was deep in thought when he saw the cars ahead start to brake and then the warning signs and blue lights.

"Oh, my God," he said out loud.

He thought of shutting his eyes for the next few hundred yards, but that was plainly impractical. Averting his head, then? Even as he contemplated this, he knew he had no choice. He had to run the gauntlet. Police and firemen were battling to clear a way through the debris on the carriageway, and he could make out a party of rescuers attempting to pull someone from a smashed car straddling the central reservation.

Then he saw the onlookers. There seemed to be many more of them now. At the rear of the group - its only splash of colour - a gold helmet glinted in the wintry sunlight.

It felt as if his heart was about to burst out of his chest. He closed his eyes and gripped the steering wheel, fighting the urge to run away screaming through the nearby fields. After what seemed like hours, the traffic began to move again. In a stupor, the blood pounding through his brain, he engaged gear and followed the vehicle in front as they crawled towards the onlookers.

He strained to look straight ahead when the car passed within yards of the silent figures, but couldn't resist a glance in the side mirror. The same female, he was certain, staring back at him. He forced out a breath, surprised. Her eyes were different this time. Somehow he knew she was smiling! Unable to make out any of her other features, he was sure of it. Nearing a bend in the road, he looked back and was shocked to see the figure holding out its arms towards his car.

Then she was gone. They were all gone.

Five or six miles along the motorway, his pulse rate finally subsiding, James began to consider what he'd seen. He was amazed he could think straight at all and felt a resurgence of his old cockiness. It wasn't everyone who got smiled at by a female ghost!

But what did it mean? He was a reformed character, he knew. Had the smile acknowledged the genuine change in him? Was the final gesture - the outstretched arms - a sign of absolution, telling him he had nothing more to fear?

THE ONLOOKERS

Suddenly he was convinced that he would never again see the figures by the roadside, never in his lifetime. He thought of Julia and the baby to come and yelled out with relief and happiness. And so, imagining his state of bliss to be a state of grace, James Brandon died almost instantly when a speeding petrol tanker struck his car in a surprise patch of winter fog.

In the split second before he went over, James understood that he'd got it all wrong. The onlooker had been smiling out of sadness and pity. Her gesture was to welcome him.

PORN

Who would have believed it of Whitescales?

Typically middle-class, almost comically English, a man so anally retentive that he'd boasted of spending more than two hundred nights on his own in Amsterdam without setting foot in any of it's several red-light districts.

Who would have believed it?

Certainly not his friend Burnside, when Whitescales was caught with his pants down - literally - in their video training room after working hours, in the company of a young prostitute he'd smuggled into the building. He might have been planning to film the whole thing. Burnside would never have credited him with the imagination.

He still couldn't quite take it in, even after he was given Whitescales' job, the other man having been sacked within days of his misdemeanour. Even on the plane over to Amsterdam for the first of many visits to their Dutch subsidiary.

There'd been rumours that Whitescales was cracking up, pressure of work, too much travel, succumbing perhaps to the temptations of the mini-bar in lonely hotel rooms. He had separated from his wife only weeks before the training room incident. It was almost as if he wanted to be caught, to be put out of his misery.

Why else would he do such a crazy thing?

Not knowing how to get hold of Whitescales, he rang the man's wife after a decent interval, when he judged the embarrassment factor had dipped below danger levels.

Although she seemed equally shocked and puzzled about what had happened, he got the impression she was holding back a great deal. She referred to her husband in the past tense. He'd left the country, she told Burnside, and she had no idea where he was. Didn't care. Even the children had washed their hands of him.

Thoughts of his predecessor were driven from his mind as he adjusted to the frantic schedule of his new job, his week shared between London and Amsterdam, except for frequent visits to the firm's sub-offices in Milan and Dusseldorf. Meeting after meeting in whichever place he happened to be.

Exhausted most evenings, he began to appreciate why Whitescales had passed up on the pleasures of the night. He quickly established a routine - an early meal, a couple of drinks, then back to the hotel room with a stack of paperwork.

At least the hotel in Amsterdam was extremely comfortable, overlooking one of the city's more picturesque canals. Consisting of several large and adjoining houses knocked together internally, it was filled with narrow staircases and

PORN

winding passageways. No two of its hundred or more rooms looked the same.

He assumed that Whitescales had stayed in a great many of them, but one day the young desk clerk surprised him by asking, "Would you like to have Mr Whitescales' room next time, sir?"

"I don't why he liked room 113 so much," the clerk went on, "but recently he always asked to stay there. Sometimes he became angry when it was not available. I notice that it's free next week, if you want to keep up the tradition." There was a sly smile on the man's face that Burnside didn't like, but he went along with the joke.

As Burnside crossed the lobby the following week, he thought he caught a look of complicity pass between two of the receptionists and, without knowing why, decided to search room 113.

In a drawer, underneath some tourist information about the city, he came across a note printed on hotel stationery. It consisted of three words in shaky block capitals.

GOD HELP ME.

A silly game being played by the hotel staff, he decided, he'd have a quiet word with the manager about it. Still angry, he switched on the television.

It was tuned to a porn channel - a mass orgy around a swimming pool - and refused to respond when he attempted to change to another station. He disgustedly switched off the set and went to bed in a foul mood, determined to blow his top with the hotel people.

He dropped off to sleep with the briefly-glimpsed images running through his head; and shuddered awake hours later, believing for a split second that there was someone in the room with him.

The next morning, however, he felt more rested than he had for months, so relaxed that he decided not to pursue his complaint. That evening, ignoring her faint look of amusement, he enquired of a girl clerk if he could book room 113 again.

It happened every time he stayed in the room.

He would switch on the TV for a moment to see the same picture, several couples happily making love around a swimming pool, and then a disturbed night would be followed by a productive and stress-free day.

Away from Amsterdam, he wondered sometimes if he wasn't imagining the whole thing. Real enough, though, was his profound edginess after a night spent anywhere else in the hotel. He understood then why Whitescales had lost his cool, was himself tempted to shout at the hotel people when told he couldn't have the room.

One evening, having been out with colleagues and drunk more than usual, Burnside watched the film a little longer. Although he found it arousing at first - the jovial, almost bucolic activities at the pool - the scenes that followed took on a darker edge, the sex more brutal, the girls looking younger and less assured.

Switching off with distaste, he vowed not to ask for the room again. He came to in a sweat in the early hours, wrenched away from visions of writhing, naked bodies. As he struggled back to sleep, the sensation of not being alone seemed stronger than ever.

The next morning, however, feeling wonderful, he shelved his promise.

After that, in spurts of morbid curiosity, he viewed more and more of the film. Eventually, he stuck with it to the end. The final scenes were almost unbearable, genuine cruelty at work, flesh pummelled almost beyond endurance, screams that might have originated in hell.

Deeply upset, he slept for what seemed like minutes before waking with a start. It was on the television set, watching him. Even in the dark, he could make out the leer on its leathery face.

His familiar.

The thing made a threatening gesture when he opened his mouth to scream - and the rest of the night passed by in frightened silence, a wide-awake nightmare. In the morning, he tried to pretend the misshapen figure wasn't there, beadily peering at him from its TV perch, but somehow wasn't surprised, only disgusted, when it hopped onto his shoulder as he was about to leave the room.

From that moment on, the creature became his constant companion. Burnside finally got the message when it accompanied him through check-in for the first time, smiling malevolently into the faces of the unsuspecting airport staff.

There was no escape.

His relationship with his wife changed at once. Although he wanted to tell her about the familiar, enlist her help, the words would never come. Instead he found himself demanding sex, almost forcing her to submit to him. In the light of day, ashamed, he was barely able to look her in the face. He could tell she was worried about him, the difference in his behaviour, yet neither of them had ever been good at expressing their feelings.

Once or twice, seeing the bewilderment in her eyes, he almost blurted out the truth, but a warning glance from the creature invariably silenced him. It was always looking on, of course, while they made love.

PORN

Burnside didn't feel so good in the mornings any more, not even when he stayed in room 113. To blot out the familar, and himself, he began to drink heavily during his stays in Amsterdam. He routinely ended up in the main red-light district of the city, window-shopping until he'd made a selection. He would sometimes go with two or three prostitutes in an evening.

During the act, the familiar would be positioned close by, the pointed tongue working over its thick lips.

Inside a blue movie of his own making, he no longer felt the need to watch TV in room 113, preferring to pick up women in bars and take them back to the hotel. The old night porter, himself turned into a familar by the passing of many bribes, expressed lascivious admiration for his exploits. "You Englishmen are all the same," he called out once in the echoing lobby. "Very big lovers. Room 113 very good room!"

Looking in the mirror in the lift, Burnside was shocked to see the familar close its heavy eyelid in a wink.

He was just about managing to get by in his job, achieved only by toiling ever harder and staying even longer at his desk. It was of some consolation that work helped to muzzle the thing on his shoulder, postponed the inevitable nocturnal debauchery.

But things were getting worse. One lunchtime he was horrified to find himself downloading pornographic images from the internet. The hollowness was speading inside him, he knew, his thoughts forever turned in the one direction.

The familiar wore an almost permanent smirk by then, only showing its anger when Burnside revealed any yearning for his old life. Then it would give a basilisk stare and dig its sharp claws into his flesh. On the one occasion he contemplated suicide - the bottle of pills in the bathroom cabinet - it caused him almost to black out with the pain.

There was no escape.

His risk-taking increased, a spell of bringing women back to the house while his wife was at her bridge evenings. Until one of them threatened to call the police when he playfully slapped her too hard. He wondered afterwards if he'd reached rock-bottom, but had the uncomfortable feeling there was still a long way to fall.

Starting to trade on the internet, he swapped images with fellow collectors around the world. Sometimes he would come out of a website only seconds before a meeting or even as a colleague walked into the room.

It gave him a thrill for a while to hold telephone conversations with the female marketing director in Amsterdam, a prim Lutheran, while paging through what had became a considerable hardcore library. But the novelty soon wore off, replaced by the need for other sensations. And all the while the familiar was getting sleek and fat, weighed him down more heavily.

It still amazed him that no-one else could see the thing. He intercepted enough looks of bafflement and concern, however, an increasing wariness of body language, to indicate that some people were beginning to sense the presence of the creature.

As the familiar prospered, Burnside could feel his own strength ebbing away. He began to lose interest in the physical side of his addiction, growing less and less satisfied with the casual encounters and sessions of paid sex. Instead his mind teemed with morbid fantasies. He became a multiple rapist and serial killer in his thoughts.

When even his dreams turned blood-red, he insisted on sleeping in the guest bedroom. His wife was both troubled and relieved. The creature was pleased with him, he could tell, but he knew that it looked forward to his final humiliation and disgrace. Then it would have him to itself.

Under its guidance, he grew careless. When he accidentally e-mailed one of his images to a major business client, the ensuing security check soon uncovered the secrets of his PC. From that moment on, he lost any prospect of returning to a normal existence.

His wife threw him out, her family threatening him with legal action if he came near her again. In their last brief phone conversation, he had the impression she was relieved to be rid of him. His job had already gone. There seemed no choice but to follow the urgings of the familiar.

They went to Los Angeles first, where Burnside hoped to break into the adult film business as an independent producer. It turned out to be as glamorous as working in a supermarket, all the talk about shifting units of product.

The female actresses were another disappointment, with their bad language and bad complexions and obtrusive boob jobs. He felt betrayed somehow, and was grateful when his companion led him westward to the East. And now it was his home, this clearing in the jungles of southern Thailand, a place in which the only industry was sex.

His former life had become a dim memory in a brain turned to mush by alcohol and drugs. He felt like a ghost moving through a world of illusions, surrounded by women who seemed as ephemeral as tropical butterflies, whose submissiveness made them appear less like flesh and blood than the slaves of his dreams. It was gratifying to see how easily their smooth skin bruised.

PORN

He would go too far one of these days, he supposed, as the familar egged him on to ever greater violence. But the town was a lawless and transient spot, where people vanished all the time. And the dank forest reached almost to his door, a vast and uncharted burial ground.

There were other Europeans living in the town, similarly employed as pimps and touts for its numerous brothels and massage parlours. It was like seeing himself when he looked into their wasted features - and he sensed that some of them, too, had stayed in room 113.

He grew convinced that Whitescales was somewhere close by, in one of the several Sodoms that dotted the region. One day, when he was stronger and his headache had lifted, he would go on a grand tour. He might even come across other friends from the old days.

He knew the familiar wasn't suffering from the same loneliness. The way it flicked its wings, as if in greeting, when strangers passed by in the street. The occasional intimate glance the creature exchanged with thin air as he slouched alongside other wraith-like figures in the dingy bars of the town, drinking through the endless watches of the night.

A familar for each of them, it only seemed fair.

Wondering what would happen when he died, Burnside pictured his familiar flapping its cumbersome way across oceans and continents, back to room 113. It would become someone else's nightmare then, another man's evil star. As for him, he would co-operate with it in every way, do whatever the creature demanded, go to any extreme.

There was no other escape.

SYMPATHY FOR THE DEVIL

Hi, everyone. I'm Ron and I'm *baaaaad*.

I haven't always been like this. To tell the truth - and that's not a word I use often these days - I was something of a geek before my luck changed. Jaywalking was one of my more dangerous pursuits. To grab a crust, I felt obliged to live my life without any risk, soldiering away at a routine job with a computer software company in Redwood, California. But, deep down, I always thought of myself as a geek with big ideas.

Did I mention, by the way, that I now own the company?

Here's how I did it.

You know those games where the protagonist gets bigger and stronger and nastier as he ascends through the various levels? I wanted to end up like that, top dog. How exactly, though, does a wage slave get to break off his chains and put bread, lots of it, on the table? Straightforward criminality never appealed to me, you can get hurt robbing a bank. There had to be less risky ways to bite the hand that was patting me on the head for being a good boy.

Even when a trainee developer named Stephanie Beazle joined the company and showed signs of liking me, I couldn't work up too much enthusiasm. Though she seemed a little reserved for my taste, I got the impression of a warm glow under the cool exterior. A chick with potential. The trouble was I couldn't take my mind off my interrelated problems of being poor and not being rich.

So there I was, working late to finish off a trivial piece of work one evening. That sounds like typical geekish behaviour, I know, but it gave me the opportunity to do some exploring with no-one else in the building, seeking out any info that might give me an edge, like the password to our payroll system.

I signed onto a video-conferencing workstation to contact a fellow slave in our sister company in Seattle (incidentally, that also now belongs to me). However, it wasn't Dougie at the other end. I thought at first it was a new guy we had taken on and then realized the background scene wasn't familar either. The open-plan office had disappeared, replaced by what looked like a plush but old-fashioned study. There was even a log fire burning in an open grate.

I was thinking the connection had somehow been scrambled when the guy spoke in a resonant baritone voice. "Surprised to see me, Ron?" This was either the most amazing coincidence or something was out of kilter. Even as a nobody, I always favoured the laid-back approach. "Excuse me, but do I know you?"

He didn't answer that one. "Just call me Nicholas," he said. I studied him more closely. Bushy eyebrows and bushy hair and bushy grey beard, but with an expensive business suit draped over his portly frame. He looked savvy and mean, and I'd seen those eyes on every sharp operator I'd ever met. But with him it was real bad. Christ, I thought, Gordon Gecko in Jerry Garcia's body!

"What's this all about?" I asked, starting to warm to the man for no good reason. Maybe because he was bringing something different into my boring life.

"I'm here to do you a favour," he said. "Several favours, in fact."

I hid my rising interest in a geek's reply. "What makes you think I want your favours?"

He seemed very sure of himself. "Oh, you will, Ron, you will," he said silkily, stroking the shrubbery on his chin. I wondered about disconnecting at that point - the guy looked and sounded several bits short of a byte. But what, I argued with myself, if he was some eccentric sugar daddy handing out cash and God knew what else to anyone he came across in cyberspace. Why should I deny him the pleasure?

There was still a huge question mark over how we had gotten through to each other, but I decided to leave the technical issues for another day. Better to concentrate on what he was offering. After all, I wasn't going anywhere, in every sense of those words. I could tell he knew I'd made up my mind. Although he smiled in a way that didn't reassure me, his question lifted my hopes. "What do you want more than anything else, Ron?" This is it, I thought, this is where Daddy Warbucks hands over a million bucks to Little Orphan Ronnie.

However, I tried playing it like I had ice water in my veins. "Oh, peace on earth, an end to global warming, Michael Jackson for President, all the usual things."

"That's crap, Ron," he said. "What you want is what everyone else wants, the best for yourself." I had to stop myself from nodding in agreement.

He suddenly became very business-like. "Come on, Ron. Let's stop playing games. What you want is health, wealth and happiness for Number One, right?"

"The health part isn't so important," I said, in a last desperate attempt to sound cool.

I was disconcerted when he took me seriously. "That's good, because health isn't really our strong suit. Now wealth and happiness ...!"

He seemed to accept my silence as a signal to go on. "Let's just say I'm in a position to do you a lot of good, but you have to agree to go along with what I propose. Is it a deal?"

"What do I get from this deal?"

"You get three wishes."

"What do *you* get?"

"Oh, nothing much," he said, disarmingly. "You have to pay a simple forfeit, that's all."

"What kind of forfeit?" I asked, suspiciously.

"Just think of it as a Go To Jail card." Yet he was smiling as he said it.

You're probably thinking I should definitely have pulled the plug at that point. The guy was nuts for sure, and I was nuts for even listening to him. But what if his offer was for real? This could be the chance I've been looking for all my life, I told myself, my blood suddenly closer to boiling than freezing. Something in me, though, the last traces of geek perhaps, held me back. "Come on, Ron," he urged. "Don't be a geek all your life." Interesting choice of phrase. Was this guy a mind-reader or what?

"One little word and it's all yours."

Even as he said this, I was shocked to see the picture start to break up. His voice grew faint. "One little word, Ron."

Just before the screen finally went black, I shouted out, "But when will I see you again?"

The words seem to reach me down a very long corridor. "When you're ready, Ron, when you're ready."

I remained at my desk - thinking - for a long time after that. We all lead fantasy lives these days. Fantasy action on our screens, fantasy money in our pockets, fantasy women in our heads. Were my wildest dreams about to turn real? OK, he didn't look as I would have expected, you know, like in the old story books. But who was I to criticise someone's appearance, or even dress sense, sitting there in my old sweatshirt?

I gave some thought to the forfeit he'd talked about. It won't be so bad, I told myself, a little on the warm side to judge from the open fire, but probably no worse than Vegas on a bad day.

I could hardly wait for the next evening, even failing to respond when Stephanie, with an inviting little smile, stopped to chat as I stood by the water cooler. I won't pretend I wasn't flattered. She was a nice-looking chick in an insipid sort of way, more than good enough to grab my attention as a rule. But it felt as if I was no longer living by the rules. I had already volunteered to work late again.

When everyone else had gone, I signed onto the same workstation and hit the buttons for Dougie's number in Seattle. I held my breath for a moment, but somehow wasn't surprised when the shaggy figure appeared once more in the same mahogany-panelled room. The fire in the background seemed to be banked even higher.

"Yes," I said to the monitor screen.

I could tell he knew what was on my mind, which seemed kind of reassuring. But he only gave me another of his wolfish smiles. I smiled back.

"Good," my strange new acquaintance replied. "Now let's get down to business." He still looked like a pensioned-off hippy, with a sharp suit and attitude. Examining him, I had a stab of doubt, but then recalled the next-door neighbours in *Rosemary's Baby*. They hadn't looked the part either. His words, too, were soothing. "No need to be nervous, Ron. This is the first day of the rest of your life. And the sooner you make a wish ..."

His voice had become a sort of purr. Even if I wanted to - and I didn't - I had no choice but to go with the flow. Funny that, since it was something I'd been doing it all my life. But now at last, I decided, the tide was getting me somewhere. I took it easy, though. That way I wouldn't feel too foolish if I'd totally misread the signs and the guy was just a fruitcake. The wish was also a basic test of his credentials.

"I want Martin Carlson's job," I announced. "Ah, the senior developer." He'd passed that one with flags flying and bands playing.

Now Carlson was the fittest forty-year old I'd ever come across. He cycled ten miles to work every day, for Christ's sake. He'd been with the company for several years and showed no signs of wanting a move. Someone had joked that it would take a stick of dynamite to shift him.

All it took was a Ford pickup driven by a hungover farmhand, in fact, and Carlson's entry into the big time trial in the sky was posted the very next morning. I didn't feel any guilt. I'd only made a wish, after all, I hadn't pulled a gun on him or anything like that. I was appointed to his job two days later, chiefly because of my recent track record of working late. Ironic or what?

A bonus of the promotion - almost better than having my own cellular office - was the interest it aroused in some of the young office chicks. As I flirted with one nubile miss, the flush of jealousy on Stephanie's cheeks seemed to confirm my suspicion of the fire inside her. Since she looked more attractive with a scowl, I put her on my mental to-do list. With any luck, she'd soon be one in a *long* queue. My new friend was going to help out in that respect. But first things first.

He looked smug when I next contacted him, more than ever the ageing flower child, high on need and greed. "I trust any doubts have now been put to rest," he said.

119

SYMPATHY FOR THE DEVIL

"Never doubted you for moment," I replied, jauntily. We exchanged smirks. The D-word was on both our minds, I could tell, but if he wasn't going to mention it then neither was I.

"What is your wish this time?" he went on in his pompous but direct way.

Give the guy his due, he didn't waste any time on useless ceremonies like hullo and goodbye. Following his example, I came to the point. "I want to be rich."

"No problem," he replied.

As the picture vanished, I half-expected to see a bag of gold materialise on the desktop.

The next day I was sifting through a load of stuff in one of the cupboards in my new office when I came across a CD in a brown paper envelope addressed to the US subsidiary of a Japanese company, a main player in the computer games market. A letter in the same envelope explained that by my late colleague Martin Carlson was offering them a game he had invented.

As I scrutinized my find, Stephanie was making liquid eyes at me from across the room. I tried to ignore her - after all I'm the boss man now, I thought - but she kept glancing over. She was dogged, I gave her that. In the end I had to shut my door.

I loaded the disk onto my PC at home that night and gave the game the once-over. I realised its potential almost at once. A whole generation of nerds are growing out of *Doom* and yet retain an interest in fancy graphics and stupid electronic music and virtual mayhem and violence. It gives purpose to their lives, I suppose.

Carlson's game was designed to attract the older, more sophisticated nerd. The extra ingredient it offered was sex, what else? Not only was the main protagonist a gorgeous amazon, but many of her opponents were also drop-dead babes, growing outrageously pneumatic and shedding ever more clothes as the game went through its various levels. There were kinky little touches everywhere.

He may have been a programming genius with a shit-hot imagination, but Carlson was still a geek. He'd have received peanuts for his program, even if it went on to make millions. Instead, I took the software to a friend of mine, a salesman with a small but progressive company based near Frisco. He was as excited by it as I was and we decided to go into partnership to patent and market the game. He sold his house to help start up the business.

The rest is history. The game, with the name I'd given it of *Bullets and Bazooms*, was a killer from the off. Within months it was a best-seller on the West Coast and then across the States. We soon moved out of our one-room operation

SYMPATHY FOR THE DEVIL

into a palatial office suite, taking on a number of bright young designers and programmers to develop new products.

With my new-found wealth I was getting all the action I could handle, of the blonde, brunette and redhead variety. But Stephanie was still giving me the moo-cow look. I promised myself I'd get around to her eventually. I'm all heart.

I resigned my job when the business really started to take off, but not before I spoke to Nicholas one more time. As well as my final wish, I wanted to have a full and frank discussion with him. Get things out in the open, ask a question or two. After all, we were men of the world - or netherworld in my benefactor's case - and surely nothing he said was going to surprise me.

In fact, I was in for several shocks.

Although the blaze at his back was now stoked high enough to cast a sinister radiance across the room, I could tell right off he was in a good mood. "Hullo, Ron," he said, smiling. That was shock number one. "You'll be a millionaire inside six months." He was just voicing my own thoughts.

"Yeh, thanks."

"No need," he said, cheerily. "Tell me, what is your final wish?"

Now I had thought long and hard about that one. It was a toss-up between being irresistible to the opposite sex and another of my cravings. Money can buy me love, I'd finally decided. "I want to be the most powerful man on earth," I said.

"No problem."

This time the picture didn't disappear. As he continued to gaze benevolently out at me, I let rip with the first of my questions. "You're the Devil, aren't you?"

"The very same," he said, looking pleased with himself and stroking his beard until it curled into a point. In spite of myself, I couldn't suppress a little shiver.

"No need to worry, Ron," he reassured me. "I've received a bad press, that's all."

He was still smiling, so I tried the one that had been bothering me. "Why are you doing this? For me, I mean."

"Let's just say you've received a *good* press." Now that really threw me.

When he saw the look on my face, he said, "You see, Stephanie likes you. In fact, she likes you a lot. She's always singing your praises, but trouble is she's shy. Kept on at me until I said I'd speak to you. Underneath that prissiness she can be *mind-achingly* persistent." I just sat there stunned. "It's quite simple," he went on, patiently. "Stephanie is my daughter." As I digested his news, and wondered why I hadn't spotted the family resemblance, he carried on talking and told me that she had decided to leave home and take up temporary residence in California.

"Perhaps it was the closest she could find to hell on earth," I joked, weakly.

He laughed at that one, but then grew serious. "It would be nice to think of her going down there as some sort of payback for what the other side did all those years ago," he said, "but it's nothing of the kind. Do you know, she actually *likes* small, furry creatures." He shuddered briefly.

"Unfortunately, she hasn't got my nature," he continued. "She never liked it here, thinks all the people are trailer trash or worse." His voice dropped. "She was an accident, you know. Her mother was a Borgia girl, I think. It's never happened before or since."

He sounded sad and disappointed and looked every bit his age. Whatever the fuck that was. It's the only time I can recall feeling sorry for anyone but me.

There was a silence when he finished. "So how do you feel about things, Ron?"

I thought about them for a nanosecond. "Fine with me," I replied, making a vow to be extra-nice to Stephanie when I saw her next. I asked if he wanted me for anything else.

"Aren't you forgetting something?" he prodded gently.

"The forfeit," I remembered.

He nodded gravely. "No problem," I joked. "I look foward to meeting up with you when I die."

"Oh, you'll do that anyway, as a consequence of accepting my offer in the first place. No, the forfeit isn't your soul." My thoughts were dwelling uncomfortably on tortures that involved red-hot pincers, or perhaps pokers, when he said, "Your forfeit is to be with my daughter."

What could I say? I didn't want to upset the old boy, after everything he'd done. There was also the danger that the wrong answer would cause him to hurl a thunderbolt up my arse. Anyway, I told myself, she's not such a bad-looking chick. And surely, given her antecedents, she would have no objections to my playing around while we were seeing each other.

"Fine with me," I said. Nicholas grinned through his beard. "You know something? You could be the best thing that's ever happened to my girl." His next words were almost the most shocking part of our discussion. "She'll expect you to marry her, of course."

So much for living in sin.

There was one consolation. Some of the sexiest - albeit most wicked - women who have ever lived were waiting for me over on the other side. Who was that ancient chick who liked to party and killed off half the population of Rome? Yeah, Messalina. I put on my casual voice. "I imagine, um, anything goes down there. You know, sex-wise?"

"Oh, no, you'll be landed with Stephanie for all eternity," he said. Then he gave a sly grin. "Though I have to warn you it might seem *much* longer than that."

As it happens, Stephanie has been content to stay in the background while I have my fun. Just so long as I tell her now and again that I love her. However, I can see what her dad meant. There's nothing more wearing than a chick who likes people and, worse, thinks bunny rabbits are cute. At least she keeps out of my affairs (of every kind).

I plan, in fact, to have one hell of a time during the remainder of my stay down here. I've discovered all sorts of talents I never knew I had; they just required to be kick-started into life.

I bought my old company within twelve months of handing in my notice. I had to force the owner's hand, it's true. Some industrial spying here, computer viruses there, a spot of jiggery-pokery with share prices, and almost any company, no matter how big, can be brought to its knees. After much practice, I have the technique down pat. When gentler methods don't have the required effect, a little brute force can work wonders, so long as it's dressed up to look like an accident or act of God. Ironic or what?

I'm growing richer and more important with every day, every hour, every minute, that passes. Computers rule: yesterday America, today the world. Everything has been mine for several years now, ever since my partner and I had a falling out. Well, he did the falling to be exact, several thousand feet from a mountaintop. As always, I was somewhere else at the time.

It hasn't just been hard work. I've had a load of laughs along the way. For instance, there was our takeover of a major software house down in Mexico. The head honcho had been particularly obstinate until an incident involving a car, a hairpin bend and faulty brakes ended his resistance. His two young sons were in the vehicle with him. How we roared when I told my father-in-law that the owner's first name had been Jesus!

We talk all the time these days. I no longer have to call him up by computer, he's in my head whenever I want to chat. Since he uses the same method to shout at Stephanie, it's truly made me feel part of the family. I know I'm only related by marriage, but it means I have a whole lot to live down to. Rest assured that I'm doing my worst.

SYMPATHY FOR THE DEVIL

Being the richest businessman in the world is simply for starters. Not long now before my last wish comes true. I'm a shoo-in for the next presidential election.

I think Stephanie understands that what I'm doing is preparation for life over on the other side. Meantime, she stays at home and out of my business - and is no doubt at this moment planning what drapes she wants for the White House.

She's a sweet girl - all the more remarkable given her background - but can be surprisingly stubborn. I would like us to have a child together; and I'm sure nothing would give Nicholas more pleasure. I don't know why, but she seems reluctant. It's about the only time she looks like her father's child, a blaze in her eyes. I'll talk her around, though, because my powers of persuasion are getting stronger all the time. I'm even developing a purr like her old man's.

In fact, I'm getting to be more and more like Nicholas. I've even thought of growing a beard, would you believe? It reflects my admiration for him. In return, he shows me a great deal of affection.

There's no secret to our relationship. I'm the Son he never had.

THE EYE

Sam Schneider and his daughter Racquel were walking towards themselves when the idea came to him.

As they stopped to poke faces at their reflections in the mirrored pillar - they were in an upmarket clothing store in a downtown shopping mall - his thoughts fast-forwarded to the end of the month when Racquel, his youngest, was to marry her childhood sweetheart Ray Manassas.

The images of the occasion, he knew from past experience, would rush by and disappear, to be recalled only from a set of staged and sometimes strained poses in a picture album. That was unless ...

"I'm getting a video camera," he announced to Racquel.

Although the young salesman was courteous and obviously loved his work, Sam understood perhaps one word in three of his technical presentation. His wife Norma wasn't of much use either, being someone who could rustle up a three-course meal at a moment's notice and yet in need of brain surgery to be able to switch on a VCR.

Later on, though, Sam had reason to recall part of the sales pitch. "It's like having another eye to look out at the world," the young assistant had enthused. "A third eye."

"Or in my case, a fifth eye," Sam had replied, pointing to his glasses. Everyone had laughed.

They were relieved to escape from the store with their purchase. "The instructions will make more sense," Sam said, hopefully.

But about all he learned was that he now owned an 8mm camcorder with an 8:1 power zoom lens and electronic image stabilizer. Sam just pointed the contraption and hoped for the best.

His eldest son Sam Jr. called around the next day, however, and gave him a lesson in the basics of using the camera. After that, there was no stopping Sam - and his wife and daughter soon joked that they were being filmed more often than some movie stars.

By the weekend he felt confident enough to give the camcorder its first run outside the house, during their regular Saturday night visit to the Italian restaurant close to their home. They'd been going there for more years than they cared to remember, first with the children and now on their own.

The other patrons, most of whom were regulars, broke into laughter and applause when Sam took out the camcorder halfway through the meal. Fat and avuncular Tony, owner of the restaurant, was more than happy to caper and mug for the camera with his waiters. Sam was even taken into the kitchen to film the chef at work.

At one point, he was talked into handing over the camcorder to a waiter, who shot him and Norma exchanging toasts with the other customers. It was the first time he'd allowed himself to be filmed and, as he watched the replay on the tiny LCD screen, he thought it might also be the last. That stupid grin!

However, the evening ended in a happy riot, one of their best-ever meals in Tony's restaurant.

Which made it all the more of a shock when the place was ripped apart by a tornado only three days later.

It was a total freak, the weatherman on the local TV station said, leaving the buildings all around the restaurant almost untouched. Such extremely localised tornados were not unknown but very rare. Luckily, the twister struck shortly after the place had closed for the night and everyone had gone home; otherwise there could have been many fatalities.

That Saturday, knowing their father was at a loose end, Sam Jr. and his brother Carl organised a family outing to a travelling fair that had just come to town. Norma elected to stay at home to put the finishing touches to the wedding dress. Racquel, as usual, was out with Ray.

Sam took along his camcorder and proceeded to film his grandchildren in every conceivable posture of excitement and terror. He was eventually persuaded to try one of the less precipitous rollercoasters for himself. Carl took over the camera and perfectly captured his father's open-mouthed expression as the train hit the bottom of its steepest descent. Back at the house the younger children especially were amused by the incident and asked for it to be replayed several times.

On Tuesday morning there came news of a terrible accident at the fair the night before. One of the rides had collapsed, killing two young people and injuring several others. A faulty strut was thought to be the cause.

The local newspaper carried a photo of the crumpled rollercoaster, a metallic tangle that could have been a giant work of abstract art. Looking at the picture, Sam was distressed and yet thankful. His family had no doubt been on that particular ride; they had tried almost every attraction at the fair.

Suspecting it might even have been the ride on which he had so reluctantly travelled with his grandchildren, his sense of relief grew.

His daughter joined him at the breakfast table. She'd obviously been watching the TV news in her bedroom. "It's no good, dad," she said, "that camera has got to go."

Sam looked at her in surprise. "What do you mean?"

Racquel laughed. "I'm only kidding, dad."

Norma, who was stirring enough scrambled egg to feed a small army, spoke over her shoulder. "What she means, sweetheart, is that you use the camera twice outside this house and something nasty happens each time. Doesn't that make you wonder?"

"I hadn't thought of it like that. You don't believe ...?" Sam looked anxiously from wife to daughter.

Racquel smiled and touched his arm. "Dad, I repeat, we're kidding you." Behind his back, she shared a conspiratorial wink with her mother.

The two women seemed to forget about their joke almost before breakfast was over. Sam, on the other hand, retired to the small room he called his study and brooded for the rest of the morning. He was an easy target, he supposed, his whole family knowing that he hated mysteries or secrets or surprises of any kind. At the same time, he was intensely superstitious.

The more he thought about it, the more convinced he became that the camcorder - although, of course, not directly to blame for the recent misfortunes - was somehow unlucky. And weren't there such things as rogue machines? Appliances, even cars, that looked exactly like the others of their type, but were forever going wrong, constantly giving problems, as if they had a will and an evil intent of their own. What if the bad luck or maliciousness extended to events in the external world, beyond the actual workings of the machine?

This final thought made him wonder if he wasn't going crazy in his old age. Now he was semi-retired he had too much time on his hands, he decided, perhaps he should take up a hobby. But he *had* a new hobby, he remembered, his camcorder. Still, there was no harm in asking the store if they would swap it for another one. Just in case.

He journeyed into town with his wife and daughter, who had some last minute shopping to do with the wedding just a week away. They were surprised to see the camcorder case slung over his shoulder. He explained sheepishly that the camera had developed a slight fault and he was taking it back to the store for repair.

"I wondered why you haven't been using it these past few days," Racquel said. Her father made no reply.

After parking the car, they agreed to separate and meet up later for lunch in a popular Greek restaurant. The women strode off purposefully towards the main shopping strip while Sam made his way to the camera appliance store. He stood outside for several minutes, thinking about what he was going to say. Would you please swap this camera because I believe it's unlucky? He pictured the salesman's face, and suddenly it didn't seem like such a good idea. Turning around, he walked away from the store.

"So they fixed it then," Norma said, when she saw the camcorder. Sam only nodded.

Following the meal, they travelled to a car dealership on the edge of town. Sam was giving the young people a new Ford Contour as a wedding present. It was meant to be a surprise, but with Sam's dislike of secrets - keeping them as well as having them kept from him - the inevitable had happened.

Racquel's main concern was with the colour of the car. However, when a smitten young salesman offered to show her around an identical vehicle to the one on order and began to explain its various features, she stood by with a look of intense concentration on her pretty face. Her parents were entranced.

Norma nudged her husband. "Get the camera out quick," she whispered. "I want everyone to see this." Knowing it would be a waste of time to argue, Sam reluctantly did as he was told.

As so often the case when the camera was pointed in her direction, Racquel went into showgirl mode. She pretended to drape herself, pouting, over the hood of the car and then sashayed in front of the showroom's display window. A Japanese couple passing by outside stopped and pointed and then started to film her with their camcorder. Sam filmed them filming.

Ray came over in the evening. Sam liked the young man, not least because he shared his surname with a favourite rock band from the Seventies. Norma insisted on them watching the recording from the car showroom, but something strange happened when Racquel went into her on-screen routine.

As she commencing posing in front of the plate-glass window, a human shape appeared ghost-like at her shoulder. The image was very faint, its hands apparently held up to its face.

Then the camera zoomed in for a closeup and the apparition's grey hair and eye glasses became evident. "Sam, it's you," said Norma. Their laughter reached hysteria levels when the Japanese couple wandered into shot and the scene became ever more surreal.

The car showroom burned down the next day.

Police reports stated that a fire had been raging in a locked storeroom for several minutes before someone opened the door. That had caused a fireball to explode like a missile across the long, low-ceilinged room, destroying everything in its path. On a busy Sunday afternoon the casualty rate had been high, including many dead. Because the smoke detection system had failed to activate there was talk of criminal charges being brought against the people running the dealership.

Sam was shocked and frightened by the news. When he raised the subject with his wife and daughter, they agreed that, yes, it was very sad, and certainly mysterious, the way these disasters kept happening - but what could they do about it? Life had to go on. He could tell they were only half-concentrating on the conversation, their thoughts racing ahead with preparations for the wedding.

Racquel hoped the fire wouldn't hold up delivery of the new car; they were counting on it for the honeymoon. Not for the first time in his life, Sam wondered why intense personal happiness and almost pathological insensitivity so often went together.

He expressed his fears about the camcorder when Sam Jr. rang later in the day. His son, who shared Norma's more practical traits, tried to reassure him. "Coincidence, dad, that's all it is. I just read about a guy who's been struck by lightning eleven different times. What are the odds on that happening, uh?"

Sam wanted to argue that the guy was obviously doomed to ill-luck, just like his camera, but didn't pursue it.

In spite of himself, Sam got caught up in all the excitement and scurrying activity of the next few days. Norma made sure he was kept busy. There were even periods - sometimes as long as a couple of minutes - when he didn't think about the camera at all.

By Friday, he'd made up his mind what to do. "It's bust again," he told Norma. "I'm going to have to take it back after the wedding."

He was relieved when she paid almost no attention to his news. "That's good, dear," she murmured, as she supervised last-minute alterations to the pageboy costumes.

There was a crowd of friends and neighbours outside the house when Sam proudly escorted his daughter along the driveway to the wedding limousine. Cameras were being aimed at them from all sides. He noticed his son Carl with a camcorder.

After the church service, they posed for more pictures in the brilliant sunlight. As he and Norma stood alongside Ray's parents, he again spotted Carl with a video camera. "I didn't know Carl had one of those," he said to his wife.

"He doesn't," she replied. "It's ours. He says there's nothing wrong with it." She gave him a meaningful look.

THE EYE

The next few minutes seemed like an eternity to Sam, while everyone meandered to the cars waiting to take them to lunch at the local country club. He felt like screaming at them to run for their lives.

He'd taken the camcorder from Carl, but knew the damage had already been done. There was a definite pattern emerging. Three days later, then two, then one. Something bad was going to happen today, he knew it.

He was relieved to see the Reverend Beeney, a good friend of theirs, lock the church doors. There were no more services being held that day, no christenings or weddings. Or funerals. He shivered in spite of the heat.

At the country club he stashed the camcorder behind an ugly but convenient urn in a corner of the room. No-one noticed his camera was missing; hardly surprising since every other person in the place appeared to be snapping or filming everyone else. Somehow he got through his speech, half-expecting to be interrupted by a telephone call to say the church had fallen through a hole in the ground.

It was still there and intact, however, when they passed by on their way home.

Although many of the guests, including all their children, had elected to stay on at the country club, where the reception was being held in another, larger room, he and Norma had agreed they needed to rest before the evening's activities. She was asleep upstairs now while he stood outside the house in the lengthening shadows.

It would be dark soon and he had to wake her to get ready for the reception. But that could wait a minute, he had some more thinking to do.

He had sneaked the camcorder from behind the urn during the meal and gone to the rear of the building, where he'd deposited it in a trash can, covered over with mounds of spoiled food. He prayed the thing would soon be compacted and spread in a thousand pieces across a garbage dump.

In spite of what he'd done, he felt sure it wasn't over. But how and where would disaster strike this time? Convinced he was missing something, he went over the few certainties in the whole terrible business for perhaps the hundredth time. They could be included in a single sentence. The incidents always took place after the camera had been used on a Saturday in a public place.

Think, he urged himself.

It was then that the truth finally struck home, a jolt running the length of his body. There *was* something he'd overlooked all along, one other factor that linked the various tragedies.

THE EYE

Him.

Each time he'd been caught on video a disaster had followed. All of a sudden, he felt sure that everything else had been incidental, even accidental, the deaths and destruction for one reason only. Some malevolent force or demon or devil - something - was trying to get rid of him, had him in its sights. Its timing had been off so far, but the thing was improving.

It was catching up with him. Growing in intensity.

The camera had been an eye alright, a bloody evil eye. Why me? he wondered, then pushed away the self-pity. Better to concentrate on what was about to happen. What misfortune would it call down today?

The roar of an automobile engine cut in on his thoughts. He glanced across to see a car bump wildly across the sidewalk and then accelerate up the lawn towards him, its driver slumped over the wheel. Although Sam tried desperately to run, his body might have turned to stone. The dying sun illuminated the windshield and suddenly he could see his own reflection there. He looked very calm, appeared to be studying himself moving towards death.

He turned his head away at the last moment.

When he heard the car thud into a solid object with a terrible ripping of metal, and then smelled gasoline and scorched rubber, he looked back. Six feet away, the stoved-in front of the vehicle was embedded in the remains of the diseased and very large chestnut tree they'd chopped down the previous summer.

The police officer told them the elderly driver must have suffered a massive heart attack, jamming his foot on the gas pedal as he died. Only the tree stump had saved Sam's life, it was a miraculous escape.

Norma put a comforting arm around her husband while they talked to the patrolman. She had already phoned through to the country club to let the family know what had happened. Their two sons were coming over. Sam felt only intense relief, certain the thing had blown its last chance.

On the way back to the house, they paused to watch some cloud formations gathering high overhead; vistas of red and orange and rose-pink, eerily backlit by the last of the sun and shot through with sheet lightning. They recoiled at a sudden clap of thunder. As a car pulled up and their worried-looking sons climbed out, he recalled Sam Jr.'s words for some reason. Coincidence, dad, that's all it is.

The storm was approaching fast, sending out advance gusts of wind to tear at their clothes. It was turning cold and the clouds had become noisy and black. Sam felt sure he could smell sulphur in the air.

There's a big one headed this way, he thought.

TASTE

My friend Veronica was always noted for her style and taste.

An elegant size 12, she only ever wore clothes made in Paris or Milan, ate Belgian chocolate, drove German sports cars. Even Lawrence, her husband, looked as if he'd been designed by some supreme arbiter of male fashion, draped in silk shirts and pinstripe suits from the emporia of Saville Row.

They were a handsome if fleshy couple, well-known in the finest restaurants of several continents.

They lived in a penthouse apartment overlooking the river. It's rooms were huge and filled with light, ideal for showing off their fine furnishings and collection of artifacts from around the world: dining table and chairs from Harrods, carpets from Isfahan, bronze heads from West Africa. They were discerning shoppers, at home and abroad.

Lawrence made pots of money out of his stockbroker job from Monday to Friday, while Veronica worked hard to make their apartment even more beautiful.

At least once a week they hosted a glittering dinner party at home. They also liked to dine out with throngs of their intimate friends in the most fashionable eateries in the West End. I was often in their company on such occasions.

Veronica loved Lawrence, but Lawrence mostly loved himself.

There were constant rumours in our circle that he was being a naughty boy with any woman who would have him. Veronica began to confide in me, complaining about her husband, his coldness towards her. As she was doing so, she often devoured several Danish pastries to ease the pain.

Lawrence, too, seemed to be eating even more, perhaps out of a sense of guilt, or maybe to keep up the energy levels for his latest fling. They began to quarrel in public, but Veronica's exquisite manners always came to the rescue, sparing the other guests from embarrassment. She would usually make her excuses and leave the party or dinner table early.

More than one of their own soirees, however, went into terminal decline because of the obvious bad blood between them. She invariably rang me for sympathy later on, usually in tears, sometimes at two or three in the morning.

Everyone knew they were growing more and more unhappy together. Then Lawrence disappeared and the police found his clothes on the banks of the river just below the couple's penthouse apartment.

Perhaps the police suspected Victoria at first, but she had a cast-iron alibi. Also, the distress on her face must have told them that she'd sooner have worn rejects from a charity shop than murder her beloved husband. The inquest concluded that, for whatever reason, Lawrence had walked away from his beautiful life.

My shoulder after that was constantly wet from Veronica's bleating about her poor lost darling. She was devouring pastries by the bucket-load and had started to look almost obese. It seemed as if she was blowing things out of proportion in more ways than one.

I spoke with her for the last time this morning. She came to my apartment for a good cry and some cream cake. I'd had enough of her moaning, to be honest, plus my stocks were getting low.

So I killed her. Now she's really gone to pieces.

The best cuts of her are wrapped in grease-proof paper in my special freezer, together with the little that's left over of Lawrence. She shared in his liver at one of my dinner parties. I'll get rid of the unwanted remains later on, then go to the police to report her missing, a concerned friend. The river will take the blame, no doubt.

While I was chopping her up, I had the occasional nibble. Perhaps it was something to do with her eating habits in the past few months, but she had a rich, sweet flavour.

Then Veronica always had taste.

WAITING FOR THE MAN

Martin Collinson was tidying his son's grave when he first became aware of the figure standing quite still in the middle distance. Squinting through the murky February light, he was shocked and frightened at first, but then overjoyed.

"I *did* see him, Rosie," he insisted to his wife that evening.

She gave him a look of concern from her hospital bed. "You need to rest, love. There's been so much on your mind lately. What with me being here. And Michael ..." After her voice trailed away, there was a long and miserable silence between them.

When Martin returned to the lonely house, he was ready to accept that it had simply been an hallucination, born of depression and the yearning for something to turn out right in his life. He had his usual sensation of having been cheated. And yet, in the moments before he drifted into a restless sleep, he made up his mind to visit the grave again in the morning. Just in case.

The next day he wondered what he was doing there, trudging along the dreary avenue between the lines of skeletal trees and frozen mounds of earth. He was very nearly alone in the cemetery, felt completely on his own in the world.

He struggled against his desolation by recalling one of their good times - Michael's look of wonder, as a small boy, when they'd presented him with a giant Mickey Mouse in Florida. He smiled inwardly, but knew it would block out the pain for no longer than seconds. The brightest of memories makeshift against the horrors of his present.

Their one and only child killed by a car at the age of seventeen. Rosie inexorably slipping away in an intensive-care unit.

Waiting for something to happen at the graveside, he busied himself in a search for non-existent weeds. Half an hour passed by, seeming more like an eternity, and he had already admitted defeat - glad in one sense, he wasn't going mad at least - when he felt a prickle on the back of his neck.

He turned to see the motionless shape less than thirty yards away. This time there was no mistaking the set of the shoulders, the tilt of the blond head, a look almost of enquiry on his son's face. He stepped forward, his eyes flickering anxiously, but in that instant the apparition disappeared.

Martin was still on a high when he visited Rosie a few hours later, so pleased with his news that he almost forget his bitterness, nearly forgave all the couples walking hand-in-hand around the hospital, the parents with their children in tow.

WAITING FOR THE MAN

"I saw him again, Rosie," he burst out, almost before he'd sat down. She gave him a warning glance, lifting her chin towards the young nurse who was checking one of the machines that helped to keep her alive.

"I *did,*" he whispered fiercely, as the girl turned away with a smile.

Yes, love," Rosie sighed. She regarded him with fond exasperation. "Are you sure you're eating properly?"

"Don't worry about me," he said impatiently. "I know you think I'm going around the bend, but he was there. Large as life."

They burst out laughing together at his choice of words, and ended up by wiping the tears from each other's cheeks. "Oh, Martin," Rosie said at last, "I really wish I could believe you."

"He was there," he repeated, aching to transfer the strength of his feelings into her wasted flesh. Anything to make her feel better.

"Almost as if ..." He never finished the sentence, afraid the words might alarm her, his own nerves jangling at the enormity of what he would be saying. He couldn't help pondering them later on, though, as he made ready for another unsettled night.

Almost as if ... *he's waiting for you.*

He went back to the cemetery every day after that; the figure was always there, just standing and watching him. Waiting.

Rosie wanted to accept his excited ramblings, he could tell, but her common-sense kept getting in the way. She'd always been the practical one in the family, organising all of their lives with her battle cry of "Will you two stop dreaming and get on with it!".

One of their friends, a practicing psychiatrist, sought to comfort him by saying that the same pragmatic streak was coming to his wife's rescue now. No point in whining about something that was beyond her control. Rosie's sister put it more simply: "She's so brave."

Perhaps it would have seemed like another defeat to her, the collapse of her mind as well as her body. He could see it plainly on her face sometimes. *You're only trying to make me feel better.*

Away from the cemetery, he wondered himself if the whole thing wasn't just a cruel self-deception, his battered emotions creating a distortion of life in that place of death. But the doubts always vanished when he saw his boy again.

He longed to talk to the silent form, to say, "Your mum is being her usual stubborn self, son. But don't worry, I'll convince her in the end."

Somehow he could never get up the courage. Rosie would have had no such difficulty. He remembered how it had been after Michael's death; he'd been close to cracking up, until she bullied him back into the land of the living, as she put it.

Yet now her toughness was working against him. He had to win her over, though, because time was rushing away from both of them. She was growing steadily weaker. After they learned there was no more hope for his wife, that she was being allowed home to die in familiar surroundings, he finally found the strength to speak to the figure. "She's coming to join you, son," he called out, falteringly. "Look after her."

Was that a smile? He couldn't be certain in the dim light, blinking against his tears.

"He's waiting for you, Rosie." The words out in the open at last, he anticipated another of her wifely admonishments.

Instead she gazed up at him and said, "I believe you, love."

He wondered at first if she was just too tired to fight him any longer. Then he saw the flicker of hope on her face, joined to the usual sorrow and resignation, and understood that he'd won the most important victory of his life. They held each other without speaking for a long time. She died the same night.

During the church service, while the vicar praised Rosie's courage and unselfishness, Martin fought against his self pity - Why her? Why *me*? - by thinking of that moment, recalling the fragile anticipation in her eyes.

And yet there was no sign of Michael when they trooped to the graveside; and Martin wanted to shout out with disappointment, felt like throwing himself after the coffin as she was laid to rest alongside their son.

Then he spotted the lone figure standing outside the ring of mourners and had to struggle not to return the youthful grin. People commented afterwards how brave he'd been, moving serenely through the post-funeral rituals.

On his next visit to the cemetery there were only the two headstones, side by side. He wasn't surprised. It was the first of the rest of his days and hurt like hell, but he accepted that Rosie would want him to keep battling on. He had his health, perhaps half a lifetime ahead of him.

They would return when they were ready, when he was ready.

The truth had struck him while everyone was slowly making their way back to the cars after the ceremony, as he glanced towards the graves one last time. The sight of the woman and the boy together, arm in arm, watching him go. Waiting for him now.

COPYCAT

At school, Lodwig was always the leader and I trailed behind. He was hermetically self-contained even then, needing my adulation but little else, and so I expected never to see him again after his expulsion for a string of offences, the last of which was to strike a teacher. We ran into each other twice more after that, in fact, and each time the course of my life changed for the better.

I dread a third meeting.

I soon followed his youthful example at school, seeking to emulate his exploits, with acolytes of my own to impress. Finally, I pushed the same teacher to the floor and joined my erstwhile friend on the school's roll of dishonour. The whole episode was a pointer to the future.

I settled down after that period of schoolboy rebellion, finding myself a steady job in the Civil Service and a steady girlfriend. Although I struggle to remember her name now, I suppose I was contented enough with her and with life in general.

Until I met Lodwig again.

I immediately recognised the figure striding towards me one rainy November day, as I scurried from my office on the lunchtime sandwich run. He was brown and confident-looking and told me in a few laconic words that he'd just returned from backpacking around Asia.

I pressed him to join me in a pub and for the next couple of hours, while my workmates went hungry, he entertained and enthralled me with his stories of strange places and even stranger people. All the old triggers activated in my brain as I listened: admiration and envy and intense feelings of hero worship.

We parted with mutual declarations of friendship, genuine on my part at least, and promised to meet in the same pub the next evening. He never showed up. Yet nothing else stood a chance after that. I felt I had no choice but to see the same places, do the same things, to follow literally in his footsteps.

I became obsessed with travel maps and timetables and spent hours locked in my bedroom, planning the best way to get from Sumatra to the Northern Territory of Australia, while my girlfriend sulked in front of the TV. She finally gave me an ultimatum, settle down with her and forget my stupid ideas - or else.

The next week, I was on a cross-channel ferry with all my worldly goods strapped to my back.

I went everywhere that Lodwig said he'd been: the bazaars of Istanbul and the fetid alleyways of Calcutta, sweltering in third class on the long train journey down the spine of the Malay Peninsula, gaping at the upswept wings of the Sydney

Opera House. I joined an ashram in Pune for food and lodging and washed dishes in Perth, but never stayed anywhere for long.

In the end, almost punch-drunk with my experiences and feeling at last that I had done as much as my mentor, I wrote to my parents asking for the money to get home.

Having traversed the world from Rome to Rotorua and stirred a minimum of feminine interest, except of the fee-demanding variety, it seemed like fate when I met Julianne on the last leg of the journey.

It wasn't the most romantic of meetings, sharing a sick bag in a force 6 gale in the English Channel, but we arranged to see each other afterwards, and unlike Lodwig, she kept her promise. We made love the same night and were married six months later.

Although we were - still are - extremely happy together, it was hard settling back into a routine; and it didn't help that Julianne soon found a permanent secretarial post, while I had to be content with a series of ill-paid bar jobs.

I was beginning to think my future lay entirely in cleaning sick from lavatory walls when Lodwig entered my life again. It was only for a couple of hours, but that was long enough.

He came into the Cheapside pub where I was providing temporary cover, looking fit and bronzed - every time I saw him it seemed as if he'd just walked off a tropical beach - and accompanied by a group of noisy friends. To judge from the expensive clothes and the fancy cocktails everyone was drinking, his travelling days were long gone, unless the journey involved business class air fares and five star hotels.

He didn't pause for breath on seeing me, picking up the threads of the conversation as if our last meeting had been a matter of weeks rather than years.

To my disappointment, he showed no interest in exchanging reminiscences about Bali, but instead talked happily about the money he made as a futures trader. I was flattered that he stayed behind after his friends went on somewhere else.

When he eventually made his excuses to leave, though, there wasn't even any pretence of wanting to see me again. As he went off without a backward glance, it felt strangely as if something of me was going with him.

Once again, however, I was snapped out of my lethargy, felt compelled to do something about my life. By an odd coincidence - and I remember wondering at the time if they really were chance, my encounters with Lodwig - Julianne heard from an acquaintance that a firm of City brokers were taking on staff. It was a company that Lodwig had recently left, where he claimed to have made vast profits for the directors and shareholders. I wrote for an interview, giving his name as a reference, and not long afterwards they offered me a junior position for a probationary period.

Now I'm a partner in the same company. We live with our two small children in a town house in South Kensington. I drive a brand-new Mercedes and Julianne has her distinctive blood-red Porsche. She remains the love of my life.

And still I can't shake off the feeling that Lodwig is lurking around the corner.

Surprisingly enough, given the fact that the City is a village, albeit a large one, I had no contact of any kind with him after I went to work there. For a time, I longed to bump into him on one of the black-tie occasions so beloved of the stockbroking community, to tell him of the skiiing holiday in Vail and how my eldest boy has been put down for one of the best preparatory schools in London. In the hope they were things he hadn't already done.

Above all, I wanted to take back the missing part of myself. To look him in the face as an equal at last, no longer a follower.

Somehow our paths never crossed. But there were frequent references to him in the broadsheet newspapers and financial websites on the internet, usually to confirm he was moving ever upwards on the business totem pole. He even made a couple of television appearances as a City spokesperson. I wasn't happy after that until I had my say about the economy on the BBC breakfast news.

Once, I thought I saw him crossing the street and hurried to catch up, only to lose him as the midday crowd was disgorged from the Bank of England. Now I would run as fast as I could in the opposite direction.

I don't ever want to meet Lodwig again.

Actually, there's small chance of seeing him at the moment, not unless he escapes from prison. He's been there for almost four years now, ever since his conviction for murdering his wife. It was a love match apparently, until he found out she was cheating on him. Then he stabbed her through the heart with a kitchen knife.

His last media appearances were the reports of the trial, Lodwig being sentenced to seven years, a light punishment even when taking into account the provocation offered by his wife's behaviour and his defence that her death had simply been a tragic mistake. Perhaps the judge owed him a favour. Nothing about Lodwig would surprise me.

He's taking up more of my thoughts as his release draws nearer. With time off for good behaviour, that can't be far away.

COPYCAT

Recent events have sharpened my musings, given them focus, and against my will I occasionally catch myself wondering what he would do in my position. And that really frightens me. Because I can't risk being influenced by him again, knowing that nowadays there's only one thing in my life I'd like to change.

Ever since the night I saw Julianne's Porsche parked outside my best friend's house and the suspicion first formed that she's being unfaithful to me.

Because even now, rich and successful as I am, the sensation persists that part of me of me is still owned by Lodwig, the same part he's always owned, ever since I was a fresh-faced schoolkid shadowing him, wanting to be like him.

Wanting to *be* him.

The other night I dreamed that Julianne was dead and woke in a sweat, imagining Lodwig to be in the room with us. The love of my life. No, I can't risk it.

At least we have enough money to start a new life, somewhere suitably distant. Australia might be the answer, and I've suggested we make a permanent move there, doing something completely different, perhaps running a nice family hotel away from the fleshpots of Sydney.

In spite of coming from that part of the world, Julianne is less than keen on the idea - I hope it's not for the reason I'm thinking. But I have to convince her. I sense my life depends on it. And hers.

In my blackest moments, I wonder if I'll ever escape from Lodwig, whatever I do, wherever I go. That even in Australia he'll walk in off the street one day, as if by accident, and ask for a room, exchanging pleasantries, wryly reminiscing about his time in jail, before just as casually going on his way.

Leaving the nightmare to begin for real.

GOLDEN BROWN

I keep telling Farley he has it made. He lives, after all, in a place where the sun shines the whole time, doing possibly the easiest job in the world, and able to indulge his favourite hobby to the full.

But all he wants is out.

We share an apartment. And while I slave at my job in Cleopatra's Court, one of the newest and biggest gambling hells on the Strip, with a towel around my waist and a smaller one on my head, Farley potters along to the local TV station three times a day, every day, and tells the viewing public that it's going to be, is, was another hot one. Then he goes home and signs onto the internet.

Seems like the barometer of Farley's existence is as steady as a rock, even though he's surrounded by people who are experiencing every kind of high and low in a city that's swept from end to end by illusion and disillusion, a world centre of emotional turbulence.

Appearances can be deceptive, however. He craves excitement alright, just of a different kind. The monotony of his job is the problem.

Not that he wants to make it as a barman or croupier or become a minister of religion and join together out-of-towners in a mock-up of the Sistine Chapel. No, you have to understand that Farley is one of the few people living in the desert town who isn't here under false pretences - "Oh, I actually own several gold mines, I drive a cab for *fun*" - he wants to get out to get on, to advance in his chosen career.

Above all, he wants some action. He dreams of forecasting real weather.

"They have fantastic climate patterns over in Europe," he once told me, a dreamy smile on his face. "Well-defined changes of season and enough extremes to keep anyone happy. Floods in Germany. Avalanches in the French Alps. Gale-force winds around the North Sea. Wonderful!"

It's funny, but the guy never looks more blissful than when he's rattling off a string of natural disasters.

He doesn't deny that women are part of the attraction. "Somehow they have more depth than the girls in this part of the world," he says in his solemn way. "Same as the weather." And that's where the internet comes in.

Although he tells me it's mainly to keep in touch with developments in his profession, studying research papers, seeking out job opportunities, and so on, I know for a fact that he spends a lot of his time just chatting with young ladies. He claims to be a killer flirt in cyberspace. I thought he was joshing me, though, when he said he'd made a romantic connection online.

GOLDEN BROWN

It was only when he started out for the airport that I realised he was serious. Seemed like the chick came from somewhere in Central Europe. Farley had been bombarding her with electronic flattery for months, working his way up to a request for free board and lodging in Transylvania or wherever she came from. But the girl had beaten him to the punch.

"Invited herself over for a holiday," he said, looking sheepish. Then he brightened. "But my turn next." And then: "Boy, I hope she's good-looking!"

Turned out that he hadn't even asked to see her picture. He was either a real cool dude or the most desperate guy I've ever met. I tried telling him not to raise his hopes, that she would probably be as ugly as the weather in Transylvania, the human equivalent of lashing rain and ice-cold winds. But I could tell he wasn't listening.

I feared the worst when I got back from the casino that evening. She was there alright, sitting on the couch next to my roommate, whose smile was finishing up somewhere behind his ears.

He was right to look pleased, I had to admit. Alright, she would never win a beauty pageant, her eyes were too close together and her legs a little short for that, but she had shining dark hair and pert breasts and a nice smile. Farley had done OK for someone whose courting had been carried out by e-mail.

She spoke good English too - although I could see her struggling to understand when Farley asked about average rainfall levels in her country. I wondered at that moment if they had any real future together.

While Farley was in the kitchen making coffee, she told me she'd always wanted to live in America; and I got the impression she wasn't planning to return to Europe in a hurry, if at all. Farley came back into the room humming the Blue Danube. I sensed then there were storms ahead.

Natasha quickly made herself at home. I was relieved that she seemed to get on well with Farley. Somehow he became a less intense person in her company, even began to laugh at himself when she made fun of his never-ending questions about the climate of *Mitteleuropa.*

"But I love the weather here in Vegas," she told him. "No fog, no snow. It is perfect!"

She spent many hours tanning herself on the roof of the apartment. Farley joined her there only occasionally - for someone whose business is the great outdoors, he seems remarkably averse to experiencing it up close.

"The sun gives me a headache," he explained apologetically when Natasha pointed this out to him.

GOLDEN BROWN

One time, she talked us into spending the day at a water park - and I couldn't help observing the contrast in my companions as we wandered around the different slides. Natasha with her honey-coloured body and my roommate looking like someone who'd spent the whole of his existence under grey skies. They'd only be happy together if they swapped continents, I decided, with the faultless logic of my Irish forebears.

So it concerned me that Farley had fallen for her. She liked him, too, but more in the way of being a friend. She shared his bed and I knew they made love - hey, the walls are thin in Vegas apartments - but there were few signs that she regarded him as anything more than the nocturnal equivalent of a thrill ride at a water park.

Farley, on the other hand, was like a small pooch that had found someone to rub up against every moment of the day.

His work suffered, as did his social life - Christ, the traffic in his favourite chat rooms on the Net must have halved after he met Natasha - but I realised it was true romance when he agreed to take her dancing.

Let's just say the club scene isn't Farley's natural habitat. The one and only time we'd hit a nightspot together, he stumbled into and overturned a table of expensive drinks, got himself threatened by a long-haired pretty boy he short-sightedly asked to dance, and suffered a massive nosebleed. All in the space of ten chaotic and very sweaty minutes. There are twisters that have made less impact in that time.

The next day, they weren't speaking over breakfast. Feeling pleased because I hadn't had to make a trip to the hospital or the local jail during the night, I attempted to lighten the mood. "The club still in one piece?" I asked my friend cheerfully.

Although it wasn't the subtlest of openings, I've found the blunt approach works best with introverts like Farley.

Unusually sullen, he tried to ignore me, but wandering around in public in a skirt can make you pretty thick-skinned. "So what happened?" I persisted, imagining that he'd fallen flat on his face on the dance floor or set fire to himself or something, the reason why Natasha sat there looking as if she'd prefer to put her melon slice up his arse than in her mouth.

"Ask her," was all Farley said, folding his skinny pale arms. But Natasha just shrugged and wandered up to the roof with her towel.

Things were more friendly that evening. A long stint of tanning always put Natasha in a good mood. I've never known anyone get more pleasure out of the

GOLDEN BROWN

sun, like she was trying to make up for twenty-four years of cold, hard winters in a few weeks. She had already gone from vanilla through butterscotch to a rich toffee colour.

There was a glow under the sheen of her skin, too, as if her insides were enjoying the change of scene as much as the rest of her.

Farley had made the first move of reconciliation, of course, a puppy dog can only hold itself back for so long.

"He brought me candy," Natasha told me with a smile afterwards. While Farley spent time with his computer - the new addiction not completely replacing the old - she confided to me that she liked him a lot but thought their relationship was becoming too serious. I said I agreed. This seemed to encourage Natasha and she leaned forward, showing a lot of brown cleavage.

"Sometimes I wish he was more ... how do you say ... more like a real American."

For a moment, I flattered myself it was a pass, but soon realised she was just talking in general terms. She, too, couldn't help drawing comparisons, this time between her boyfriend and all the hunks strutting their Venice Beach muscles along the Strip.

Seemed that Natasha had a fancy for body-builders, thought they were the only true representatives of the American race. People like me were almost but not quite there, ultimately just a European with an accent and a suntan. Farley partially missed out even on that score.

It was her obvious interest in some of the other male dancers that had sparked off a row at the club the night before. But now all was forgiven, Farley practically romping around her feet for the rest of the evening. There was no missing the gleam in Natasha's eyes, however, whenever a big, good-looking guy appeared on TV.

The storm clouds, I felt, were gathering overhead.

Natasha had been with us for a month when Farley started to talk about meeting her parents. I think it was a genuine attempt to formalise their relationship - in his innocence, he probably pictured a wedding in a pine grove with toasts in spiced vodka and gypsy violinists playing afterwards - but also a first move towards his ambition of leaving Vegas for a world of rollercoaster atmospheric conditions.

It was no surprise to me that Natasha showed zero enthusiasm for the idea. "But I like it here, honey," she pouted. She was beginning to sound as well as look

144

the part, bronzed to the point of reflecting back the sunlight, brimming with health, looking as good to eat as a basted turkey.

She grew angry when Farley kept on about going back with her to Europe. The inner effulgence I'd already noticed became more obvious at such moments, as if some sort of volcano was smouldering away inside her.

The eruption wasn't long in coming. It was bad enough that my friend didn't look American - but not wanting to *be* American. Natasha could never forgive him for that. When she finally exploded, it must have been heard at the Grand Canyon. Farley was upset enough to come to Cleopatra's Court to tell me, almost weeping, that Natasha had moved out. It was probably the first time he'd been in there or any other casino. Hell, he might not even have realised until then that Vegas is a gambling town.

When I got back that evening, he was in his room and I could hear the clicking of the computer keyboard. The Net, an ever-present solace in times of trouble.

He never referred to his ex-girlfriend again. I was secretly pleased, no longer worried I might have to find a new roommate, still bearing a grudge against Natasha for implying that I wasn't a true-blue Yank.

Because I didn't want to rake up the past, I never mentioned it to Farley when I saw her one more time, driving past as she strolled along the sidewalk with her new beau, a side of beef in singlet and cut-off shorts, the statutory brush of greasy blond hair reaching almost halfway down his back.

It was mid-afternoon, a time when all right-thinking people in the desert town have long since found air-conditioned heaven, and the pair of them looked as hot as hell.

Natasha had turned a deep charcoal; and I remember thinking her sun-broiled skin could have been used to toast bread.

Farley was back in the groove by then, a little work, a lot of "research" on the internet. He'd taken the break-up hard for a time, making no reference to a spell of weather in the Alps so atrocious it had even reached American TV screens, the sort of climatic aberration that normally has him wetting himself with excitement.

I knew things were on the mend, however, when he enthused to me about a blizzard that had hit the Low Countries. Reeling off a list of similar disasters in the past twenty years, he looked happy for the first time in an age.

Now he's racing along the information superhighway again, even tells me he's found a new girl over in Europe. Seeing the look on my face, he said, "Don't worry. I checked this one out good. She hates hot weather and flying. My perfect woman!" He must be confident of getting across there; he's asked for an extended holiday from the TV station.

I wish him well. I'll soon be on my way, too, to the City of Angels. Oh, didn't I mention that I'm really an actor, just resting up in Vegas for a while?

There's one farewell present I won't be giving him, any mention of a bizarre little piece in the local rag about a deeply-tanned young woman who suddenly burst into flames and burned to a crisp in a downtown supermarket. Some speculation that it was a rare case of spontaneous combustion.

There was a follow-up story a few days later, saying how strange it was that no-one had come forward to identify the woman. Not if she was an illegal immigrant and didn't really know anyone, I thought.

It would be unfair to share my suspicions with Farley, not when he's about to set off for his Brave Old World. The last thing he needs is that sort of baggage, a painful reminder of his track record. And perhaps, this time, his luck really has changed.

I wouldn't mind betting, though, that one part of Europe is in for the *mother* of a heatwave ...

MOBILE

Jane Dublin stood back to admire the Company logo shimmering in primary colours on her kitchen table. Her brand-new PC. She was tempted to call up her sister Christine on the other plaything.

Not brand-new, she remembered from that afternoon's conversation.

Jane was a single mother, a status arising from the death of her husband Stephen more than twelve months earlier. Her employers, a medium-sized Cambridge-based insurance firm, had recently introduced a scheme to enable staff to work from home. It was intended to benefit anyone considered still worth employing, but unable or unwilling to get to the office on a daily basis.

Jane had immediately placed her name on the waiting list. An experienced claims assessor, she qualified on all counts.

Her son Jonathan came in from the garden followed by Blackie, the cat owned by the elderly spinster who lived next door. Blackie was decrepit and balding - just like his mistress, Jane sometimes unkindly thought - and smelled powerfully of the many tuna meals he had consumed in his lifetime. Nevertheless, she felt a kind of exasperated affection for the animal and always gave him a saucer of milk when, all too frequently, he wandered into the house. She busied herself doing that now.

Jonathan was eight years old and very proud of his mother. None of his friends' mums knew anything about computers. He picked up the mobile phone. "What's this for?" he asked.

"Put that down," she said. "It's not a toy." She turned away to hide her smile after she said it, thinking of her own excitement a few minutes earlier.

"They gave me that so I can stay in contact with people in the office even when my PC is linked to the mainframe at work," she explained. Jonathan nodded sagely, as if he understood exactly what she meant. A child of the computer age, she thought.

Jonathan went away to watch television in the front room. Blackie had already finished his milk and disappeared, leaving behind traces of his body odour.

She switched off and unplugged the PC, thinking that she'd move it into the box room after supper. Although small, the room would be a good working environment. It was filled with light on sunny days and, importantly, contained a telephone jack point to enable her PC to be connected to the mainframe database at headquarters.

That it was Stephen's old study somehow comforted her and made her think this new venture would be a success. She started to repeat the mantra of the homeworker: "Self-discipline, self-discipline, self-discipline."

MOBILE

Still chanting, she picked up the phone and was about to put it to one side when she noticed its lighted display panel. Jonathan must have switched it on by accident. She was surprised to see a message scrolling across the tiny screen, <<<YOU HAVE A DIVERTED CALL>>>. She consulted the reference manual and pressed a button.

There was a blast of electronic jumble from the earpiece and she hurriedly held the mobile away from her. She could just make out a tiny voice submerged in the waves of static. The man - about the only thing she was sure of - could have been calling from the moon. The noise ended abruptly.

She stared thoughtfully at the silent phone. The signal must have strengthened towards the end because she'd caught a couple of scratchy phrases.

"Sandie, for God's sake ... must see you." Even through the stew of interference, the pain and desperation had been obvious. She recalled what she'd been told that afternoon.

She had gone along to Human Resources to sign for the receipt of the PC and mobile. "I hope the phone brings you better luck than the last person we loaned it to," the young woman in HR had told her. She must have looked alarmed because the girl had laughed and said, "Don't worry, it's not as bad as all that. It used to belong to Sandra Chalmers, remember her?"

Jane had nodded, having known her by sight, even been faintly jealous of the woman's unsubtle and yet striking good looks. Because she worked for Sales and Marketing, out on the road most of the time, Sandra Chalmers had made only infrequent appearances at headquarters. When she did, it was evident that she was very well liked, especially by her male co-workers.

Owing to her popularity, there had been a great deal of gossip when she suddenly handed in her notice. There were rumours about her involvement with some man or other - she was obviously very good at keeping secrets because nobody seemed to know the identity of her lover - and it was known that she and her husband had sold up and left the area shortly after her resignation.

At the conclusion of their business, Jane had ventured a weak joke with the woman from HR. "A mobile for someone who's not going to be very mobile," she'd said.

The other's answer showed that Sandra Chalmers was still on her mind. "Better than being too mobile, like some people."

Jane was thinking, Sandra. Sandie. Extra-marital affairs. Strange, passionate phone calls. The lives some people lead. Feeling a little sorry for herself, she got on with preparing the evening meal.

MOBILE

It was only later, when she was watching TV after Jonathan had gone to sleep, that the call struck her as odd in another way. It had certainly been made since her meeting with the woman from HR. No diverted messages had shown up when they'd switched on the phone to ensure it was working.

Yet Sandra Chalmers had resigned and handed back the phone more than six weeks previously.

The caller - this man who was so frantic to speak to her - obviously didn't know that. Where had he been all this time? Where was he now? Still running the possibilities through her mind, she went up to bed.

Jane settled into a routine in the days that followed. To school with Jonathan in the mornings, then three to four hours' work on the PC. A light snack for lunch, sandwiches or a salad, and another two or three hours of work before picking him up. It was predictable but satisfying, and she soon decided that she'd made the right choice.

She went to headquarters once a week to attend briefings with the rest of the team and to discuss any problems and plan her forthcoming work schedule with her boss. She looked forward to those outings. Discussing business on the phone was all very well, but it was nice to see people face-to-face occasionally.

Her use of the mobile phone was limited, calling the office perhaps a half dozen times a day, usually to clarify some point relating to the case currently displayed on her PC screen.

Incoming calls were even less frequent. Which was why she was surprised to hear the machine's distinctive bleat when she opened the front door after one of her visits to headquarters. Not least because she thought she'd switched it off before leaving the house that morning.

The voice had a metallic edge to it, but was stronger now through the surrounding din. "Is that you, Sandie?" Jane couldn't think of a suitable reply. She could hear his panic return. "Please, Sandie, this is Tony."

She had to speak. Feeling very foolish, she said, "I'm afraid this isn't Sandie, I mean Sandra. She's left the company."

Only static for several seconds. Then the voice again, sounding young and confused. "I - I don't understand. Where's she gone?"

She suddenly felt very sorry for him. "I wish I could help you, but I really have no idea where she is."

"You mean she's left me?" Although it was difficult to be sure with that awful noise breaking against the earpiece, she suspected the man was crying. She, too, felt on the point of tears. Stupid, stupid, she told herself, for someone you don't even know.

His next words astonished her. "You seem like a very kind lady. I hope you don't mind me saying so."

She was flustered, but managed to say, "No, not at all."

He seemed resigned now. "I knew she'd go off me. Which is why ... never mind. I'm sure I'm boring you. I'm sorry."

He sounded so lost and alone, she wanted to throw her arms about him.

The interference abating, he sounded much closer all of a sudden. "It's been nice talking to you. I feel better now. Would you mind if I phoned again?"

Somehow Jane had been expecting the question and said, "No, please do." Wondering at the intensity in her own voice.

"Goodbye then."

"Goodbye, I hope we get a better connection next ..." She broke off when the words came echoing back to her.

Although she would never have admitted it, not even to herself, the phone call made Jane feel like a different person. She realised what she'd been missing since Stephen's death. The attentions of a man.

Never mind the unfortunate circumstances and the fact he was a total stranger, someone she had never met and was never likely to meet. She didn't care about any of those things. He'd brought some drama into her life and she found that she couldn't stop smiling.

Jonathan thought his mum greater than ever. Blackie was given double helpings of milk now when he called around. She kept the mobile switched on all the time, even when she wasn't working on the PC.

It was over a week before she heard from him again.

She was suffering from a cold and had already reported in to the office to say she wouldn't be doing any work that day. Feeling listless and bored, she kept glancing at the mobile resting on the arm of her chair. Even so, she was shocked when it started to ring. Steady on, she told herself, it's only someone calling back from the office.

But she knew it wasn't.

"How are you?" The connection *was* much improved, the radiophonic splutterings reduced to a more acceptable level. It no longer seemed as if he was speaking from the far side of the moon or the depths of an ocean. The rust had almost disappeared from his voice; he even sounded quite cheerful.

She felt better already. "I'm fine, thanks." She remembered he didn't even know her name. "I'm Jane, by the way."

"Hullo, Jane. I'm Tony. Tony Truro. Silly name, isn't it?"

"That's a coincidence," she said. "My surname is a town as well."

"Don't tell me, Oxford?"

She laughed, decided he was definitely getting over Sandra. "No, Dublin."

"You'd be easy to find in the phone book then, just like me. You're a local girl, Jane?"

"Lived in Cambridge all my life," she replied, recalling that Sandra Chalmers had talked with a South London whine.

He sounded very young again. "I'm sorry about last time, but I know I'm getting over it. My problem, you see, is that I grow too attached to people. I find it hard to let go ..."

His next words were lost in a sudden upsurge of background noise.

She was afraid the signal would be broken and that she'd never hear from him again. "Hullo?" she repeated several times, starting to panic. She was relieved to hear him speak again, but much fainter now.

"I have to go, Jane," he said, "but I want to meet you. I'm sure you're very beautiful."

Jane, who knew herself to be motherly-looking, plump and a wearer of unflattering glasses, said nothing. An overwhelming screech cut into his next words. "I promise I'll ..."

The violent and inconclusive ending to their conversation unsettled her; and she found it difficult to sleep that night. Due in the office next day for a team briefing, she was determined to make it in spite of her worsening cold.

It was time she took the initiative.

Sandra Chalmers had cultivated a special female companion at work, one Tracey Wilkinson, who was younger and much less confident than her friend. On Sandra's occasional visits to headquarters, they had always lunched in the staff restaurant, heads together, whispering and giggling. Men colleagues had gathered kudos just for being at the same table.

Jane had gained the impression there wasn't much the two women kept from each other.

After the briefing, she went to Tracey Wilkinson's office on the second floor. The girl was alone apart from an office junior, moodily entering statistics into an electronic spreadsheet. As he wandered off in search of coffee and excitement, Tracey looked at her.

"Can I help you?" Her accent was a mongrel blend of Cambridge and South London. Her friend's influence, no doubt.

Jane knew the odds were extremely long. After all, not one word of rumour had reached her - or anyone else, so far as she knew - concerning the identity of Sandra Chalmer's boyfriend. Perhaps Tracey wasn't such a confidante after all. But she took a deep breath and said, "I know all about Sandra Chalmers and Tony Truro."

The straightforward approach worked. She could see the girl was too staggered to put up any sort of defence.

"H-h-how do you know about that?" Tracey stammered. "I never told anyone. Sandie will kill me, she hates people knowing her business." She looked so frightened that Jane wondered what hold Sandra Chalmers had over the young woman.

She tried another question, wanting to confirm her suspicions. "She broke it off because of the age difference, didn't she?"

Tracey, still in shock, nodded dumbly. "Sandie's not as young as she lets on," she mumbled. Her face indicated that this revelation was the final betrayal.

And now for the million dollar question, Jane thought. "And you know where Tony is, don't you?"

She was astonished when Tracey started to cry. "I know, I know," she sobbed. "But it wasn't all Sandie's fault. He was only a kid. I could tell he was taking it too seriously, he was that type. I told her, but she wouldn't listen." For the first time, Jane noticed the strain on her pretty features.

The young woman was staring back at her. "But how do you know about Tony?" she said. "No-one here knows, except me."

Jane debated whether to tell her the truth. No, the girl would think she was a sad case, searching for a man because he'd accidently phoned her a couple of times! "I need to see Tony," she said.

Tracey gaped at her, horrified. "You must be mad! They'll never find his body after all this time!"

The secret was out now and she couldn't stop talking. "How was Sandie supposed to know he'd drown himself? Just because she finished with him. That's why she left here after it happened, she can't bear people knowing ..."

Her words were no longer registering. It was as if the lights were going out in Jane's brain, one by one, and then she began to fall, her glasses sliding down her nose. The last thing she saw before she blacked out was the puzzled look in Tracey's wide-open blue eyes.

MOBILE

She was alone at home a week later, Jonathan having gone to the pictures with Christine and his cousins, a long-promised treat. Christine had begged her to go with them, but Jane still felt unable to leave the house. Reluctantly, her sister had gone off with the kids.

The day after her faint in the office, Jane had returned the mobile phone by registered post, together with a letter of resignation. Her boss had called around to the house, but left shortly afterwards, mystified, cradling the PC in his arms while promising that her job would be left open in case she changed her mind.

Jane now sat staring blankly at the book she held in her hands, strange thoughts racing around her head.

One image in particular: a watery figure trudging across the fields of East Anglia, towards the city, towards her.

Stupid, she told herself, the poor devil was rotting in the North Sea, he wasn't going anywhere. Anyway, he was a very modern ghost. At the very least, he'd come in a phantom car. She only stopped laughing when she recognised a rising note of hysteria.

The same thoughts, the same words, over and again. *I grow too attached to people. I want to meet you. Easy to find in the phone book.* A modern ghost indeed. She glanced at the directories stacked beside the telephone in the hall. No, I'm not looking to see how many there are, she told herself, it would mean I *am* going mad.

It was dark outside when she went into the kitchen to get a glass of water. As she stood at the sink, there was the sound of scratching at the back door. Jane remained very still, but the noise continued, growing steadily louder. Then a strong whiff of fish reached her through the partly open window. She hoped it was Blackie, come for some milk.

But she knew it wasn't.

153

HELL

It's not nice being stuck between four walls. Sometimes I think, this is what Hell must be like. But I try not to dwell on it. Won't be long, I tell myself, before I'm out of here.

I have a theory about bed-sitting rooms, that they have a time limit. A stay-by date. It varies, but ten years is absolutely the max. By then you're a terminal case, on your way to the scrap heap or the funny farm. I'm worried the rot is setting in early in my case. I swear this room is getting smaller.

I visit the local pub to get away from my thoughts. A lot of the flotsam and jetsam from the house are regulars. Old Henderson sits in the corner on his own, never speaking to anyone, except for the occasional remark to himself. He scares me, not least because I have visions of becoming like him.

I usually chat with my best friend from the house, Peter Doromo, who serves behind the bar. He's different from most of the others, confident and full of life. He makes it plain that he isn't going to be around for long. Moving on up, as the song says.

He makes fun of our fellow-lodgers behind their backs, giving them derisive nicknames. The maddo saddo, he calls Henderson. I laugh along with him, but can't help thinking, only a couple more years to go.

I try to avoid old Henderson, just about managing a "hullo" when I encounter him slouching towards me, hunched against the cold even in the middle of summer, mumbling into his dirty grey beard. He must be the loneliest person in the world. Never gets a letter, never makes or takes a phone call. A study in social isolation.

Yep, we're each in our own little hell.

I sometimes suspect all the people who live here are either damned or deranged. Or soon will be. Old Henderson, for one, appears to be clinging onto reality by his blackened fingernails. I wonder if he's done something in a previous life to deserve this. I wonder if I have.

Peter doesn't believe in any kind of religion. He still mocks me for letting on that I flirted with Oriental spiritualism in my teens. He's taken to calling me Buddha. It's all in good fun, though.

There's a stir of excitement in the house at last. Her name is Cassy and she's down on the second floor, in the room next to old Henderson. Probably can't believe her luck. All the no-hopers have been sniffing around, but only Peter has had the guts to ask her over to the pub. He's going to be my role model when I get out of here.

HELL

Cassy is pretty - for this place anyway. We chat at the bar while Peter is busy serving people. I think she likes me. But that makes me even more depressed. I can't help remembering how long it is since I last had a girl-friend. I don't stand a chance against Peter anyway; he already acts as if the two of them are an item.

It's a Saturday night and the house is silent, as if no-one else is here. Peter has taken Cassy out for the first time, to the movies. I'm too down even to fancy a beer, but the sensation that the walls are closing in finally drives me out.

I exchange words with a few of the regulars and then notice old Henderson, on his own as usual. Peter has recently changed his nickname, rather mysteriously referring to him as Stan. He won't say why, obviously a private joke.

For a moment, I feel a pang of sympathy for the old man, even think about sitting down with him. Then he shoots me a look, the evil eye, and I shake my head in alarm and disgust. Perhaps I really am going mad.

I meet Peter on the stairs. He's full of himself, leering at me when I ask how the date went. However, I notice there are scratches down one side of his face. And Cassy no longer comes to the pub.

I've just had a shock, a pleasant one for a change. Cassy is in my room, explaining why she hasn't been for a drink lately. Seems that Peter was less than the perfect gentleman on their night out. Tried it on, in fact.

There's a gap in the conversation after that. Eventually, to fill the silence as much as anything else, I ask if she'd like to go for a meal or something. I'm conscious of my cheeks burning as I stumble over the words, but astonishingly Cassy accepts my offer. It feels as if she's turned up in the nick of time. Even the room has stopped shrinking.

Peter has taken the news well. After our third date I decided that I really ought to tell him about me and Cassy. I get up the courage in the pub after an unaccustomed stint on the whisky.

"No problem, Buddha," he reassures me. As I'm throwing up in the filthy toilet afterwards, I feel a sort of love for my friend.

I'd like me and Cassy to move in together, a nice flat somewhere. Heaven or hell, it should be no contest.

And yet I can't bring myself to ask her. It's fear of change, I suppose, the unknown. But there's another reason. Peter has hinted that Cassy is seeing someone else behind my back. I tell him that's nonsense, the only person she's seeing more of than me is old Henderson.

To my mind, it's the one flaw in her. She fusses over the man as if he's her father or something, always popping across the passageway to see how he is. More than once I've been on the point of speaking out. Even in my head, though, it doesn't sound brave or make sense. He scares me, Cassy.

She says she feels sorry for him.

I'm talking to Peter in the pub. Old Henderson is in his usual corner, with his usual sour face. Peter asks if I've ever wondered about "Stan the Man", as he puts it. I don't know what to say. "Don't you think he looks like a Stan?" he asks. Now I'm even more confused. Peter just laughs.

Peter was right. It seems there *is* someone else. He's some sort of hippy, a drug user, who lives in a squat across town. Cassy explains that she's moving there to look after him. She says she's sorry for giving me the wrong idea.

She says she felt sorry for me.

I'm glad she's gone, otherwise I might have done something bad to her. I could tell she was upset when I wouldn't even say goodbye. She should count herself lucky.

I'm spending more and more time in the pub, anything to get out of my room, the walls closing in again. Peter supplies me with free tots of whisky; I'm even getting a taste for the stuff. In fact, I'm changing in lots of ways. More than anything right now I want to punish someone, hurt them. Just to get my own back.

One night, as we're staggering back to the house, Peter lets me in on a secret. His face is a yellow mask under the street lamp, not the slightest trace of a smile. I wonder for a moment if he's gone mad, or I have. Or both of us.

He tells me that he believes old Henderson is the Devil's representative on Earth, recruiting for his master. It's only a joke, of course, but he says it with such a straight face! He's constantly urging me to be careful of old Henderson, to the point where I can no longer look the man in the face. Peter has changed his nickname again, re-arranging the letters.

Now he's Satan.

Even though she's made me hate her, I defend Cassy. She couldn't have been one of the old man's recruits, I argue, too kind for her own good. A stupid bitch, yes, but she would never hurt anyone. Peter gives me a look. All at once there are doubts in my head.

But I have so many questions! Peter answers them non-committally with an easy smile. He won't tell me how he knows about old Henderson, just asks me to trust him. As he says the words, I notice a red light in his eyes. Then it's gone.

Peter's theory is playing on my mind. It seems to confirm that my first instincts about the old man were right. Catching the acrid whiff of his shabby overcoat as I edge past him in the street one day, I find myself wondering if that's how sulphur smells.

The doubts are in my head. In fact, they're taking over.

Peter says we have to do something, before he corrupts anyone else. The pieces are falling into place. Peter says it's why he doesn't get any mail or phones calls, being able to communicate with his boss in other ways.

When he urges me to look at the old man in the pub, I watch him with growing horror out of the corner of my eye. Mumbling, a pause, more mumbling, just as if he's holding a conversation. "See, Buddha," my friend hisses.

Peter says I have to do something about the old man.

I sense that things are coming to a head. My head, Peter's words running over and again in there. When I shudder awake in the mornings, it feels as if I can touch both walls without extending my arms.

Things *have* come to a head. Someone has moved into Cassy's old room, a young woman. Peter tells me it's not a coincidence. He says I have to act with speed. I find myself in the hardware store down the road.

Peter explains it's the only way I can escape from the house. "Won't be long," he reassures me, sliding another double across the counter, "before you leave here for good." The strange glow is back in his eyes, for seconds, as if a fire has flared up inside him.

He's my only friend in the world. I want to be like him.

Old Henderson's smell seems to be everywhere in the house, even my food tastes of him. It's as if I've turned into a cannibal. I stop eating. I saw them both going out the other morning. She held the door open for Satan and smiled. I worry that she's already been contaminated.

I spend my days in my room now, listening out for their noises from below. The place has become so small that I can get to the door in one step if I have to. I don't even go to the pub any more. Peter smuggles out bottles of whisky for me.

Peter confirms that it's too late to save her. He says they'll both have to face the music. I show him the axe I've bought. "That's sharp," he says with approval. Because my hands tremble so much, it's become his habit to button up my shirt. He does that now. "One last time," he jokes. He's my friend.

"Remember, it's your only escape," he reminds me, as he stands in the doorway. The light in the passage throws his shadow against the wall. It looks huge, misshapen. The red glint is in his eyes again.

After he goes, I sit on my bed and test the edge of the blade with my thumb.

HELL

There are noises from downstairs. They're both in, Peter told me. The smell is growing stronger, seeping under the door. I have to keep myself from retching. It's the stench of evil alright. This place is definitely the ante-room to Hell.

Thoughts of Satan and the girl and revenge fill my skull. I'll go down and see to them in a minute.

SHOPPING

Gerald regretted volunteering his services more than ever when a thick mist descended on the motorway.

He slowed the car to a crawl and switched on its headlights. The murkiness ahead became solid, a grey wall, and he had the uncomfortable feeling it was pressing hard against the windscreen. Threatening to buckle the glass inwards.

He wondered why he'd done it, agreed to take her on this shopping trip. He normally hated going to such places, huge sheds on the edge of nowhere, packed to the rafters with people whose idea of fun was to become footsore while looking at things they usually had no intention of buying.

Wendy, of course, thought they were heaven.

Over the years she had visited just about every major out-of-town shopping complex within a hundred miles of their home with her friend Ruth. Now Ruth was dead, many years of thirty cigarettes a day having caught up with her.

Although he suspected Wendy's sense of loss was mainly to do with being deprived of a chauffeur - she had never learned to drive - he felt sorry for his wife and said he would take her the next time she wanted to go on a shopping expedition. Hoping it wouldn't be for weeks if not months, not until she had gotten over Ruth's death.

Instead she'd pointed to an advert in the newspaper and said, "There's a new place that's just opened up - the biggest in the country, it says here." When she started making plans for the coming Saturday, Gerald had his customary trapped feeling.

As the fog continued to obstruct their progress, his thoughts turned from Ruth to his father, also now dead. He couldn't seem to shake off his memories of the old man. Funny that, seeing they'd just about lost contact down the years. Even when his father had moved into sheltered housing just a few miles away, Gerald had hardly ever visited. Too busy with one thing and another.

Wendy had ignored the old man completely, never talked about him, apparently never even thought about him. Only on his death, when they learned he was worth a little money, had she shown any interest.

Then she had conducted an undignified and protracted legal squabble with Gerald's elderly aunt; most of the money, inevitably, had ended up going to their respective lawyers. Gerald, feeling guilty and ashamed throughout, had stood aside from the battle and said nothing.

He heard Wendy gasp and shook himself out of his reverie. There was a lorry right behind them, much too close, its fog lights burning into the rear view mirror. Blinded for a moment, he looked down at the speedometer, which revealed they had dropped below twenty miles an hour, dangerously slow even in bad weather.

When the boom of a klaxon horn added its own note of menace to the few feet of clammy air between the two vehicles, Gerald, never the surest of drivers, could feel himself slipping out of control.

He wrenched on the steering wheel - better to slam into the protective barrier at the side of the road than to be crushed beneath a juggernaut - and then, as if by a miracle, they found themselves careering up a slip road and away from danger. Even the fog had cleared, replaced by a misty drizzle.

He drove automatically, still in shock, looking for somewhere to stop the car while he recovered his composure.

"Over there," Wendy said.

He saw a large building in front of them. It was surrounded by a great expanse of tarmac and, turning off the main road, he steered with exaggerated care into a parking space.

Sirens sounded from the direction of the motorway as they slowly got out of the vehicle. "What is this place?" he asked, but knew the answer when he saw the look in Wendy's eyes. She was obviously feeling better already.

"It's a shopping mall," she said, in the tone of voice some people might use on first seeing Chartres Cathedral.

"But where are we?" Gerald complained. "Nowhere near where we're going, that's for sure."

"It doesn't matter," Wendy chided him. "We could have a quick look around here while we wait for the fog to clear." As he trailed behind her, he knew that she actually meant they'd be there for the rest of the day.

The parking lot was huge and they seemed to walk forever through its numerous zones. Although the place was unusually full of cars for the time of morning, they saw no-one else during their trek.

As the mall got nearer, Gerald was impressed in spite of himself by its enormous size. They had to walk for several more minutes around the building before reaching the front entrance. He was surprised that there looked to be no other way in, not even a side door or loading bay.

A coach was disembarking its complement of elderly passengers when they reached the entrance.

The sight of all the rinsed hairdos and plastic macs lowered his spirits still further; but it was of some comfort that the pensioners appeared to be feeling as miserable as him about the coming experience, trudging in a moody crocodile towards the sliding doors. The weather was enough to get anyone down, he decided.

The entrance foyer was surprisingly small, totally out of scale with the rest of the building, and filled to bursting point. At least people had cheered up now they were indoors. Even the old folk had found their voices, presumably animated by the prospect of all the retail therapy that lay ahead.

After much pushing and shoving, they finally squeezed through the ridiculously inadequate inner doorway into a broad avenue lined on either side with shop fronts. This was also thronged with people, but seemed almost deserted after the crush they had just left.

Gerald tracked his wife as she began to window-gaze.

It must have been years since he'd been in one of these places, he thought, but things hadn't improved much in all that time. Although the shops themselves seemed prosperous and well-stocked, the lighting everywhere would have been more suited to an underground car park, harsh and fluorescent.

There'd been no attempt made to soften the effect by deflection or concealment - had they never heard of false ceilings? Even their local supermarket could do better.

As a result of the over-illumination, the passers-by all looked as if they had a prison pallor. His own ashen features stared back at him from a shop window, crow's feet turned into fissures.

Almost the worst thing was the way the glare reflected off the plastic-coated posters that littered much of the plate-glass.

These were many and various, advertising reductions and special offers, and in some places covered almost the entire window. They were all tricked out in the most hideous and clashing of primary colours - green on red was a particularly favoured combination - and began to hurt his eyes after a while.

It was funny that no-one else appeared to mind these inconveniences. Small groups were chattering among themselves, comparing prices, pointing out especially good buys, oohing and haaing over the bargain bins that stood outside many of the stores.

After a while, though, he noticed a few individuals with preoccupied expressions and had the feeling that, like him, they were thinking - what am I doing in this place? Wendy certainly wasn't one of them. He followed her into a department store, which was stacked from floor to ceiling with expensive-looking clothes of every kind. She was muttering appreciatively over a cashmere jumper when he caught up with her.

SHOPPING

"I'm hungry," he complained. She didn't even look up. Rather than argue, he said, "There's bound to be a food court somewhere here. I'll see if I can find it."

He left her cooing to herself as she rifled through a rack of silk blouses.

Wandering down one garishly-lit avenue after another, glancing into various shops where people pushed by each other without ever establishing eye contact, it struck him that he had yet to observe anyone making a purchase. For that matter, there were no sales assistants anywhere to be seen. And no window dressers. No security guards. They couldn't all be at lunch, surely? And where was there to eat in this place anyway?

It felt as if he'd been walking for hours and yet he hadn't come across a food outlet of any sort, not even a cubicle selling cookies or icecream.

He was becoming tired and would have welcomed a seat, even the kind of uncomfortable bench normally found in any shopping mall. Usually in the central area serving as the focal point of the complex, the spot where all the indoor streets came together. But first he would have to find the heart of this particular building.

Gerald realised he was lost when he entered a street that appeared exactly like the one along which he'd just traipsed. He had the feeling he was going around in circles.

The place was a giant maze, its geography a mystery to him. How was he ever going to find Wendy again? And where was the way out? He couldn't remember seeing an Exit sign anywhere on his travels.

He continued to walk - there was apparently no other choice - and then saw his father going into a bookshop.

He was doing that all the time these days, seeing his father. In the street, in shops, once on a train. It couldn't be his father, of course. His father was dead. The trouble was, he had decided, all elderly men looked the same with their silver hair and apologetic body language. He passed the bookshop without a sideways glance.

He rode an escalator down to the next floor. More excessively illuminated corridors that appeared to go on for ever, lined with what could have been the same clothes shops and gift stores.

There was a definite sense of being subterranean here, but even at ground level there hadn't been any windows. Surely the newer malls were designed with atriums and glass roofs, so that people could at least see the sky?

In spite of the look of the shops, their luxurious fittings and glossy displays, the place generally had an old-fashioned feel. He guessed it had been around for some time.

SHOPPING

The crowds were thicker at this level and seemed to be shopping - or rather browsing - with an even greater intensity. He saw two women squabbling over an item of clothing, both of them practically screaming with rage; strangely, they were doing this without even looking at each other.

He still hadn't seen anyone make a purchase.

Gerald's feet were already hurting him, a huge blister on one toe, and now a pain was coiling around his forehead, making it difficult to think. He felt it was important to think. Something was wrong here, he knew. But he kept on walking.

People all around him were chattering away and for the first time he noticed that many appeared to be talking to themselves.

He passed one old lady, her face drained of colour, who was looking through her purse and remonstrating bitterly with no-one in particular. Perhaps it was his headache, but he could make no sense of her fretful accusations.

He began to eavesdrop on other conversations - monologues - and soon realised they were all the same. The words emerging as an angry and unintelligible mess. Everyone gabbling away to themselves. No-one communicating.

He suddenly felt disorientated, afraid. It was as if he'd crash-landed onto a strange planet, with people talking in a hundred, a thousand, different alien languages. Attempting to quicken his stride, he cannoned off the oncoming shoppers until their weight of numbers compelled him to a stumbling, wheezing halt. No-one paid him any attention.

He forced himself to calm down when he found himself on an escalator descending to the next level. At least his own mind was still in working order. The others might be mad, but he was OK.

Two thoughts were uppermost: I'm in danger and I have to get out of here. But first he had to find some way of going back up. Telling himself not to lose concentration, he pushed his way forward.

He was in a shop examining a rack of slippers. Wondering for a moment what he was doing there, he thought it must have been to get away from the crowds. It was worse even than on the upper floors, people crammed together in the passageways, flowing in great competing tides, looking, touching, squabbling. But never buying.

He thought he'd seen his wife - what *was* her name? - as he looked around frantically from what had become almost a stampede. She was in a boutique, holding a dress against her body and prattling into a mirror, but there was no way he could get to her.

SHOPPING

He realised he hadn't seen or heard anyone laugh since entering the mall. How long ago was that? Days? Weeks? By now, every face seemed to be tired and drawn, unsmiling, painted a deathly hue by the merciless luminescence. And still they shopped on.

When he caught himself jabbering unintelligibly at the brocaded slipper he held in his hand, he dropped it with a gasp of horror. He mustn't lose concentration, he mustn't! It was his only chance.

He forced his way back into the swarm and eventually found a passageway that was, perhaps, less crowded than the others. It was getting harder and harder to think rationally, but he understood that his marrage had been a sort of preparation for all this. To his consternation, he began to sing a crazy little song, its lyric consisting of the one word.

Trapped. Trapped. Trapped.

He was joined by someone else, another man, who stood gazing into the same shop window. Somehow Gerald understood that he would never again be able to look directly at another person - only objects, goods, things - but for a fraction of a second their eyes touched in the glass.

He knew at once what the stranger was thinking.

The same notion came to him on the escalator to a still deeper level, where everything and everyone was bathed in an even more ghastly light. It was true, he thought mournfully, as a hubbub of quelerous voices rose to meet him.

Shopping *was* hell.

HELPING HAND

Everybody is given one chance of real happiness, Colin thought bleakly, and his had come and gone. He wondered where Sally was at that moment, while he sat on the edge of the bridge in the cold night air. The water looked inky and sluggish beneath his dangling feet. It seemed a long way down.

He still couldn't believe it. They were made for each other, everyone had said so. Even her mother, who always hated him, had seemed to be coming around to a reluctant acceptance of their relationship.

The woman was a witch. She had tried everything to break them up, pouring poison into her daughter's ear at every opportunity. He'd often wondered how his sweet-tempered Sal could have emerged from such a nasty old crone. But, together, they'd beaten her.

And right at that moment, when he thought things couldn't get any better, Sally had walked out on him. She'd smashed his world to pieces. Never mind, she would soon have cause to regret her actions. When the police turned up at her door - wherever that was - with their news and their questions. Do you have any idea why he did it?

She would understand what he'd been through then, with people staring at her afterwards, whispering behind her back. There she is, she drove that poor man to his death ...

And yet it could have been so different, if only she'd explained how she really felt.

"We'll get married one of these days, Sal," he remembered telling her.

"I believe you," she'd replied, laughing. "It's not easy, I know, for someone who takes ten minutes to make up his mind about what tie to wear."

"It's only a piece of paper, after all," he used to say, teasing her. "Just being with you is enough for me."

He'd always assumed that Sally felt the same.

As the temperature continued to drop, he pulled up his jacket collar and then laughed out loud. Wouldn't have to worry about the cold where he was going. He studied the river, imagined his body floating in the dark.

There was the shuffle of feet from behind him.

The shock of it almost sent him tumbling into the void, having to grab frantically at the clammy ironwork to stay upright. After he regained his balance, his heart still pounding, Colin took a timid sideways look at the other person. He could only make out a shadow, standing beyond the range of the dim street lamp. But who was this on the bridge at two o'clock in the morning?

HELPING HAND

Someone else, perhaps, with death on their mind. Suicide. Or was that *murder*?

As he started to tremble, the figure spoke. "Is anything the matter?"

The voice was mild, sounded worried, and Colin breathed out with relief. Then he remembered what he was doing there. "Please go away," he said, trying to summon up some aggression. Even to his own ears, the words carried little threat.

That had always been his problem, acting with conviction. Indecisive, his boss had written in his last staff report, before he'd been given the sack. Wishy-washy, Sally's mum used to call him.

"Anything I can do to help?" the man asked, stepping into the light. He looked ordinary and a little embarrassed. Colin thought of shouting at him, but instead silently shook his head. He suddenly felt glad of the company, his bravado gone, imagining the sensation as the freezing water surged into his throat and lungs.

He shuddered. "No-one can help me," he said, tears starting to dribble down his cheeks.

While he snivelled quietly, the man stared at his feet. When their eyes finally met, Colin could tell there was concern on the stranger's face. He felt touched that someone he didn't know, a passer-by, was prepared to help him, show sympathy.

Which was more than could be said about anyone else after Sally had left him.

"I've no idea where she is," her mother had insisted, a look of triumph on her face, "but I do know that she doesn't want to see you again." Finding the strength from somewhere to stand up to her at last, he'd insisted on seeing Sally. Her spiteful little eyes had merely glinted with amusement.

"If you don't go away from here at once, I'm calling the police," she'd said.

Defeated, he had turned on his heel. "I'm not giving up, you know," he called over his shoulder, the show of defiance surprising even himself.

The witch had fallen silent for a moment, but then answered back, saying, "Stay away from her, do you hear?" Her voice reaching a crescendo of malice as he stumbled away. "Wishy-washy!"

The stranger was still watching him. Blowing his nose on his sleeve, Colin felt compelled to offer an explanation. "I've got problems, woman problems." He attempted a manly laugh, but quickly gave up the pretence. "Seven years we were together," he lamented, "and the trouble is I can't stop thinking about her. I told her, I'd do anything for you."

166

"Anything but marry me," Sally had replied, when he finally tracked her to a friend's place.

"But I thought we were happy as things stood," he'd defended himself weakly.

"Couldn't make up your mind, you mean. Didn't want to make a decision." She was extremely composed, looked determined, and he wondered how she had changed so much in a few short weeks.

Before then, during their time together, she'd been as diffident as him, not pushy at all. He had always thought it explained their attraction for each other. "It's not too late, we can still get married," he remembered saying, trying to keep the desperation out of his voice.

Sally, shaking her head resolutely, had countered, "No, Colin, I've moved on. Why don't you do the same?"

Well, she would have her way soon, he mused, staring down to the black water. I'll be moving on all right. Then she'll be sorry. He steeled himself to jump, but was held back by visions of the river rushing to meet his body, his overwhelming terror in those last few seconds. He began to cry again.

Hed almost forgotten the man was there, but the soft tones were sympathetic. "I can tell you've had a hard time of it."

"The worst," Colin replied, thinking about the previous few weeks.

It was the supreme irony, but he'd been moved to extremes of emotion for the first time in his life, waiting for hours outside the house where Sally was staying, watching all night sometimes, following her to the supermarket and the gym. He had tried pleading with her, in floods of tears, but his ex-girlfriend seemed determined not to budge. Even submerged in his self-pity, he could make out the strain on her face.

On one occasion Sally's mother caught them talking, arguing, outside her daughter's place of work. As the old witch screeched her way towards him, he had had to beat a hasty retreat.

Even his stalking turned out to be ineffectual, a failure, and a letter from Sally's lawyer had soon threatened to take him to court. Worse was to follow when Sally resigned her job and moved away.

"She said she's not coming back," her friend had told him. "I've no idea where she's gone." The woman's big and watchful husband had deterred any thought of Colin pursuing the matter.

His own work had suffered since the break-up; he'd fallen asleep at his desk more than once. He knew people at work were laughing about him when he wasn't there, in the rest rooms, around their desks. Losing his temper, he'd ended up screaming at one of his tormentors. The company had said there was no option but to let him go.

The shouting match in the office had taken all the fight out of him; and so he'd come to this ice-cold bridge, determined to end it all.

No-one would miss him, he'd told himself, no-one gave a damn.

And yet a stranger had shown him that the world wasn't all bad. It might have been the man's act of kindness - or maybe his imagination would anyway have stopped him from taking the final leap. Either way, he was too tired to care. He just wanted to go home.

There was scarcely any feeling left in his limbs and he turned his head to the good samaritan. The man was already stepping forward, obviously realising he needed assistance to get down from the bridge. "Thanks for your help," Colin said.

"That's what I'm here for," the other replied. With that, Colin felt a hand push him gently but firmly in the back.

He heard the same courteous voice, much louder now, as he plunged in terror through the frigid night air. "She said to give you a message."

The shout carried to him from high above, almost lost in the roaring in his ears as he struck the arctic flow of the river.

"Wishy-washy!"

NO MORE HEROES

Malinowski is smiling at me again, attempting to keep my spirits up. Instead it makes my skin crawl.

The others are getting noisier outside, vodka circulating as usual after a brush with the enemy, while we sit with our all-too-sober thoughts in this shadowy cabin. Earlier on I asked Malinowski if it was alright to turn the lamp down because the light was hurting my eyes. Neither of us has spoken since. Even Malinowski has run out of words. My own tongue feels swollen and useless.

Time is dragging. We seem to have been sitting in this room for days and weeks, not hours. The silence is profound. Hard to imagine that only yesterday we were the best of friends, Malinowski chattering away in his gruff peasant voice, me just glad to be in his company. There was always something that marked him out from the rest of our band. The bold look in his eyes, perhaps.

That's why we're here together, in this mess. Every time Malinowski gets up to stretch his powerful limbs, it feels as if invisible chains are tugging between us.

The skirmish this morning is already a distant blur to me. The rattle of gunfire as we struggled to get away. Prudowicz's scream as he fell dying. We didn't stop to retrieve his body, just desperate to put distance between ourselves and the Germans. Everyone fleeing for their lives.

Except Malinowski.

He'd held his ground, kept on firing long after we forded the stream which lay between us and safety. Attracting attention to our position. The chief had to strike him to get him to stop. Meantime I was cowering behind a giant fir tree, bleating something about my mother. When one of our comrades retrieved me, there was laughter all round because I'd soiled my pants.

The laughter ended when the inquest began.

I've never seen the chief look so angry, the veins standing out like cables on his neck. "What if everyone behaved like you?" he screamed. "How long do you think we would have lasted?"

He's right, of course. We've stayed alive because of his tactics. Hit and run. Mostly run these days, heavily outnumbered and outgunned by our pursuers, confined to these forests, chased from one God-forsaken part of eastern Poland to another.

We all know that things will not go well if they ever lay hands on us. At best, they shoot prisoners out of hand. Their worst still makes me shiver, recalling the time we came across the mutilated body of one of our captured comrades. Strung up and left there as an example and warning.

NO MORE HEROES

After ranting for several more minutes, the chief decided that death was the only penalty - to stop the rot from spreading. I closed my eyes at that moment, anticipating the blast of his heavy pistol.

I should have known better. He's an old fox, always coming up with the unexpected. He glanced from me to Malinowski with cunning in his reddened eyes. Of course, he knew we were the best of friends. He gestured at me with contempt. "You can look after him," he snarled, "until the moment comes for his execution." No-one dared to ask when that would be.

And that's why we're in this room, me and Malinowski, in a flickering half-light.

Although our comrades outside are swapping crude jokes, I can tell there's an edge to their laughter. They're thinking about what's going on in this cabin, just glad they're not with us. It seems interminable, the wait for the moment when the chief is ready - and drunk enough - to carry out his sentence. It's torture for them too, this sadistic delay. Our leader's message loud and clear, everybody will be made to suffer for the sins of one man. Never behave like him.

It feels as if if I have a fever. Seeing me shiver in spite of the evening warmth, Malinowski speaks up at last. "Don't worry, Bronislaw," he soothes me. "Things will turn out alright, you'll see."

Not for the first time since this morning I wonder if, deep down, I've always hated Malinowski. I recognise now that what I took for his simple peasant ways was actually a severe lack of brains. The man is a moron - believing the chief was ever going to forgive and forget! That at any moment he'd say that everything is fine, come outside and have some vodka!

No, the only thing that holds our band together is fear. The fear of dying. The chief knows that. He also knows the only way he can retain our utmost loyalty is to make an example every so often. This is what happens when you disobey me. We are easily cowed, after all.

Except Malinowski.

He is smiling at me again in his boneheaded way, muttering words of encouragement. Perhaps that's the thing about being brave, you think the worst is never going to happen. I don't have that consolation, a born pessimist and born-again coward.

I curse Malinowski in my mind. If it wasn't for him I wouldn't be stifling in this cabin, suffering like this. Wary of his huge hands, the hands I've seen almost knock a man's head from his shoulders, I keep my thoughts to myself.

NO MORE HEROES

He saved my life in one of his fits of bravery, carrying me through the long grass as I bleated from a leg wound, until we had outpaced the Germans. Thinking about this day of torture, of what will happen at any moment, the dark stain on the earth, I wish for a moment that he'd let me die back then.

Because I can tell by the lowering of the voices outside that the terrible finale is not far away. I expect the chief to call out at any second. I am quite literally shitting my pants. "Courage, Bronislaw," Malinowski says.

That's easy for him to say, the lion-hearted imbecile! Malinowski is smiling to himself and I know exactly what he's thinking. Too many hours spent in his company for it to be otherwise. That craggy open face always easy to read. His expression saying, in a few minutes only one of us will be alive.

Finally, he's realised! Until now, Malinowski has told himself, and me, that the chief was simply playing a cruel game with us.

I can almost see it, the body lying on the dark earth with a bullet in its head. The sweat breaks out again in my armpits.

And yet when Malinowski touches my shoulder tenderly, it really feels as if some of his courage is passing into me. I experience an upsurge of my old feelings towards him. "It'll be fine," I mutter through cracked lips, ashamed of my earlier thoughts.

"We're still friends, then?" he asks, rather anxiously. "Of course we are," I respond. His heavily muscled arms engulf my shaking body.

The sound of boots on the wooden steps outside. The rap of knuckles against the door. The chief's muffled roar. "Come out and meet your fate!"

Malinowski looks at me, and for the first time there is dismay in his eyes. But it is soon replaced by a peasant gaze, impassive, accepting that what will be will be. He takes my hand in his giant paw. "Goodbye, old friend," he says in a firm voice. I am too overcome to answer.

Our comrades are in a crescent facing us when we go outside. I can tell, even in the gloom, that many of them wish they were anywhere but this forest clearing.

It's getting late and everyone is obviously the worse for drink and lack of sleep. Only the chief looks determined, his eyes redder than ever in the lamplight. "Our work is never done," he jokes to the second-in-command. There is uneasy laughter in the ranks.

Looking across to where the two of us are standing to attention, he gestures me forward. When I stumble to a halt with a pathetic attempt at a salute, he says, smirking, "As a fitting punishment for your cry-baby display back there, I sentence you to latrine duty for the next month."

Someone shouts out from the back, "I have your shovel here!" Several comrades snigger and snort.

The chief's voice is still jovial. "And now for the final job before we turn in." Suddenly no-one is laughing.

As if gauging the mood of the men, the cunning old fox changes his tune. All at once his voice is benign, even patriarchal. "I should have seen that you were always too bold, my son", he says. "But we are still alive today not because of impetuous courage but because we know when to be cowards, when to run away."

His voice still has a paternal ring. "Now, my boy, come and meet your fate."

There is a protesting groan from someone in the ranks. Malinowski was always a popular comrade. As he steps forward, his head held high, I can feel the tears on my cheeks.

The chief's voice is higher now, sounding angry, as if he's whipping himself up to do the deed. "You could have cost us everything with your confounded bravery." He stares at all the faces in the shifting light. "This is to show that when I say retreat, I mean retreat." The last thing I see before I close my eyes is the heavy pistol being raised.

When I open them again, the body is lying on the dark earth. The chief is addressing us in a voice which holds both regret and resolve. "Remember this lesson well."

As we drift in silence to our rough beds, I catch his aside to the second-in-command. "Too brave for his own good."

THE SEER

As Joe lay dying, his thoughts were full of the seer. The things he could tell!

Not that anyone would listen. They were talking about him now, two nurses. "See the old guy over there? He's a hundred and five. Isn't that brilliant?"

He closed his eyes again, and was back in France. As so often, it was that morning in July 1916 when he'd first met the seer, only days after another futile attempt at a push. There, in a hell of mud and blood and broken lives, their shattered battalions had been merged to form the semblance of a fighting unit.

They were reinforced by drafts fresh from England; and his new comrade - his name was Edgar but Joe never thought of him as anything but the seer - was going around the frightened boys with words of encouragement. On seeing Joe, he smiled and said, "Hullo, young 'un."

He mumbled something back, but liked the man right away. The penetrating eyes continued to study him, as if they could see through his lie about his age. Joe almost blushed. He was so green!

They all were at first. Even after two savage years of war, thousands of deaths, perhaps it was only at the Somme that the poor bloody infantry realised how terrible was to be their sacrifice on the alter of incompetence and stupidity.

But even though disillusionment had seeped into their very bones, they were still able to laugh and joke, were still willing to die for King and Country. Atkinson, the self-appointed company clown, a street urchin from South London, summed it up. "This show is bleedin' shite, lads, but we can't let ol' Jerry win."

After their first meeting, Joe followed the seer around like a puppy dog, feeling safe in the presence of the older man. The seer let slip that his lie had been in the opposite direction from his young comrade's. On learning his real age, Joe looked at him in wonder. "Wouldn't you rather be with your family?" he asked.

The seer was matter-of fact. "Oh, I shall be all right."

He quickly took Joe under his wing, began to act almost like his father, protecting him as best he could, as anyone could, from the worst consequences of their awful situation. It felt to Joe as if the older man was keeping him alive. "Why are doing this for me?" he asked in his naïve way.

"Because I want us to get through this together" came the reply.

The seer was soon promoted to corporal. And somehow they continued to survive. Neither man suffered so much as a scratch, in fact, as the months of slaughter went by, with a multitude of bodies rotting on the barbed wire. The casualty rate in the rest of the company was meantime running at more than two-thirds.

THE SEER

Their comrades didn't begrudge them their good fortune, however, the general opinion being that everyone was going to buy it sooner or later. Envy was reserved for fellows with a Blighty one, injured badly enough to be sent home. Even losing an arm or a foot was deemed worth it.

"I'm not so sure about my bollocks," Atkinson announced, to general amusement.

The seer, in spite of his kindly nature, was strict with them. "I have to be to keep you buggers alive," he told them one day, as they toasted each other in cheap red wine in an estaminet which was a hope-inspiring distance from the front line.

Atkinson seemed to speak for everyone. "Maybe we'll get through this bleedin' awful mess yet."

But, of course, many didn't. And Joe began to notice some of the men looking at the seer with apprehension, as if nervous and even afraid of the corporal.

He soon realised that whenever he caught someone watching the corporal in that strange way, like a pet which had just been kicked by its master, they were invariably dead within twenty-four hours.

He grew fearful himself. "Imagine," he muttered. "People trying to kill me all over the place. And there I was afraid of the one man who was working to keep me alive. Imagine!"

He opened his eyes at that moment and caught the startled glance of a young doctor. Dismissing him with a feeble gesture, he drifted back to the Somme.

He felt close to breaking at that point. It would have been so easy to let his mind go. Shell shock was the common name for it. Men were court-martialled and shot for throwing their weapons away after a pounding by the big guns. He'd seen good comrades screaming their heads off, mad with fear.

The worst of it was that he couldn't discuss his fears with the man who had become the most important person in the world to him.

What saved him was his first battle wound. It happened as they were crossing No Man's Land, hunched against the usual storm of machine gun fire, the German forward trenches virtually untouched by another ineffective artillery bombardment. A piece of shrapnel caught him in the upper arm and he fell to the ground in shock and pain.

"Are you alright?" The familiar voice, sounding anxious. He could feel his injury being roughly dressed.

They were ten hours in a bomb crater before managing to get back to their own lines after dark. And all the time the seer was doing his best to lift his spirits. Joe felt ashamed of himself. "I'm sorry," he said. To his surprise, the seer seemed to know exactly what he was thinking. "Apology accepted," he said in his gruff way.

"Are we going to die?" Joe asked, his voice small.

"No, we're both going to get back to Blighty, you'll see," the seer reassured him.

Joe was more puzzled than ever, but knew one thing for certain. This man would never do him any harm.

Their friendship grew even stronger, more equal; Joe joked that he was now the better man, with one more wound than the corporal. But he still noticed his comrades looking at the seer in that cringing sort of way. And still they continued to die.

It was only when poor Atkinson bought it at Arras that he finally got up the courage to raise the subject with the seer. They were in the rest lines once again, sitting by themselves this time, watching the world go past from a cafe table.

They were both in a good mood, laughing almost like in the old days, like they were on holiday, and he was beginning to believe that perhaps his friend was right about them surviving.

The seer was so cheerful that he asked him right out, "But how do you know we're going to get through?" It felt as if he was asking his father to tell him there wasn't something nasty under the bed. The seer looked at him for a moment and then laughed once, sharpish, and began to speak.

"If I say I can read death on the faces of our comrades, would you believe me?" he asked. Joe waggled his head, too afraid to say a word. "The trouble is there seems no way I can hide that I know," the seer went on. "Somehow the men always sense it. I wish they couldn't."

"But what can you see?" Joe asked.

His question must have sounded so child-like that the seer laughed again, though it finished up more like a sob. "Too much," he muttered. "I see the manner of their end. I even know what their final words will be."

"Do you see it on my face?" Joe asked, alarmed.

The seer looked at him with real affection. "No," he said, and Joe somehow knew he was speaking the truth.

He asked if the seer always knew that Atkinson was going to die. When his friend nodded, he grew agitated again. "Or does it suddenly appear? Perhaps I'll look different tomorrow?"

The seer pulled gently at his sleeve. "You have nothing to fear," he said. "You will lead a long and useful life. You see, I know who will live and who will die. It only comes on me strongly just before it happens - that is when they sense it from my face. But the feeling is with me all the time. I *always* know."

His voice trailed away so that Joe could hardly make out the last words.

They were silent for a long time after that; and a guardsman watched them curiously from the next table. Joe looked to see if he could make out any death signs on the fellow's face, but could read nothing there. That pleased him.

He felt a great pity for his friend. "Why haven't you gone mad?" he asked.

"I don't know," the seer replied. "Perhaps I'm already mad. Isn't this whole thing a madhouse?" He gestured around and Joe found it impossible to disagree with him. The guardsman, after catching a glance from the seer, had walked away slowly, his head bowed, as if he was already trudging towards the machine guns.

"I have always had the gift," the seer went on, "but coming here has sharpened it, made it a thousand times stronger. I'm in a place where the about-to-die are everywhere." He sighed. "No, I am not mad, but I would certainly blow my brains out if I wasn't going to get through this alive. I *must* carry on, for the sake of my family."

Later on, when they passed a column of wounded prisoners, Joe noticed at least two of the men flinch away when the seer looked into their sullen faces. "Germans, too?" he asked. Again the seer nodded.

Not long after, the seer was made up to sergeant and transferred to another battalion in a different part of the line. He tried but failed to get Joe posted with him.

Joe remembered thinking he wasn't sorry. The man was his best friend and had almost certainly saved his life, but to know what he was going through every single day and then to have to serve alongside him. On top of everything else. It would have been too much. Too much.

They kept in touch, though, and even managed to meet up once or twice when their battalions were in the same sector of the line. Joe was relieved to see that the seeker was holding up remarkably well. He was an officer by then, but their relationship remained the same.

He recalled joking to the seer the last time they met in France. "I must be one of the few people in the British Army who don't fancy a Blighty one," he chuckled. "After what you told me."

Peace came, and demobilisation at the age of barely twenty. He wondered if he would ever see his friend again. Then he received a letter from the seer.

"I wish he hadn't sent me that letter, I was still just a boy," he groaned.

THE SEER

"Are you OK?" a passing nurse asked him.

"I wish he hadn't done it," Joe croaked to her.

"Yes, yes," she soothed him. "We'll be giving you your medicine soon."

Joe closed his eyes again. At once he was back in that spartan room, more like a cell, listening in horrified fascination to the seer.

It turned out that his friend was being detained in what was popularly known as a loony bin. The doctors said he had a severe case of shell shock. He was a danger to himself and everyone else, they claimed.

There were short periods at first when the seer was lucid, almost his old self. After they stopped, so were any visits from outside. The seer seemed to know it was the end for him, the last time he would ever see Joe. "Everyone thinks I'm barmy," he said, urgently. "But I saw something out in France, something frightful. More frightful than you can imagine."

Joe tried without success to think of anything worse than spending four years on the Western Front with the power to foresee the death of every man you came across.

"It was just before the end," the seer said, with a wry smile about his bad luck.

He had been in charge of a fighting patrol, sent out to test the opposing front line near Ypres, when he was captured by the Germans. A group of the enemy stood watching as he was escorted to the rear. In his customary way, almost casually by then, his senses dulled by years of slaughter and privation, he looked into the haggard faces of each of the men in turn.

Then he stopped dead in his tracks.

Joe suddenly knew he was shouting. "Shut up," said the man in the next bed. But Joe continued to scream until a nurse came and held his hand. "Every word of it was true," he told her, his voice growing weak. "He had the gift, you see."

Even as darkness washed over him, he shuddered in memory of the seer's final narrative.

One of the bystanders had caught the seer's attention, a hollow-cheeked NCO with a dark moustache. The way he told it, the seer sensed right away that there was something badly wrong with this individual. When he looked more closely into the German's face, he was horrified by what he saw there.

"I knew that life for this one man meant misery for everyone else. The whole dreadful business all over again. War and starvation and disease, the death of civilisation."

THE SEER

Noticing the seer stare at him, the enemy soldier stepped forward, his features contorted, and raised his hand as if to strike the prisoner. Most of his comrades seemed amused by the show of ill-temper, but an officer with them snapped out what must have been a warning. The man dropped his arm.

The group walked away, with the moustachioed NCO trailing morosely in the rear. The seer, in almost the last words he spoke to Joe, swore that the German was ringed around by shadowy, apocalyptic figures, swirling in a protective cordon. When the man half-turned to look back at the seer, the officer admonished him again.

"Nein, Adolf."

KEEP ON RUNNING

When Henry first acquainted him with the mysteries of the Hash, he made it sound like something from a Sherlock Holmes story. "It's time you joined the HHH of KL."

But even as a newcomer to the office and the country, Tom was able to break the code. He had earlier spotted the piece of paper on Henry's desk, a timetable of future runs, and overheard his colleague on the phone, discussing arrangements for that evening with one of his cronies.

After work, they went to the bar located on the ground floor of their office building, one of the most modern in Kuala Lumpur. Over drinks - brandy and ginger was Henry's favourite tipple, Tom following suit - the younger man was given chapter and verse on the Hash House Harriers.

Listening to Henry explain that the club had been founded between the wars by a group of foreign residents in the humid Malaysian capital, Tom wondered at his companion's enthusiasm.

It's just a glorified paperchase, he thought. The older man, at least twenty-eight, seemed to read his thoughts. "This isn't kiddies' stuff, you know," Henry admonished him, before going on to recount tales of the Hash with a child-like glee. Encounters with snakes and other jungle animals. Runners getting themselves lost and not turning up for days. How - Henry appearing serious for a moment - two of their members had recently died after colliding with a tree, driving home from a run along an unlit dirt road.

But he concluded his litany of mishaps with a happy laugh. "Don't look so worried, old son. If we had a motto, it would be: 'A little run followed by a lot of booze'. You'll love it."

As he staggered out of the bar some time after midnight, Tom had already changed what was left of his whisky-shattered mind.

The Hash was just *greaaat*.

He felt like grabbing Henry and giving him a hug of thanks. But somewhere between the beer wagon and the curry house and the series of girlie bars along Jalan Chow Kitt, his workmate had disappeared. "Probably off to see his latest totty," one of Tom's many new friends had explained with a bleary wink.

This was confirmed by Henry the next morning, during their coffee break. "Some of the others have no choice but to pay for it," he said. "Brothel fodder." He chortled derisively, but then tried to look modest. "Luckily for me, it's usually on offer somewhere or other."

Not long after, seeing Henry work his charm on one of the locally-employed secretaries, the captive look on her face, Tom began to understand what the other man meant. In a different way, he could feel himself falling under his colleague's spell.

Henry's hold over him became complete during another meeting of the Hash. "Like to go on a double date tonight?" came the casual question, as they towelled themselves down before wandering over to the beer wagon that stood like a beacon at the end of every run.

Tom was filled in with more facts as they made their way to the rendezvous, Henry aiming his car nonchalantly through the chaos of the market district.

"You know I'm married, don't you?" Tom nodded, not sure what to say. The other gave his boyish grin. "It's OK, she's not some terrible secret I keep locked away in the attic. It's just that ... well, we have an agreement. I don't embarrass her and she turns a blind eye to me having a bit of fun."

While they escorted their dates towards KL's trendiest discotheque, the latest Abba hit pounding at them before they got through the front door, Henry whispered in his ear. "Remember what I told you. If she asks - yes, I'm definitely getting a divorce."

That night Tom was introduced to a different kind of hash, *ganja*, and other strange and wonderful things by his new girlfriend. As they sat on the balcony of his hilltop apartment, naked, sharing a fat joint, contentedly staring down on the lights of the city, he knew he had never been happier. A lot of that was due to his best mate, Henry, he decided. There was nothing he wouldn't do for the man.

Even though his head was spinning, he took another deep puff.

Dawn was luscious and loving and able to wrap him around her little finger. When she smiled at him, he more than half-believed in Henry's breezy justification for playing around, that some local women possessed sexual powers unknown in the West, could make themselves irresistible.

But Dawn was in a temper a few weeks after their blind date at the disco. Henry had just told her friend, Sandra Leung, that he no longer wanted to see her. "She has broken heart," Dawn seethed in her almost fluent English. "He is a butterfly, landing on many women. One of them will take away his wings, you will see."

For a while, Dawn seemed to believe she was that woman. Tom had to work hard to persuade her not to lay a complaint against Henry with the company, only getting her to calm down with the promise of a long weekend in Penang.

When he mentioned it to Henry, his friend looked panic-stricken. "The bitch!" he exclaimed. "I know this is the Seventies, changing times and all that, but the firm still has some funny ideas, a bit old-fashioned. And what would Jean say?" That thought appeared to frighten him more than anything.

Their friendship was sorely tested in the next few minutes, as Henry called down all the furies of hell on Dawn. But Tom felt he had to make allowances. And the other man apologised for his outburst later on, while they sat drinking in the Paramount bar.

"Suppose I'd better play it safe from now on," he added, morosely.

At the next drinks party they both attended, Tom was encouraged to see Henry in a scrum of male friends and not practicing his seduction technique on one of the several attractive girls in the room.

Jean was standing close by, which may have been an influencing factor, but that hadn't always stopped his friend in the past. He mentioned this to Dawn, looking like a crimson flame in her best cheongsam. She let out a Chinese snort of disbelief.

It seemed symbolic of his friend's new regime when Henry invited him to dinner, "Just you and me and Jean."

He hardly knew the woman, aside from a few quick party conversations, had always felt his friendship with Henry was in a similar category to the man's affairs. Not for divulgence to the wife. Henry had hinted at the reason when talking about the essentials for the successful adulterer.

"Always remember, careless talk costs lives."

Now he was being admitted into Jean's presence. It could only mean one thing, that Henry genuinely meant to reform. He was tempted to ask if Dawn could come along, too, but realised even a Henry freshly sanctified by the Pope wouldn't be able to take that much of a risk.

As the three of them sat down to dinner in the comfortable bungalow in one of KL's smarter residential districts, Tom was in a state of mild shock. In his own home, Henry the macho drinking man, the imperious womaniser, had been transformed into a humble fetcher and carrier of dishes.

Jean, drab-looking in a floral-print dress, issued her commands in a quiet voice and Henry rushed to obey. Tom was put in mind of a naughty boy, trying his hardest to please his mum. It seemed the key to their relationship.

Henry escorted him to his Mini at the end of the evening. Tom saw him glance over his shoulder as if to ensure that Jean had already gone back inside. "Thought that went pretty well," Henry said, the assurance back in his voice.

The next words were spoken more quietly. "The truth is, old son, she's heard one or two rumours about me. She doesn't like that. Not so much the doing, but the being talked about, if you know what I mean." Henry leaned confidentially towards the open window, until his handsome blond head was almost inside the car. "Seems that one of her friends has told her we've been knocking around together. There've been other bits of stupid gossip. And somehow the old woman got it into her head that you're a bad influence on me."

Tom hesitated between laughing out loud or saying a very rude word and his friend rushed into the gap. "Yes, I know, crazy." he said, soothingly. "But, anyway, it doesn't apply any longer, now she's met you. She thinks you're OK." Tom finally swore when Henry's large hand reached in and pinched his cheek. "In fact, she thinks you're *sweet*."

As he drove away, still shaking his head in resigned amusement, a loud chortle seemed to pursue the car through the muggy night air. The naughty boy had obviously decided he'd got away with it again.

Tom understood that he'd been conned along with Jean when, a few days later, he spotted Henry chatting to the new assistant in the flower shop that occupied one corner of the marble lobby of their office building.

The girl's pretty face was tilted towards his friend, almost as if she was offering him her lips, and Tom knew they weren't discussing the price of orchids.

"She's the one, old son, I've finally hit the jackpot," Henry enthused not long afterwards. They were trotting down a narrow track towards a lush valley from which steam was already rising, even in the relative cool of the morning. Tom adjusted the heavy satchel on his shoulder.

"You certainly had me fooled," he said, grudgingly. "I really thought you'd turned over a new leaf."

Henry's laughter caused several birds to flap, startled, from the surrounding trees. "Sorry about that, but I had to throw the old woman off the scent," he said. "Talking of which - what do you think?" He waved a proprietary arm around him.

They were almost into what looked like secondary jungle, the track sinking into a tangle of wet undergrowth, and Tom felt glad they were smothered with anti-mosquito repellent, a vicious hum from the gloom ahead of them.

"It's great," he replied, flattered all over again that Henry had chosen him to help with a task that was only ever assigned to senior members of the Hash: laying the trail for the run later in the day.

"One of the old messengers in the office told me about this spot," Henry boasted. "It's almost like a secret place. Close to the city centre, but not too many people know about it. We've never had a run in these parts before, the chaps are going to be impressed."

KEEP ON RUNNING

No harm in him really, Tom thought, as he caught the juvenile note in the other man's voice. Just wants to make everyone happy.

Henry's elbow broke in on his reverie. "Come on, old son, start earning your keep." The tall figure was already laying about with a parang and consulting the compass in his other hand. Tom, hurling down pieces of white paper, followed on.

That evening, in their favourite curry house, after they were ceremoniously toasted for the success of the run, Tom heard some more about his friend's new love.

"Eva's the most smashing bird," Henry confided. "Passionate ... you know. Taught me a few new tricks, I can tell you." There was a shine on his face that didn't just come from drink and sweat; and Tom couldn't help speculating about the woman's sexual powers, able to dazzle even a well-practised philanderer.

Henry made his excuses and left shortly afterwards. Tom experienced a stab of envy, seeing the other's look of intense anticipation, but felt better when he thought about Dawn waiting for him at home.

All the same, he paid closer attention to the flower shop girl the next day. Eva was a beauty alright, with shapely legs and a shining bob and exquisite face. Any man might fall for her. As he watched, however, she served a customer - male and middle-aged and obviously smitten - with a cruel little smirk on her full red lips. She almost tossed his change at the man.

There was a sulky glow about her, Tom now saw, an all-consuming blaze of self-regard under the warpaint. He wondered if he should warn his friend, be careful or she might burn away your wings, but knew it would do no good. A reckless butterfly.

Jean had started to come up to him on social occasions, referring to mutual acquaintances and joking in her humourless way about the drawbacks of the domestic staff she seemed to change every few weeks. She never once asked him about Henry, what they got up to on their drinking bouts or with the Hash. It seemed that her spouse had learned his lesson, was keeping his new girlfriend well under wraps.

Henry continued to be on his best behaviour. No longer flirting at parties - even with the totty at its thickest - and meekly following orders whenever Jean decided it was time to go home. Some of their cronies at the Hash reckoned, only partly in fun, that he'd lost the knack. Henry normally answered with a V sign and another swig of Tiger beer.

After Henry's initial burst of enthusiasm in the curry house, Tom could never get his friend to open up about Eva. A couple of times Henry changed the subject with the words, "Careless talk, careless talk!" Tom amused himself by wondering if all the new-found restraint came from the onset of maturity - or not wanting to upset mummy.

One morning, following Henry into the lobby, he saw the other man clatter past the flower shop without so much as a sideways glance. As Tom marvelled at the evidence of iron self control, Eva came out of the shop and stood watching his friend's back in the queue for the lift. Even from several yards away, he could see the hunger and fire in her eyes.

Henry dropped his bombshell on the next run of the Hash.

"I'm asking for a transfer," he said. Tom, struggling to keep up with his companion, had only enough breath to let out an astonished grunt.

Without breaking stride, Henry shrugged his shoulders. "Been here long enough, over three years. And Jean keeps pestering me, she's never really liked the heat."

While his friend accelerated towards the front of the pack, apparently embarrassed by his admission, Tom was forced to slow down and lean against a tree, taking in gasps of warm air along with Henry's news.

Much later, as they watched a cockroach skitter across the bar counter of the Kowloon bar, Henry said to him in a slurred undertone, "KL sheems like a modern place, a shlightly dirtier and more exotic version of Croydon, wouldn't you agree?"

Tom gave a sleepy nod. "Don't you believe it, old shon," Henry went on vehemently, sounding very drunk. "Dark forces at work all around ush. Magic. Things that can be bought on any street corner. Potions, you know ..."

What could have been minutes or hours later, Tom heard his friend mutter, "Too much for me ... got to get away."

He persuaded Henry to go on one of their lunchtime hair of the dog sessions the next day. Fiercely hungover, wondering if perhaps he'd dreamed the whole thing, Tom broached the subject at an angle. "I hear that Gerry Bryson is looking for another job because there's been some talk about sending him home. He can't bear the thought of leaving KL."

"Good luck to him," the other man said, grimly, "but I've had enough of it."

Tom was too perplexed to attempt any more tact. "But I always thought you loved it here. The climate, the Hash, the totty ..."

Henry broke in. "Ah, now that's the problem." His friend's look was one that Tom hadn't seen too many times before, a properly grown-up expression. This is serious, he thought.

So it was woman trouble, no other sort of predicament with Henry. He kept his probing gentle. "Everything, um, OK with Eva?"

"Unfortunately, it couldn't be better," the other replied, sounding more miserable than ever.

Henry read his face and laughed sharply. "Yeah, I know it doesn't make sense. She's crazy about yours truly, doesn't give a fart about me being married. Only one subject on her mind. One subject on *my* mind, when I'm with her. You wouldn't believe some of the things ..."

Henry's voice trailed away, as if even talking about Eva exhausted him. Tom spoke up tartly. "So what's the problem?"

The older man forced another laugh. "The problem, old son, is that I've finally come to appreciate the truth of the old saying. You know, too much of a good thing."

The next words came out almost in a whisper. "Sometimes I think she'd like to *eat* me."

Tom broke the silence. "Still, it's a bit drastic, isn't it? Leaving KL, I mean. Why don't you just finish with Eva?"

"Tried it. No can do. Impossible to keep away from her. Lost my interest in other women." There was astonishment all round at that moment. "No, the only answer is to do a flit. Luckily, the old woman agrees it's time for a change."

The dog's hair must have been working the power of recall in Tom's mind. "You were talking about magic in the Kowloon last night. Love potions and things. You don't think ...?"

His companion was shame-faced. "Oh, that must have been the drink talking. All rubbish."

More than one secretary burst into tears when the imminent transfer was announced to the world.

Henry, however, seemed to be very nearly back to his old self; and Jean was obviously thrilled, looked almost pretty when Tom was invited for another meal, tribute to his special relationship with Henry. A much grander farewell party was planned for the following week. Henry joked with him in private that Eva wasn't on the invitation list.

Tom was in bed on his own - Dawn away visiting her family in Ipoh - when the phone rang a couple of nights later. Henry's voice emerging from a ghostly crackle. "Tom, I need you to get over here."

It was close to two o'clock, even noisome nocturnal KL growing quiet, when he found Eva's apartment. Henry led him without a word into the bedroom, where something lay on the concrete floor, covered with a sheet. Tom felt a shock of horror to see bloodstains on the thin material.

Henry spoke at last, calmer now, straining to be matter-of-fact. "I've cleaned the place up. But we've got to hide her somewhere." It sounded like an order: you're on burial detail. Seeing him frown, Henry grew anxious. "You will help, old son?"

They stood for a moment gazing down at Eva. Less out of curiosity than to fill the void - the bedside clock ticking towards an explosion - Tom spoke up. "What happened?"

That seemed to animate Henry, the words escaping in bursts. "She found out. You know. About me leaving. Seemed to go berserk. Said she'd do herself in. Tried to do *me* in. It was an accident, old son. Just trying to get it away from her, honest."

Suddenly he held out his hands, like a child before being allowed to sit at the table, and Tom saw the ointment-smeared cuts on both palms.

"Knife must have slipped, straight through her heart." There was the hint of an apologetic smile. Sorry about the cock-up, it seemed to say.

The idea came from somewhere inside Tom's befuddled head, after it became obvious that Henry wouldn't go to the police, arguing stubbornly, "No can do, old son. You know what they're like out here. They'll carve me up for sure. A foreigner."

Tom had tried using logic. "But someone's going to miss her, surely? At the shop?"

"No, no. She was always leaving jobs without any warning. Just not turning up. She'd already threatened to resign, getting bored with it."

Tom had made one last desperate attempt. "But what about her friends and family?"

Henry could have been a contestant in some macabre quiz show, his answer off pat. "She didn't have any. Friends, I mean. Close ones anyway. Said that every girl was jealous of her. Don't know about her family, she never mentioned them."

Tom had slumped into a canvas-backed chair by then, no more questions except one: where's the door? As if claiming his prize, Henry had quietly asked, "Will you help me, then?"

Seeing the desperation behind the shaky composure, remembering Dawn and the Hash, fighting against every instinct of self-preservation, Tom voiced his brainwave. "Your secret place."

Henry looked as if he'd unexpectedly been given the day off school. "Nice one, old son!" he exclaimed.

KEEP ON RUNNING

They dug Eva's grave in the evil-smelling soil, taking turns with the spade Henry kept in his car for Hash emergencies. "I should be in the boy scouts. Always prepared," Henry said, with a jarring touch of pride.

When Tom made no reply, the torchlight was switched to his face and the other's voice grew placatory. "Not to worry, old son, they'll never find her here. Do you know how quickly things disappear in this climate? There won't be any trace of her in a month's time."

Except in my head, Tom wanted to say, but Henry's mind was already on other matters. "Don't forget, if the old woman asks, we were at your place all night, playing cards." A note of triumph. "Good old Jean."

As they trudged out of the jungle, Henry sighed with satisfaction. "One more week and I'll be back in good old Blighty."

But I won't be, Tom thought unhappily, the suspicion deepening that he'd been taken in again. A violent urge then to spoil his friend's good mood. "So much for her magic powers." He spitefully mimicked Henry's words. "Poor old Eva." There was the satisfaction of hearing the other man cough with embarrassment. They walked on in silence.

Henry was talking again by the time they reached the cars. "I'm looking forward to tomorrow," he said. When Tom stared at him, his friend grew gently reproving. "You haven't forgotten? The Hash. My farewell appearance."

Tom stumbled over his words. "But ... I thought ... after tonight ..."

In the dim glow from the dashboard, Henry wore a noble look. "I know. It's going to be hard, but I can't let the chaps down. Wouldn't be right."

Tom shifted the night's madness, scene after scene, through his tired and frightened brain on the way home. He could almost hear the phantom chuckle in pursuit of the car. And yet the next day he nodded his head, even manufactured a smile, when Henry asked if everything was OK for that evening. He was relieved to learn the run would be in a scruffy patch of abandoned plantation several miles from the burial site. His friend didn't seem to think it was important.

The run had attracted a larger than usual turn-out, people travelling from all over the place to pay their respects to the man of the hour.

"Let's make it a good one," Henry said, with his boy's wolfish grin, before racing away at the head of the pack. Tom trudged along towards the rear, feeling more than ever like just another insect, helpless against a bright light.

There was no sign of Henry when he finally reached the beer wagon.

"The silly sod's got himself lost," one of their cronies chuckled. "On his last run, too!"

KEEP ON RUNNING

Everyone had a good laugh about Henry's misadventure, and after several unproductive sorties back along the trail, they set off in convoy for the curry shop. The shutter of darkness had already fallen.

"Not much we can do for now," one of the old hands explained. "The authorities will start looking in the morning if he still hasn't turned up. He'll be alright, though. Good man, Henry."

Tom called Jean to let her know the situation. She sounded calm enough, a veteran Hash widow. "He'll just stay where he is until it gets light," she said. Tired of listening to maudlin toasts to absent friends, Tom went home early.

Unable to sleep, a wriggle of concern inside him, he returned to the start of the run at dawn. Henry's car stood in the same place. One or two of the others were already there and someone told him a helicopter was on its way. By evening, with still no sign of his friend, the worm in his head had turned into a serpent. The next run of the Hash was cancelled, while the search continued with diminishing hope.

Everyone sympathised with Tom because he looked so ill. The company gave him several days off work, and Dawn overwhelmed him with love and foul-tasting Chinese medicine. The snake had grown immense by then, constricting his thoughts with a dreadful certainty.

And still he told no-one. What would he say? I know ... somehow he *knew*.

When a friend telephoned to say that Henry had been found dead, Tom remembered in time to pose the expected question. "Right where you had your run," the man answered. "But what was he doing there?"

There were rumours and counter-rumours concerning Henry: that he'd been discovered with marks of violence on his body, or smiling peacefully, or even in a fallen attitude of prayer. Tom shut them all out. Jean, who had insisted on identifying her husband, was soon flown home, apparently suffering from some sort of breakdown.

He knew the same words were being expressed a hundred times, a thousand. "What was he doing there?"

Tom could have told them - following a trail of ghostly paper to the dark and shining grave. A butterfly to the end.

The serpent had mutated into a fearsome Oriental beast. Tom began to have bad dreams, a recurrent nightmare of staggering along a moonlit track, heart pounding, the fearsome figure of the dead woman suddenly bursting out of the dank earth to confront him.

After putting in for a transfer, he agonised about breaking the news to Dawn. The conviction grew that he should leave without telling her, just get on the next plane out of KL. He could scarcely bear it now when she attempted to soothe away his terrors in their air-conditioned nights, had even grown fearful of her words of endearment as they sat on his small balcony high above the treetops.

"I love you very much."

Loud echoes of boyish laughter seeming to sound a warning then, flying out of the black jungle ...

MOMMY'S GIRL

Even as a little girl she wondered about daddy's secrets.

The look on his face at her innocent questions like he'd swallowed some poison and couldn't spit it out, the words stuck in his throat.

When she was still very small, a lady visited the house and looked at daddy in a sloppy kind of way, but he wouldn't talk about his business even with her. One day the lady asked why there were no photos around the place. Daddy had grown *soooo* angry and that was the last time their visitor called.

She'd been happy to have him to herself again, but couldn't help thinking the same as the lady sometimes. While everyone she knew at school had brothers and sisters, aunts and uncles and cousins, her family consisted of daddy.

One thing especially bothered her, until one day she came right out with it. "Where's my mommy, daddy?" she asked. Daddy gave one of his sick stares and told her to go and watch television.

He threw a party for her fifth birthday, but it wasn't a great success. The jello turned out runny and some of the girls pulled faces behind daddy's back. Everyone wanted to go home early. She really missed having a mommy then.

At last she got to learn about one of daddy's secrets. He talked in his sleep.

He slept a lot, daddy. Almost every night, tucked into her little bed, she would hear him creak up the stairs, splashing noises from the bathroom. Then she would tumble into her dream.

It was always the same one, a crowd of people having fun in a great big room with red walls. None of them paid her any attention. She couldn't see any of their faces, but somehow knew she was among family.

Because he liked to sleep so much, daddy wanted her to do the same, shooing her to her room with the chant, "Early to bed, early to rise, makes a girl healthy, wealthy and wise."

He was forever warning her, too, about wandering around the house at night. She might fall down the stairs.

But one time she was forced to go to the bathroom and heard daddy's voice through his half-open bedroom door. Peeping inside, she saw he was asleep. The night light by his bed puzzled her, though, grownups weren't supposed to be afraid of the dark.

His talk didn't make much sense either, the same words repeated every few moments. "Marie. Marie. What have you done?"

She listened at the door for several nights running, but it was never any different. She was only a kid, just turned seven, and couldn't hold it back any longer. "Who's Marie, daddy?" Daddy went as white as a sheet. When he started to moan, catching hold of his stomach, she grew frightened.

"I heard you say the name in your dreams, daddy," she almost screamed.

He seemed happier after that, but kept glancing over his shoulder for some reason. Taking a dusty bottle out of a drawer, he poured himself a large glassful of what looked like medicine. Must be for the pain in his belly, she thought.

Then, for the only time, daddy talked to her about the past, the words coming out hot and confused like the sickness had reached his brain. She couldn't keep up with him.

Marie was her mommy, she understood that part, daddy saying it in a funny way. A terrible thing had happened, causing him to run off, taking her with him. Somehow mommy's family were to blame.

"The craziest bunch you could ever imagine, something out of a nightmare."

Those words stuck in her child's mind, but nothing else made much sense.

He even showed her a picture, a beautiful woman with red lips and long black hair, and she cried on realising it was her mommy.

That set daddy off, too, huge tears rolling down his face until he couldn't speak any more. When he fell asleep on the couch, she covered him with a blanket and lay down on the floor next to him, her small hand clutched in his fist.

The next morning daddy looked tired beyond belief. She asked him in a tiny voice, "Is my mommy still alive, daddy?"

He told her to go upstairs. From then on, even in the hottest weather, his bedroom door was closed at night. He refused to talk about her mommy again and claimed he'd lost the photograph.

It made no difference, soon everyone in her dream had a face like mommy's.

She was ten, but still treated like five, when daddy found another woman friend, the first since her toddler days. He even went on a couple of dates, leaving fat Mrs Standish from next door to babysit her.

Seeing his look when he kissed her goodbye, she wondered why he bothered to go out if it was so painful. Both times he came back early to tuck her into bed.

He asked his friend over to the house for a meal. Her name was Stella and they worked together in the post office. Daddy wore a troubled smile when he introduced the two of them, almost as if he felt ashamed that she was his only family.

She expected the worst, thinking about the runny jello, but daddy's cooking must have improved because Stella kept praising him after they started to eat. That gave her the chance to examine the woman. Although Stella was pretty enough, she couldn't help comparing her with mommy. It was their guest's turn to look worried, when she realised she was being watched.

Surprised by the woman's confusion, she decided to stare harder, deliberately making her eyes grow wide as saucers. That worked even better. They finished the dessert course in almost total silence. Soon afterwards Stella made an excuse to leave.

That night the mommy-faced people seemed to take in her presence for the first time. Some of them even began to smile at her.

She wasn't surprised that daddy didn't go on any more dates with Stella.

And so her life dragged by, the days creeping into weeks and months and years. Nothing much seemed to change. Not in her dream, not anywhere. Neither of them fitted in, she knew, and yet daddy appeared determined to make the most of things in the small, dull town that seemed to be on the edge of the known universe.

But she could tell he wasn't really happy, not for a single moment. She had given up asking questions, though, mostly to avoid seeing the sickness on his face.

When she reached her teens, some of the boys at school began to taunt her, calling out, "There goes Little Miss No Date". That bothered her, but she would cheer herself by imagining that the bullies were only shadows, less real than the characters in her favourite cartoon shows. It was a creepy but comforting sensation.

She had periods of wondering if everyone in the town was a sort of mirage, in fact, even daddy. The people in her dream seemed more alive somehow, always laughing and fooling around.

She was getting restless and bored, tired of being treated like an infant by daddy. No boyfriends, no parties, no fun. Early to bed, early to rise.

She yearned to talk to someone, an adult, about the changes that were coming over her, but knew it would be a waste of time. Growing pains, her teacher's answer to everything. Daddy would only give one of his hurt looks. She was missing her mommy more and more.

Daddy's nerves seemed as bad as ever. She was beginning to hate his stupid curfews. He finally allowed her to attend a school dance - she was gone fourteen, almost an old maid - but only after she'd moped and pestered him for days.

He insisted on picking her up afterwards, *soooo* embarrassing. Daddy looked tense driving back to the house through the lamplit streets, and she suddenly thought it must be because he hadn't been out so late in a hundred years.

Back home he watched her in a relieved sort of way and said, "I'm very proud of you."

"Then stop treating me like a baby," she burst out, stamping up the stairs before he had the chance to tell her to go to her room. Daddy just stood there with his mouth open. She felt sorry and pleased at the same time.

She had the sensation of being grown up in her dream that same night, finally allowed to share in the joke with the others. She couldn't remember any of it in the morning, however.

Mommy was constantly on her mind from then on, a vision of glossy red lips and shining black hair in the moonlight. Strange, but now she only ever pictured mommy in the night-time, laughing, in a party mood, and wondered if that was her woman's intuition.

Could it be why daddy hated the dark so much?

In spite of his instructions, she took to wandering about the house after lights out, sneaking past his bedroom door and sitting downstairs in the blackness for hours, just thinking about her life.

One night she was disturbed by a noise from outside. Peeping between the drapes, she saw a group of boys a little way down the street, clowning around, revving a car engine too loud. The glare from a street lamp caught the long blond locks of Billy Hollander.

They'd eyed each other from a distance at the dance. Although he was much older than her, seventeen at least, and had a reputation for drinking and fighting and worse, that only gave an edge to her fantasies.

The tension built in her for days, images in her head of doing crazy, wonderful things with Billy Hollander. The final act seemed out of focus, beyond her imagining, but she sensed it would it be the most fun in the world.

When she heard them outside again, she didn't hesitate. She was already wearing her street clothes, the sexy top she'd bought with her own money. They were surprised to see her at that hour, she could tell, suspicious stares on one or two of the tough-looking faces.

Billy, though, immediately put an arm around her shoulder, as if he owned her. She wasn't pleased about that, but held her tongue.

"Like to come for a ride?" Billy asked, while the rest of the gang exchanged grins. She nodded, too excited to speak. She felt that mommy would be proud of her at that moment, doing something freaky at last.

An older boy drove the battered car, two others crammed alongside him in the front. She wasn't happy about the company, but went along with it, allowing

Billy to paw her in the back seat.

They quickly reached the scrub that surrounded the town and parked by the side of the road. Then, as the others stood around laughing and jeering, Billy pulled her out of the car and began to mess with her some more. She could smell the beer on his breath.

She humoured him at first, thinking he was just being boisterous, mommy's people, her own, would be no different. A wild bunch, according to poor daddy.

But she grew angry when Billy tugged frantically at her top. She knew exactly what she wanted to do with him then, the picture all at once sharp and brightly-coloured in her mind. Her mommy was there as well, smiling with satisfaction in the background.

She was about to whisper to Billy that they should go somewhere quiet - she could tell by his eyes that he would be all for it - when one of the others shouted out, "Cops!"

As a car with flashing lights approached, the boys scrambled into their own vehicle. Billy tried to pull her inside, but she resisted, fed up with his bullying. They drove away in a shower of small stones, leaving her by the roadside.

The policeman was very kind. He asked about her age and what she was doing there. Grown very calm on the surface, she anwered all his questions with a bewildered little smile. Inside, though, she continued to boil. The blood was pounding in her ears. She sensed, too, that mommy was no longer pleased with her.

So, when the policeman turned his head away to make a radio call, she bit through his neck with one swift movement, tearing and chewing until he was completely dead.

As she walked back to town afterwards, she felt fantastic - it *was* the greatest fun - but couldn't quite believe what she'd achieved, running her tongue in wonder over her small, soft teeth.

Still, she'd always guessed she was different, out of the ordinary. "Thank you, mommy," she said gratefully to the night air.

She looked forward to meeting up with everyone in her next dream. It would be a very special one, she knew.

She wondered what to do about daddy. Poor, sad man, he'd always been so frightened all her life. Scared for her, she had always thought. Terrified *of* her as well, she now realised, of what she might become.

In spite of everything, his betrayal of mommy, she would probably allow him to live. Because, after all, blood was thicker than water. But he would have to tell her the truth, no more family secrets. Then she would go and find mommy for real. She hugged herself with excitement, gazing up at the red-streaked sky.

She was *soooo* happy.

MONKEY

When Monkey lifted the laptop computer from the unlocked motor behind Sloane Square he never mean to keep the thing. There were plenty of faces in the boozers around King's Cross who'd hand over ready dosh for a class piece of high-tech merchandise. Enough to pay the back rent on his bed-sit, keep him in pills and drink for a time.

Then he had second thoughts.

He was sick of being a sneak thief and chancer. An insect preying on other insects, scuttling in circles to avoid the flat feet of the Law, or worse still, being chewed up by the heavy-duty bugs that swarmed all over in his line of work.

He'd learned about computers on one of his rehab courses, but that had only sharpened his appetite for lifting them. Yet he knew more than one lucky sod was making a fortune from the internet with nothing except some technical know-how and a bright idea. There had to be a doorway into the cyberspace treasure vault for a smart operator like himself.

That was the answer. He'd go respectable, no more skulking about in the street. Millions of bits of useful info floating about the ether every day, names and addresses, credit card numbers. Bound to be mugs all over the place, in every corner of the planet, only too ready to be gulled out of their hard-earned dosh. Even the words had a nice safe ring to them: white-collar crime.

While he waited for the bulb to light in his skull Monkey went to work on the laptop, catching up with its twists and turns, pleased to discover he had a natural way with the thing. Connecting himself to the internet he prepared to make a killing.

Trouble was the grand idea, the master scam, always seemed just a click away.

He created a website but wasn't sure what illusion to peddle there. It had to be something that would drive the punters into a feeding frenzy, a flood of money coming to him, until the stupid bastards made out they were chomping on empty promises. He'd be swimming towards his next scheme by then.

Although porn seemed the obvious answer, he guessed there would be stiff competition in that particular field. He sniggered at the thought, but then grew depressed as he examined the opposition and saw that every preference and perversion was already covered in a hundred different ways.

They pissed him off for another reason, his trips around the back streets of the Net. Monkey had never had a proper girlfriend. Too busy ducking and diving, his excuse. Now, as the images danced in his skull, he began to feel a sense of loss. He wanted some romance in his life.

MONKEY

He'd always been a loser with the fair sex, crap at dancing, too pushy in one on one situations. His nickname didn't help, even the barmaids in his favourite boozer suspected of laughing behind his back.

Somehow the moniker had stuck after a local leader of fashion had clocked his stooping walk and long arms and told the world that all he needed was a tail.

But no-one knew him on the internet, he could be anyone he wanted. In the chat rooms he began to enter, still seeking the edge that could lead to riches, he called himself Roland Mills. It sounded nicely middle-class.

He put three inches on his height and changed his hair colour to blond. Soon he had a whole new biog, a job in the City instead of petty crime, boarding school in place of Borstal. One little birdy in particular seemed to take to him. She told him her name was Sondra and that she lived in New York City. Monkey was impressed.

Although he had a passport, in case he needed to do a serious runner, he'd been abroad only twice, on booze-collecting trips to the hypermarkets of Calais with a nutcase known as Thumper. The partnership had ended after a falling-out over the proceeds of the second trip. He'd been forced to lie low for a while until Thumper lost interest.

Sondra told him she *loved* the British style. She used upper case and italics a lot. Monkey enjoyed the attention, her girly chat, the novelty of being admired.

She started to mail him daily and he replied when he felt in the mood. After taking one of his pills was favourite, he could plaster on the compliments then, let his imagination run away with him.

One time he invited himself over to New York for a visit, joking that he might stop with her for several months. Sondra immediately sent a long screed about the things they'd see and do together in the Big Apple. She gave the impression of being serious.

But Monkey still had a living to earn with his internet dreams on hold. One day, mooching through Soho, he saw that a mug punter had left the window down and a shining leather briefcase on the back seat of his flash motor. There was a thick wodge of crisp twenties among the loads of useless documents.

Monkey splashed out some of the dosh on clothes, the sort of gear he imagined an upmarket chancer like Roland Mills would wear.

Sondra sent a picture of herself. *THIS IS ME*. It showed OK features and long straight hair. She wasn't a beauty, but good enough for Monkey. He wondered about her breasts. Another mail asked to see his picture. Back from the boozer, a comforting buzz in his bloodstream, he said it would spoil the surprise when he turned up at her front door.

The messages kept coming, like everything in her life, her skull, had to be transmitted to him. Reports of her activities, hefty digs about her feelings. *Went to the college dance last night but can't stop thinking about you.*

His zonked-out replies only seemed to crank up her interest, a dozen mails in his intray the next time he looked. Eventually the one-liner: *I LOVE YOU.*

Monkey, flattered, mailed back that he felt the same way and then wondered how to milk the situation. A straight request for dosh probably wouldn't go down too well, even in her besotted state. He started on the draft of a combination lover letter/business plan.

Then he got some bad news.

The word on the street that feelers were being put out for the reprobate who'd filched a briefcase in Soho. The stolen article belonging to a top-notch villain in the drugs trade, a monster bug. The disrespect regarded as beyond the pale, no quarter to be shown to the offending party.

He wished then that Monkey wasn't just a name, so he could make for the trees and vanish into the high foliage. Instead he did his usual insect dance, scurrying around in search of a hidey-hole for a week or two until the fuss died down. But this time it was different, he could tell from their faces. Geezers scared even to be seen with him. He sensed the snapping jaws were close behind. Time to do a serious runner.

He risked going back to the bed-sit to gather up his new clothes and passport, the laptop, and then did a twitchy scuttle to Heathrow. At the airport for something to calm his nerves he went into his intray for the first time in days. There were fifty-eight messages from Sondra.

The most recent of them said *PLEASE SPEAK TO ME! PLEASE!!!*

And he thought he was having a bad time! It wouldn't do her any harm to stew, he decided, make her all the more pleased to see him. He shut down the laptop and boarded the plane for New York.

He found himself a fancy hotel near Times Square and, after buying some hair bleach and an adaptor for the computer, changed into his Roland disguise. Feeling relaxed, convinced all his troubles were over, he fancied a spot of sightseeing before contacting Sondra. She'd be at boiling point by then. With a hot flush of his own coming on, he spent the afternoon in a porn cinema.

When he finally opened the intray it contained more than a hundred unread mails. He wondered at that moment if Sondra was quite right in the skull, but it was too late to turn back. It made him shiver just thinking about the searching soldier ants at home.

He didn't bother to read her messages. He had no address or telephone number, didn't even know her last name. Only one way to get in touch. He kept it short and sweet to double the impact. The name of his hotel and then, come and get me. He pressed the Send button and went down to the bar.

That night, after admiring his newly-golden locks in the mirror, Monkey had a panic attack. What if she was peeved about his silent treatment, didn't want to know? His remaining dosh wouldn't last more than a few days and he didn't fancy chancing his arm in Manhattan. The coppers with enough firepower to start a war.

The laptop was silent on the bed, no new mails from Sondra. He took a couple of pills to relax but still felt on edge. When the phone rang he did a passable imitation of one of his furry brothers, jumping halfway to the ceiling light.

A girly voice, sounding American. "Is that Roland?"

He had to think about it for a moment. "Yes."

"Can I come up and talk with you, please?"

He was checking his appearance, wishing he'd bought some shoes with lifts. "Please do," he said happily.

He opened the door to her minutes later, an ugly tart with curly hair and glasses. She's been having me on, Monkey thought angrily, can't trust anyone these days. He forgot about being upmarket. "You've been telling me porkies, Sondra."

She looked confused, but then picked up on the name. "You don't understand, Roland. I'm not Sondra. My name is Cherry. I was Sondra's room-mate."

She went on, "This is going to come as a shock."

He was already reaching for the duty-free Scotch. "I can guess," he whinged. "She's sent you to tell me to get lost."

There was a strange look on her mug. "You really don't understand, Roland, do you? I said I *was* her room-mate. Sondra is the one who's lost. She killed herself a few hours back."

While his gob fell open with a smack the woman's voice turned cold. "You should have stayed in touch, Roland." He felt a tickle in his belly. It could have been guilt, he wasn't sure.

"Been busy," he muttered. "Thought it'd be a nice surprise, me just turning up."

199

MONKEY

Silence, the bird still giving him the evil eye. This one's not taking to me at all, he thought. He offered her a drink in the hope the buzz would lighten her mood. She drained it quickly and gave a big wet sigh. "I suppose she told you she went to lots of dances?" she asked. He nodded, too down to speak.

"Lies, all lies. My ex-friend Sondra lived in a fantasy world. She couldn't even walk, Roland. Been in a wheelchair for the past three years."

"Shit," he said.

"Shit indeed," Cherry echoed.

The stare she gave him, Monkey felt like a specimen in a bottle. "She never did have any luck with men. That's how she ended up in the chair, jumped in front of her last boyfriend's car after he split with her. She always took any relationship way too seriously, even a stupid virtual one."

He asked, "How did she snuff it ... die?" Thinking about his own messy exit if he had to return to the Smoke.

"Well, she always was a drama queen, no slipping away quietly for Sondra. Got out of her chair and crawled to the window of our apartment, threw herself out from six floors up. A very determined lady."

Her specs had an accusing glint. "I got back from the hospital and saw your mail, came straight over. Thought you ought to know about your part in her downfall ... cheers, Roland." She snatched the bottle from him and gave it a pasting.

At least he made her laugh, trying to tap her for some dosh. The tight bitch was still smiling about it when she wished him a goodnight in hell.

After she left he finished off the whisky and popped some more pills, but couldn't shift the sickness in his guts. No Sondra, no smoochy hiding place. No strength to move either, like Cherry's story had punched all the life out of him.

She seemed to be having another go at him, getting him back for her friend. A mail appearing in his intray: *I'm coming to get you*. Trying to put the wind up him, must think he was a shit-arsed kid. The trouble was he didn't feel so good.

Even though he'd shut down the laptop, some instinct against sending a mouthful to Sondra's mail address, like taking the piss out of a corpse, he had the spooky sensation the messages were piling up in there. A pinging sound in his skull every time a new one arrived.

He told himself it was just a bad trip. Then he jumped when he heard loud voices outside in the corridor. Jesus, he was twitchy. Thinking about the creepy-crawlies on the hunt for him. He felt trapped but was too scared to leave the room, like it was the only safe place in the universe. He'd stay there until they forgot about his naughty, watching the cartoons on TV, ordering from room service whenever he needed any grub.

To prove his point, not even hungry, he picked up the phone and asked for a burger. He went back to staring at the ceiling. That Sondra, she was a strange one alright, a psycho, he was well out of it. The whole tub of shit was down to her, on his tod in a strange city. All her fault. Bleeding cripple.

A funny thing but he seemed to be having troubles of his own in that department, his pins too wonky for him to stand for long. A bad bad trip, the ghost mails arriving every few seconds, pumping up the volume.

Then the noises really started to kick in, going faster and faster, louder and louder, until all at once they shot through the roof, making a din like a dozen alarm bells. He upped the decibels on the TV, but it was like striking a match in a burning gaff. Curled up in a sweaty ball, his skull coming apart, Monkey finally sussed that Cherry had got her wish.

Then things suddenly went quiet, apart from the shouting voices on the box. He wondered if it was a trick at first, but finally wept tears of relief. Bad mistake, Sondra, he thought, filling up the intray so it can't accept no more messages.

He switched off the telly from the remote, still too shuddery to test his pins, feeling good about silence for almost the first time in his life.

There was a sound in the corridor. The creak of wheels, getting closer. "Shit," Monkey said.

The noise stopped outside his room, then a muffled female voice. He saw, horrified, that Cherry hadn't shut the door behind her. As it began to creak open, his head jerked frantically from side to side.

The waitress almost dropped her tray of food when she saw the not-so-wise Monkey crouched behind a cupboard. Eyes shut, hands over his ears, trying hard not to scream.

HAUNTED HOUSE

It was a mixed blessing, Mervyn decided, when he tripped over a step and banged his head against the garage wall. The benefits had been four blissful days spent off work, his wound treated with smiling care by a beautiful young nurse.

On the other hand, he had begun to see dead people everywhere.

He was used to them by now, eighteen months on, as they lurked at street corners or paced along busy roads, looking uneasy and preoccupied.

They had good reason to be upset. Take the female figure he saw on his way to the office, who stood outside the newsagents in the High Street and showed every sign of having just missed a bus. Except that a bus hadn't missed her. Five years ago. He remembered reading about it in the local paper.

They were all like that, he'd soon realised, unfortunates who had met an untimely and often violent end, struck down by acts of God or man. The victims of car crashes and fire and flood, noisy murder and quiet suicide. Some were unmarked, but most bore evidence of their passing, crushed limbs and broken heads. All were morbidly pale. The first time he sat next to a ghost on a train, he concluded that death didn't really improve anyone's looks.

They were sinister enough in winter, but at least it shrouded them, merged them with its general gloom. Sometimes he almost forgot they were there as he drove to work or the shops.

Summer was the worst. Their wounds always looked more horrific, bloodstains a brighter shade of red, their agitated eyes reflecting back the sunlight. And it was then he came across new ones, travelling around with his mother.

On tour in Scotland the previous August, they'd encountered a phantom hitchhiker, his outstretched thumb dangling by a thread of sinew. Nearby, oblivious to his ghostly neighbour, a young man with the flush of life on his cheeks had held up a card showing his destination. Mervyn hadn't stopped to pick either of them up.

He was fortunate to have a restriction on his dead people, he supposed, no-one who had died of illness or old age. They'd be everywhere otherwise, in supermarkets and private homes, jockeying for position around hospital beds. But somehow he didn't feel lucky.

He had grown accustomed to his condition, accepted that no-one could help him. The one time he broached the subject with their family doctor, the man had prescribed a course of tablets. It couldn't be anything but disconcerting, however, to picnic six feet from the bloated shade of a long-deceased bather with his mother saying, "Have another egg sandwich, dear."

HAUNTED HOUSE

It was now the second summer since his accident and the old lady wanted to get away for a break. The problem was finding a place where he would feel at ease, confident that everyone he came across was still breathing. The beach was out - too many treacherous currents and bad swimmers. And so were the mountains, for obvious reasons.

He didn't dare to contemplate the horrors of abroad, shuddered at the possibility of being in a plane with someone dripping blood on a long-haul flight. Luckily, his mother had her own fears about overseas travel, although in her case they centred on eating anything that contained garlic.

They'd gone on day trips to familiar places that he knew were sparsely populated with ghosts - praying there hadn't been a coach crash in the meantime - but were starting to feel the need for somewhere different, some novelty.

The TV advertisement for a theme park provided the answer. Perfect for a long weekend, it even contained its own four star hotel within walking distance of all the attractions. The ad made it out to be a happy sort of place, where people strolled everywhere, full of children and laughter. Surely nothing bad had ever happened in such a paradise?

Sunlight was glinting off the metal framework of the white-knuckle rollercoasters when they checked into the hotel on a Friday afternoon.

Everything appeared to be very new, Mervyn noted with pleasure, the site probably consisting of empty fields before the advent of the park. Nonetheless, he couldn't help looking around cautiously when they tried a few of the less intimidating rides the next morning.

He began to relax after lunch, having seen nothing more scary than the greasy hamburgers they'd eaten in a fast food restaurant. If I'm going to see any dead people, he decided, it's going to be in that place.

There was a moment of fright later on, when he spotted a gore-streaked figure dressed in rags near the entrance to the haunted house. But it turned out to be a park employee playing a ghoul.

He felt amused and a little contemptuous in the darkened building, listening to the screeches and gasps as their little train trundled between the tame mechanical devices and mildly-alarming optical illusions. No-one had ever heard him yell out, after all, even with his whole world turned into a haunted house.

It was warmer still the next day, hot enough for his mother to remove her cardigan. They watched some pretend jousting in an open-air arena complete with mock battlements. Mervyn loved it, knowing the realistic-looking armour and weapons were made of plastic or tin. The park was nothing but illusions and make-believe horrors, he now knew, a fun palace. It made a pleasant change from his own freak-show.

Much less pleasurable was the area containing the thrill rides. While they watched the rollercoasters twist and tumble at breakneck speeds, plunging with their shrieking cargoes to within feet of the ground, he marvelled that people chose to put themselves through such agonies. He knew spectres who were pictures of health compared to some of the holidaymakers staggering wild-eyed off the cars.

Seeing the enormous superstructures judder under the stress, he tried not to speculate how long it would be before the park had its quota of restless spirits. Studying his fellow spectators, their thrill-hungry faces, he wished for a moment he could open up his haunted house to the general public. At least their screams would be for real then.

His mother was already complaining about her feet when they arrived at the entrance to the circus big top. The park truly had everything except ghosts, Marvyn thought, while they waited in the semi-darkness of a canvassed vestibule for the next performance.

The edges of the tent were lined with trick mirrors that turned people taller or shorter or fatter or thinner. Some distorted their features in alarming ways. Mervyn was pulling faces in front of one such contraption when a red light came on overhead to signal the start of the next show. He stared into bulging eyes and a tongue that lolled from between thickened lips. Blood everywhere.

He could have been a corpse.

Mervyn wasn't perturbed, however, only confirmed in his belief that the dead didn't make the most attractive of companions. Somehow it added to his enjoyment of the circus; and he noted with particular satisfaction the quality of the safety net used in the trapeze act.

With a pang of regret as they drove away, he said, "We'll be back." His mother only nodded, too tired to speak. The early evening sunshine was in their eyes when they left the carpark.

He must have been more weary than he realised, after days of tramping and queuing in the heat. Certainly his mother was snoring next to him before they came to the bend in the road where a ghost prowled. He'd made a note of it on the outward journey; the figure of a biker wearing a silver helmet, anxiously searching for his lost machine. A clue to his status was the lack of both arms.

Mervyn, half-asleep at the wheel, didn't see the mutilated figure until the last moment. Blinded by the glare off its helmet, he pressed hard on the brake and the car went into a slide. There was an enormous thump as they hit a lamp-post, and then came the impact of other vehicles running into the back of them. He had the impression of people rushing about in a panic, before coming forward to help.

He was out of the car now, looking around for the biker. There was no sign of the apparition. Then he realised blood was trickling down his face from a knock on the head. And yet he experienced no pain, felt wonderful even.

He was cured!

But why was his mother screaming like that? He had to go to her. And what were those people doing, gathered around the driver's seat of their car? They seemed to be attending to someone. As he watched, one man turned away and shook his head grimly; he mouthed something to a knot of onlookers. Unable to make out any of the words, Mervyn wondered if his hearing had been affected by the crash. First ghosts, he thought, then deafness, it's one damn thing after another.

But worse than that, he was turning numb all over. No longer felt in the least bit wonderful.

In the next instant, as he guessed the truth, a spectral howl building in his throat, he caught the eye of a teenager being helped from one of the cars involved in the collision. Although there didn't seem to be much wrong with him, only a livid bruise on the temple, the young man looked in fear of his life.

Mervyn understood the reason at once. He was no longer in charge of the haunted house. Just another of its attractions.

THE CROSSING

Although he'd often pondered what it would feel like to kill someone - he hoped the deed would be glorious, in the line of duty - Stevens had to be told about it when his daydreams became a reality.

It was the merest nudge that had sent the cyclist careening into the ditch near the level crossing.

He'd been driving the unmarked police car too fast as usual, in a hurry to get to the station after a detour on his way back from investigating a late-night disturbance on the Bessington Estate. Already on a last warning about breaking the speed limit on non-emergency business, he knew that Sergeant Ecclestone would take malicious delight in having him thrown off the force.

Funny that, since it was the fat sergeant's wife who had occasioned the detour.

There was nothing quite so stimulating as a quickie on the living room carpet, he had decided, seconds before hitting the cyclist. He'd accelerated away from the scene without stopping, certain the man hadn't seen his number in the rain and dark, grateful the level crossing had recently been converted to automatic, no longer the watchful eye of some railwayman to observe what had happened.

The cyclist's body was spotted by a passing motorist the following day. It looked as if the man had banged his head on a tree after leaving the road. He might have had a thin skull, anyway it would all come out at the inquest.

"Poor bastard," Sergent Ecclestone said, breaking the news to him as they got ready for the evening shift, the smile on his rubbery lips making a mockery of the words.

Stevens said nothing, only thankful he was presumed to have been several miles away at the time.

Later on, though, he called Joanie, Ecclestone's wife, to make sure her feeble brain wasn't attempting to put two and two together. He was reassured by her sleepy non-comprehension of his guarded questions. As if she had time for anyone else's misfortunes but her own! Looking into her husband's stupid and malevolent face, Stevens could see her point.

The day was on-and-off sunny when he next passed the old signal box. Watery light shifting across its broken windows gave the illusion of movement inside, which prompted him to offer up silent thanks to the decrepit hulk and everyone who had ever worked in it. He couldn't help feeling the place had saved his bacon.

THE CROSSING

But the memory of the incident had begun to fade when he first encountered the cyclist's widow. He was on another callout to the Bessington, a daylight mugging this time, and suddenly realised the dead man had lived in the next street.

Out of curiosity, wondering if he had noted the man's address from the dossier with more than just a copper's reflex, he pulled up near the house, a shabby semi in a long line of shabby semis.

And then he saw her, knew it was the wife even before she opened the peeling gate and walked up the short garden path. The look on her face was the give-away, proclaiming that something terrible had happened to her. For all that, she was youthful-looking and pretty. He drove away in a thoughtful mood.

Two days later, off-duty, he was back outside the semi, wondering how he could get to meet the woman. Ring the bell and say, "Hullo, I'm the copper who killed your husband"? He could think of more persuasive chat-up lines.

His problem was solved not long afterwards by an aggravated burglary a few doors away. The standard procedure being a quick house-to-house in the immediate vicinity, he volunteered for the job and wondered at his nervousness as he knocked on the door in its cracked council green.

She didn't look so young close up, worry lines clustered around her eyes, but the blonde hair was fine and her lips nicely shaped if unsmiling.

After a couple of cursory questions, to which she gave the expected negative responses, he was about to lapse into silence when he noticed the framed picture on the television set.

It was hardly subtle, but there seemed no other way to kick things off. "Excuse me," he said, pointing to the portrait, "but don't I know him?"

Anticipating a rebuff or perhaps tears, he was gratified by her matter-of-fact reply. "He was my husband," she said. "He died."

Stevens pretended recall. "Of course," he lied. "I was at the morgue when they brought him in." He shook his head. "Terrible business. They reckoned he fell off his bike, didn't they? He'd had a few pints that night."

She looked steadily back at him and he was disturbed at being the first to look away. Her technique could have come straight off a police training video: *How To Interrogate Stupid Coppers*.

"He rode that bike everywhere," she said, scornfully. "He never came off once, not even after a skinful. No, someone knocked him into that ditch." But if the thought upset her, she didn't show it. Cold bitch, Stevens thought, wondering what she'd say if he told her the truth. It crossed his mind that she might even thank him.

THE CROSSING

Puzzled by her lack of emotion, he nevertheless felt convinced there was a spark of response, a quick glance from under her eyelids, when he said, "Well, if there's anything I can do for you ..."

He knew there were few women who could resist his well-practiced charm at full blast. "I'll see you, then," he said on the doorstep, wondering if she would understand the meaning behind his words. When she gave a small nod, it seemed like the clearest of signals. All the same, he had to play it careful, mustn't rush into things.

After all, for Christ's sake, he'd just killed the husband, even wondered if that was half the attraction. Then there was the woman herself, did she possess any warmth at all under the glacial surface? Still, it would be nice trying to find out.

He was unable to stop thinking about her in the days that followed.

The affair with Joanie was an early casualty of his preoccupation with the widow. When she pestered to see him, he frightened her off by hinting that Ecclestone suspected something. If it came to a choice between his embraces and the fat sergeant's fists, he knew, there was no contest.

Unable to wait any longer, he went around to the Bessington. The woman gave an enquiring look at the door, seemed barely to recognise him. When Stevens pretended concern for her welfare, she was polite but detached. They talked for a while and then she offered to cook him something. Later still, they went to bed and made love three times.

In the morning, studying her sleeping face, he realised it looked just as troubled in repose. Christ, even her lovemaking had sounded as if she was about to burst into tears!

Still, it hadn't seemed to affect her enjoyment. It certainly hadn't affected his. When he slipped out of the house before she awoke, however, he had little intention of returning for more. To be honest, he liked his females with more sparkle.

He was back the following evening, and the evening after that. The woman gave a quizzical look on the doorstep each time, before letting him in without a word. He was starting to enjoy the routine of waking to her sulky features.

The next time he called around he was carrying a holdall of spare clothes, which the woman hung up for him in the cupboard in her spare bedroom. In order to make space, she had to remove her husband's shirts and trousers and a single shabby-looking suit. Stevens was pleased when she folded these neatly into a couple of bin bags, explaining that she would give them to the Oxfam shop in the morning.

THE CROSSING

Encouraged by Stevens, she began to talk about her husband. He hoped to hear the dead man had been abusive, that she was glad to be rid of him. It would have turned the accident into something positive, even an act of chivalry.

But she had nothing bad to say about the man, in fact, nothing much to say at all. He'd cycled a lot, drank a lot, worked as a fitter in a local factory before being made redundant. They had got on alright. People spoke with more passion about their pet birds.

He began to stay over on the weekends he was off-duty; and one Saturday morning found a bicycle in the garden shed, realising with a shock that it fitted the description in the dossier. Without knowing why, he asked the woman if it would be alright for him to ride it - he'd been thinking about doing something to keep fit. She simply shrugged and carried on with her cleaning.

Their affair should have been an ideal arrangement, every philanderer's dream, a woman who demanded no commitment and requested no favours. Always ready and willing when the rest of his harem was otherwise engaged.

The only snag was that his other concubines had all done a runner, tipped off by the unreturned phone calls and cancelled assignations, hiding out with husbands or boyfriends or seeking refuge in television and chocolate. He wasn't bothered. She was enough for him.

He wondered, though, when he would finally break through the ice. She seemed to have so many layers!

He believed he'd cracked it, torched her into life, when she murmured "Darling" into his ear during one of their climaxes. The next evening, however, when he phoned to say he couldn't make it, working overtime, she sounded almost relieved.

That was the other thing troubling him. Was there someone else on the scene, another man who'd walked in off the street and been accepted straightaway as a bed partner?

With any of the others he'd have come right out with it, anticipating a lie. This woman's reply would be brutally honest, he just knew, and the wrong answer would trigger his code of honour, obliging him to ditch her. He couldn't take the risk.

One evening, he saw some older lads banging on his car outside her house and warned them off. As they sneered away, he heard someone mutter, "Filth". He realised word must have gotten around, too many crooks on the Bessington for it to be otherwise.

THE CROSSING

There were yobs and vandals all over the place. Only hours before, on his way to see the woman, he'd passed the old signal box. Offering it his usual soundless homage, he'd got the impression of someone lurking inside, a shadowy face staring back at him. Little bastards messing about, he told himself, in too much of a hurry to stop and investigate. Eager to see her.

He knew he could handle any number of young thugs, but there was no point in asking for trouble.

"I'll use the bike from now on, the exercise will do me good," he told the woman. She just gave him a look.

The next night the word FILTH was painted on her front door in red letters. Although the woman seemed almost amused, Stevens immediately went to the home of the lad he knew to be the leader of the gang. The boy's father, a small-time criminal, answered the door and refused to let Stevens speak to his son. His mistake was to mouth an obscenity as the policeman, cooling down, turned to walk away.

Stevens hit him hard in the stomach, leaving the man to throw up his dinner on the squalid driveway. He was confident that no-one would report him, the family least of all. They wouldn't want the police meddling in their affairs.

Unfortunately for him, one of their neighbours happened to be among the few law-abiding citizens in the area and had seen everything. Worse still, she remembered Stevens from a previous burglary investigation, when she believed money had gone missing after he'd been in her house. Combining righteousness and revenge, she went to the station the next day.

Stevens was suspended on full salary pending an internal investigation.

One of his colleagues confided there were other charges in the pipeline, following complaints from small shopkeepers that he'd taken things without paying for them. He laughed disbelievingly at that one, wasn't it a perk of the job?

At a later interview, a superior officer said his relationship with the woman was inappropriate. He found that amusing, too, given the fact she was single and unattached, conditions that couldn't be ascribed to many of his conquests.

To pass the time, he began to use the cycle even when he wasn't visiting the woman.

The countryside outside the town was criss-crossed by narrow lanes that led to well-groomed villages where the small cottages were more likely to house computer professionals than farm labourers. But that meant there were well-stocked pubs everywhere, serving good food and a variety of beers.

THE CROSSING

He had never been a connoisseur of booze. Alcohol was simply a means to an end, sufficient to loosen the tongue and then the knicker elastic. Now, for the first time, often hot and sweaty after a long ride through the August sunshine, he began to take pleasure in drinking for its own sake.

"He used to do that," the woman said, when he told her about a place that sold a particularly fine selection of real ales. "Spending money he didn't have in pubs. He must have been in every one for twenty miles. Only he held his drink better than you."

Stevens didn't resent the inference that the dead man had been better than him. It was the living ones you had to watch out for.

Although he still hadn't caught out the woman, he felt convinced there was another boyfriend. They continued to get on well in bed, but her affection for him seemed to begin and end there. Given what he suspected about the volcano under the ice, she had to be treating some other bloke better than him.

The only time she'd shown any admiration for him was after he punched her neighbour. He remembered a remark made in passing by a female colleague about the dead cyclist, before Stevens had met the woman. "Bit of a bully, that bloke, but he didn't deserve to die."

Now he wondered what she'd meant. The husband had no criminal record. Perhaps she'd come across him on a domestic call-out? Had he been handy with his fists? He raised the subject with the woman. Finally, exasperated by her non-committal answers, he asked point-blank if her huband had mistreated her.

"If you mean, was he paranoid," she replied. "Yes, he was. Just like you." She refused to say any more, even when he grew angry. She appeared to be inviting his aggression. Would she enjoy it? Was that why she didn't respect him, because he hadn't beaten her?

He began to imagine himself hitting her, in the same way he'd once dreamed of killing criminals. A small inner voice said she would deserve it. To prevent himself from being tempted, he was spending more and more time on his bike. He was discovering pubs he didn't even know existed, had never come across in all his years as a policeman.

Had he ever been a policeman? His previous life seemed more like a dream. Something in his head wondered how it would feel to work in a factory.

He took to calling on the woman at odd times, frequently in the small hours, hoping to catch her with the other man. He never did, but often got the impression she'd only just said goodbye to someone else and was secretly laughing at him as they lay together in the dark.

THE CROSSING

He had the sensation now of crossing into enemy territory every time he cycled past the old signal box on his way to see the woman. He wondered if squatters had moved in there, vague figures in its dark interior, the notion he was being watched. It darkened his mood still further.

The worst thing was that she appeared to be unaware of his erratic behaviour. Confronted with her expressionless face, he began to understand what her husband had gone through. He often felt as if he was being punished for what he'd done to the man. Sometimes it felt as if he *was* her husband.

And so he drank even more, drowning himself in beer. But he could still remain steady on his bike, able to hoodwink his erstwhile colleagues as they passed by in their fancy cars.

When he boasted about this to the woman, she said, "You've changed a lot lately." Wearily, as if it wasn't the first time she'd spoken those words.

He didn't tell her when he received the letter sacking him from the police force. What would be the point? It didn't seem real even to him. He thought he shouldn't see her any more, the urge to do her serious harm growing more powerful every time he entered the semi. Knowing it to be filled with her mocking laughter when he wasn't around. Instead he cycled into the countryside, looking for a public house he hadn't yet visited. The same voice inside him said it was important.

He saw a crimson light in the distance. The old signal box. Shouts and screams reached him on the strengthening wind. Must be having a party, he thought.

He eventually found himself on the edge of a tiny hamlet he'd never heard of. For some reason, though, the pub looked familiar. The room was cheerless and almost empty and even the few regulars looked miserable about being there. No-one spoke to him.

As he sat with one pint after another, pondering his misfortunes, he concluded they had a single cause. The woman. It was her fault he was broke and friendless and without a job. And now she was sneering at him behind his back with this other man, whoever he was. Well, he'd show her, the sour-faced bitch.

When he left the pub, the voice was drowning out everything else in his head.

Rain was sluicing down, but he set off confidently into the darkness. The voice seemed to be directing him along the unlit track and it came as no surprise when he emerged from a series of lanes to see the level crossing ahead.

Somehow he knew exactly what would happen next.

THE CROSSING

The car was travelling too fast for the conditions, its lights ablaze, and came alongside him in a rush of cold air. His front wheel went perilously close to the edge of the ditch as the vehicle brushed against him. Then, beaten, it retreated into the distance while he calmly carried on pedalling towards the Bessington.

He looked up to acknowledge the shades, silent now, as they watched from the old signal box. They returned his salute. Something inside him said the crossing was complete.

He admired the way his grip felt strong on the handlebars. The voice continued to encourage him, saying how lucky it was that he'd put his hands to good use in the factory all these years.

They were required now to perform the one last task. His unfinished business ...

THE FACE

Have you ever woken to find a strange face on the pillow next to you? Have you ever stared for a moment into panic-stricken eyes? Have you ever jerked upright in bed in shock and alarm?

What if you blinked and the face went away? What if it happened more than once?

Would you think you were going mad?

Richard Millman, fearful of just that, was advised by his doctor that the cause was most probably stress and the depression inevitably brought on by the death of his wife. Sally had only been gone six months. Richard decided to follow the man's advice and give it time.

When, a week later, he emerged from a drug-induced sleep to confront the same apprehensive gaze, the face inches away from his own, he screamed once more and then told himself his mind was simply playing tricks.

And yet she seemed so real, just for that split second! When the same thing happened again and then again, he knew he had to get professional help.

The psychiatrist was very thorough - not to mention expensive - but all her probing could find nothing in Richard's past or present to account for the visitation. The stranger was no-one he had ever met or even seen. In spite of her air of calm assurance, Richard sensed that she too was beginning to think of him as just a loony. He rang her to call off their next appointment.

He had no-one close to turn to. His mother and father were both dead and he had no siblings.

No children either, he mused bitterly, they'd never got beyond talk about starting a family. Sally's own relatives lived on another continent. He skirted around the subject with various friends at work, hinting that he was having more than just bad dreams, but always stopped when he saw the onset of disbelief or amusement in the other person's eyes.

The next time the woman appeared, he worked hard not to blink and took in her face for a second or two longer. It was then, for the first time, that he realised the apparition was effectively a snapshot. Unmoving, unblinking.

A shouted question was on his lips when the frightened countenance disappeared in an instant. Whoever she might be, his tormenter was youngish and good-looking in a careworn sort of way. It crossed his mind that something terrible must have happened to her.

She began to appear to him first thing every morning. He conjectured why - if such weirdness had to happen at all - he wasn't waking to Sally's sweet-natured features.

THE FACE

Then the strangest idea came to him. Maybe there'd been a mix-up. Perhaps another man was exchanging startled glances with Sally and wondering why it wasn't his late wife he saw. For a moment, Richard was convinced he *had* gone mad.

Partly to keep such notions out of his head, he determined to treat the mystery as a problem capable of being resolved by reason, by analysis and deduction.

First, he had to make up his mind what it wasn't. Couldn't be that the house was haunted, too new for that, they'd been its first occupants. Anyway, he refused to believe in things that went bump in the night, much too old and cynical.

He felt certain it wasn't some sort of after-affect from a repeated nightmare. Much too vivid. And, anyway, even as a kid he'd never suffered from an over-active imagination. In spite of everything, he was functioning as best he could in every other aspect of his life, which seemed to indicate that he hadn't lost his marbles.

So what *was* happening to him?

The next step seemed a logical one. He stopped taking the stuff to make him sleep.

Fortified by black coffee, he spent the night with a book, occasionally staring at the starless sky through his undrawn curtains. It was half past three when he last looked at his watch; then he must have drifted off because there was an orange glow at the window when he jolted back into consciousness.

The frozen, wide-open eyes were staring into his. Just for a second or two. Just long enough for him to yell out with terror and frustration.

He made his bleary way into the office, too conscientious to miss work, not wanting to be on his own. It happened when he passed a sandwich shop where he often went for his lunch.

He saw the face.

The woman, dressed in a white coat, was working behind the counter of the shop. Richard stood transfixed, staring at her for several seconds, the blood pounding through his brain.

When his heartbeat finally subsided, his first instinct was to charge into the shop and confront her. He had already taken a step forward before a series of thoughts occurred to him. She'll think I'm mad. Everyone in there will think I'm mad. How exactly do you go about accusing a stranger of haunting you?

Instead, with the feeling of being incredibly brave, he went in and ordered a sandwich. "T - tuna mayonnaise on brown, please," he stuttered.

THE FACE

Up close, he only became more positive it was her. The same tiny wrinkles around the same grey eyes. The same nose and lips. Even the way she made up his order, with a slight frown, added to his certainty; he'd somehow grown convinced that that a puckered brow was his dream woman's more usual expression.

He jumped a little when she took his money and their fingers touched. "You new here?" he asked, struggling to sound casual.

Her reaction was a timid nod. "Yes," she said with a blush, evidently believing he was trying to flirt with her.

With an excuse about not feeling well - which happened to be true - he finished work early. The sandwich shop closed at half past two, after the lunch-time rush. The woman emerged in a drab brown coat. He stayed close behind as she caught a train to another part of the city, then followed her to a block of flats.

He took time off work - not even bothering to phone in, there didn't seem much point in making lame excuses when it felt as if he was going out of his head - and saw a lot of the woman in the next few days.

After waking to her face in the morning, he spent hours, surreptitiously, in her company. He trailed her after work and around the shops, to school to pick up her kids. There were three young ones, noisy and unruly, no wonder she looked permanently harassed. Her husband didn't appear to be a great deal of help, spending much of his spare time in their local pub.

He learned her name, Tina, from a colleague in the sandwich shop on her day off. She seemed like an ordinary, decent female, no different from thousand of others in the city. So why was she plaguing him?

One evening, he manouvred himself into conversation with her husband in his local, winning over the man with a couple of rounds of drinks.

When he brought up the subject of families by saying, honestly, that he had none of his own, his new acquaintance was soon in full flow about his wife. "Silly little thing," he confided. "Afraid of her own shadow." But Richard learned nothing of any apparent importance. She was ordinary, ordinary, ordinary.

The people at work were no doubt wondering what had happened to him. He was likely to lose his job. And for what? Absolutely nothing had changed. The expression on the fleeting image of her face. His predicament. The horrible suspicion that he was stuck with her for the rest of his days.

He rose early the next morning and made his way across the city, determined to spend as much time with Tina as possible, still hoping for a clue in her behaviour, something she did.

THE FACE

As they made their glum-faced way towards the railway station, he was reminded of what the husband had said. She *was* a timid little thing alright, constantly darting her head to left and right. Once she even stopped and looked back over her shoulder. He had to dodge sharply into a shop doorway.

Waiting nearby while she bought a magazine from the station kiosk, he could feel himself trembling with tension and barely-suppressed rage.

It was all the woman's fault. He followed her onto the crowded platform with tears of self-pity stinging his eyes. Then, taking in the slight figure in front of him, recalling his hunch that something terrible must have happened to her, his distress broadened out to include his quarry. Well, it's something binding us together, he thought wryly.

She was still peering about her anxiously. His own nerves felt like red-hot wires.

It suddenly came to him that he'd gone about things the wrong way. He should have spoken to her, explained about his little problem, not acted like an inept and unproductive spy. They could have sat down and talked it over, discovered what had brought them together in this way, where exactly their lives intersected.

But it wasn't too late. Impulsively, driven by the need to resolve matters, he walked into her line of sight. He saw Tina jump, a flash of recognition in her eyes. She knew him, he felt certain, and not only from their brief encounter in the sandwich shop.

Somehow she knew him! For an instant the answer to the whole puzzle seemed just around the corner.

As he stepped closer, about to speak, the woman's face changed, her features taking on a grotesquely familiar expression. Startled, stunned, scared. He shuddered violently.

"Why have you been following me?" she implored. He was conscious that several heads had turned in their direction.

"Please ..." he croaked, stretching out a hand to reassure her. The woman screamed and cringed away from him. She stumbled backwards onto the track.

Any number of people on the platform had caught the fright on the woman's face, had heard her cry out. They'd watched as his arm jerked forward, just before she fell into the path of the express train.

More than one of them, talking to the police afterwards, interpreted the gesture as a push. He had been seen hanging around the sandwich bar for days on end; and his friends at work were forced to admit that he'd been acting strangely in the period leading up to Tina's death.

Even the testimony of his doctor and the psychiatrist only strengthened the case against him. All the evidence pointed to the presence of some kind of paranoid delusion which had driven him to kill. Most likely brought on by the loss of his wife.

The dead woman's husband hammered down the lid of the coffin when he recalled their chat in the pub.

In the days following his arrest, Richard certainly gave every impression of being in a profound clinical depression. He was actually almost catatonic with bewilderment, wondering why the truth had never occurred to him.

Because for all his attempted analysis of the situation, the search for hard facts, he had completely overlooked what had, literally, been staring him in the face. It seemed so obvious now the woman was dead.

The vision had been the shape of things to come. Not from his past but his future. A presentiment.

In the weeks and months that followed, of interrogation and incarceration, Richard continued to see a lot of Tina. She often appeared in his nightmares or at unguarded moments during the day. Her blurred features were sometimes mixed up with those of his equally dead Sally.

Things could have been worse, he consoled himself. He had escaped one horror at least. He no longer saw a strange face when he woke up.

DANCING IN THE DARK

He fell in love with graveyards as a boy, seeing distant figures dance among the tombstones as he walked past their local church with his parents one fine Spring evening.

He mentioned his experience to no-one and wondered afterwards if it had happened in a dream - for a period in his early teens he spent every night in a dimly-glimpsed but apparently enormous cave, unseen creatures everywhere about him, the sensation more vivid than anything in his waking life - but didn't think so.

That first sighting was just prior to the sudden death of his fierce-looking maternal grandmother, a fact he remembered much later on.

He couldn't decide who had been secretly more pleased when the old woman died, him or his dad. Walking through the cemetery, as he did almost every day after school, he always avoided the path that would take him close to her resting place.

His obsession continued after he went to the local college, searching out country churches every weekend in the old Mini given to him as an eighteenth birthday present. When he came across a particularly interesting gravestone, he would take its picture and paste this in a cheap album.

He soon had several volumes of photos. Showing them to his pal Gary one day, he felt disappointed that his enthusiasm wasn't shared. Their friendship ended a short while later when he told Gary that he'd spent the whole of the previous night curled up against a crypt, happily sipping from a bottle of wine.

At home, it was increasingly as if his unlamented grandmother had been resurrected. His dad began to spend more and more time in the garden shed, away from his wife's never-ending censure. She disliked almost everything about her husband, but especially the way he always buckled under her criticism.

"Spineless, no wonder you've never been promoted."

Her son, on the other hand, she regarded with unqualified approval. He occasionally wished he could return the feeling.

Father and son bore their different crosses stoically, the one loathed, the other loved, both staggering under a crushing weight of words. Anything for a quiet life. Perhaps it was the silence of the grave that attracted him, he sometimes thought on his all-night vigils, still watching out for the dancers.

He had invented a hobby - night-fishing - to explain his nocturnal forays, only glad that his mother never commented on the lack of any product from his supposed efforts.

His father, typically, had added two and two and made five. "Don't worry, I won't say a word," he said, winking and touching a finger to the side of his nose.

DANCING IN THE DARK

And then, miraculously, he *did* have a girlfriend, a fellow student, falteringly approached at a college dance and thrillingly responsive to his stumbling overtures. Laura was frivolous and light-hearted - everything his mother wasn't - and seemed to promise another way out of his existence. He even began to cut down on his churchyard visits, although it was of some consolation that he had to cross the municipal cemetery to get to the flat Laura shared with several other girls.

He debated whether to tell his dad the news, knowing it would please but also depress the old man, make him think about the even harder times ahead when the three of them became two.

In the end he decided to keep silent, but tried to encourage the mildly-rebellious streak that led to long hours spent in the shed, away from the nagging tongue. He said nothing to his mother because he sensed it would be a fatal mistake.

It was a couple of months from his nineteenth birthday when he encountered the dancers again.

He'd left the house after a blazing row with his mother. She'd come across a picture of Laura in a cupboard in his room and accused him of deceit and betrayal. They might have been a married couple instead of mother and son. His dad had fretted on the edges of the quarrel, endeavouring not to draw attention to himself, his eyes filled with wonder at the boy's noisy defiance.

As he slammed out of the house, he could hear the whiplash of her voice turn against the old man. Only recently, exasperated that his campaign to stiffen his father's resistance was failing, he had asked him outright, "Why do you stay with her?"

The old man had looked puzzled for a moment, raising hopes that he'd got through at last, finally triggered some doubts about a doomed relationship. When he realised it was the question itself that had thrown his dad, he knew he was talking to a lost soul. Someone who perhaps had always yearned to be lost.

So, returning home the next day, he was more distressed than surprised to learn that his father had killed himself during the night. The real shock had come as he lurked in the municipal graveyard, grateful for its comforting embrace, not wanting to see anyone, not even Laura.

It was in the pitch-black of the early hours, while he dozed fitfully against a headstone, that he'd heard them stirring all around. The faintest of rustlings at first, then more audible scratchings and scrapings. The noises had rapidly grown in strength and purpose, until all at once he'd got the impression of many forms coming together in the dark, twisting and writhing in a ghostly saraband.

DANCING IN THE DARK

The dance had lasted only minutes, followed by a profound silence; sudden fragmentary moonlight had revealed he was alone in the cemetery. He'd felt no fear, only disappointment at not actually seeing the dancers.

The funeral was symbolic of his father's life and death, unobtrusive and low-key, hurried and furtive.

There were few mourners and general relief when it was over. His mother's choice of the municipal cemetary rather than their local churchyard for the burial seemed like a deliberate insult. He continued to endure her cloying attentions, but told himself he would get away as soon as he decently could.

Neither of them mentioned his girlfriend again. The relationship had anyway cooled, Laura saying she was too young to commit herself to one person.

Her rejection had upset him, but at least it meant he could spend more time in the cemetery. He had taken to sneaking in there in the early hours to watch over his father's grave, waiting for the dancers to return. Wondering why they'd appeared on only the two occasions more than twelve years apart.

The incident with the dancers had only just preceded the other thing, the lonely ending in the garden shed, and he sensed that they were somehow connected, the visitations and the deaths of his relatives. It was almost as if he'd been given leave to attend as they were danced into the tomb.

The thought was exhilarating; and he felt flattered that it seemed to be happening only to him, all his love of graveyards being repaid.

The cemetery had become his real home, he decided, a place of refuge when his mother was asleep.

He hardly spoke to her these days, could barely stand to look at her, her features beginning to remind him of his grandmother's much-dreaded mask. It only made things worse that she continued to indulge him in every way.

When Laura approached him in the student restaurant and said she wanted nothing more to do with him, he knew at once that his mother was involved.

"I can do without the hassle," Laura said, her anger ebbing when she looked into his face. "Being called names in front of my friends. Just keep her away from me, that's all."

As an act of defiance, he had gotten into the habit of stopping off for a couple of pints at the end of each college day, before dragging himself back to the house. That evening, several drinks over his usual quota, the unaccustomed whisky making him feel sick, he decided to make a detour through the municipal cemetery.

He hoped it would give him the strength to confront her.

DANCING IN THE DARK

He would keep the whole thing dignified, a minimum of name-calling, but would very firmly place the blame where it belonged. Especially for his dad's death. A glow of anticipation warmed him, imagining her reaction when he came down the stairs with his suitcase.

He glimpsed them through a stand of trees as he approached the cemetery. Writhing and whirling to some sepulchral but unheard melody, hundreds of vague figures cavorting in the twilight.

He staggered into a run, but they had disappeared even before he made it through the main gate. Stumbling to a halt, he cursed his luck, then decided that the sighting was an omen, urging him to get on with his life. He rushed off, more determined than ever to go through with the confrontation.

The meaning of what he'd seen only percolated through the alcohol haze as he let himself into the house. The dancers were concerned with the dead, not the living. His mother ...

He felt uncertain whether to be relieved or disappointed, hearing her in the kitchen as he opened the front door. Then he grew furious, thinking that she'd disproved his theory about the dancers. When his mother appeared at the kitchen entrance, her welcoming look turned his stomach and everything after that happened in a nightmarish blur. His carefully-prepared speech rapidly turned into a tirade.

She followed him around as he gathered up his clothes and shovelled them into a case, pleading with him to stay. Things were turning dark around him, the walls of the small house expanding into a huge cavern, his mother's gargoyle face at every turn.

So dark that he could scarcely see when he barged into her at the top of the stairs as she attempted to block his way.

He had her buried in the municipal cemetery, not far from his father's grave. There were even fewer mourners this time. Most satisfying, however, was knowing that his instinct about the dancers had been proved right.

It was the evening of his nineteenth birthday and he was on his tenth pint, reluctant to go back to the empty house.

Nothing had turned out as he'd imagined.

Laura still didn't want anything more to do with him; the last time he'd visited her flat, a strange man had threatened to punch him if he bothered her again, while Laura and her friends had giggled in the background. Though he would never admit it, he even missed the sound of his mother's voice, talking through his favourite TV programmes.

Above all, he was depressed to think that he would never again see the dancers. He had no remaining close relatives that he knew of; his mother and father had been only children, his grandparents were all dead. Although he still visited the occasional graveyard, it was more out of habit than anything else and he often left, dejected, long before the sun fell.

His life had lost all purpose.

When he left the pub, rain was sluicing from a moonless sky. He staggered towards the municipal cemetery, not wanting to return home and having nowhere else to go.

He decided drunkenly to call on Laura in the hope she would take pity on him. In his light clothes he was soon soaked to the skin. After clambering unsteadily through the gap in the railings, he stumbled blindly across the waterlogged grass, heading for the main path through the cemetery.

Suddenly he was falling, plunging headfirst into liquid mud. As he lay winded, staring up at the blackness, he realised that he was at the bottom of an open grave, freshly-dug for a funeral the next day.

Giggling to begin with, stupidly inebriated, he attempted to scrabble up the sides of the pit. But all his efforts were defeated, the mud sliding through his fingers, the quagmire under his feet turning into quicksand as the rain continued to hammer down. Finally, he collapsed to his knees, too exhausted even to call out. And anyway there was no-one out there to hear him, he knew, his body already turning numb with the cold.

Fighting to stay awake, he was tempted by images of sleep, curled up in his own silent world, a warm and private place. He closed his eyes at last.

He woke with mud in his mouth and his heart like a block of ice, turning over feebly in his frozen chest. The rain had stopped and everything was quiet except for the rattling sounds coming from deep inside him.

The first soft noise barely registered on his dimming consciousness, but it was soon joined by others, as if hundreds of small animals were simultaneously burrowing to the surface.

As he listened, the disturbances grew louder. He pictured great mounds of earth being pushed to one side. Frigid night air being gasped into non-existent lungs. Spindly limbs unravelling.

When he heard their footsteps rustling across the sodden earth, he smiled. He only wished he was with them, dancing himself into the grave.

PARTS

Clements was a strange one alright, silent as the grave most of the time and then piping up with his bizarre notions of justice. A lot of people in the office thought he was more than a bit creepy.

I'd never had much in the way of a proper conversation with him - no-one had - but gleaned that he lived on his own, was unmarried, and liked to collect things. Stamps, old postcards, the sort of comics that have green-skinned men and yellow-and-red explosions on their front covers. I pictured them stored away in carefully-labelled plastic envelopes.

The only time he got out of the house, apart from coming to work, must have been when a collectors' fair was held in town. It didn't seem much of a life. Since I have loner tendencies myself, it probably explains why I tried so hard not to judge him.

He never came for a drink with us after work. Most of the others were only too pleased about that, but I would have been glad of the chance to get a drop or two of the hard stuff down him to see if it opened him up.

I suppose I was intrigued by him, more than a little curious about his inner life. I try to write novels in my spare time and like to think I can get to the bottom of what makes most people tick.

But Clements was a puzzle to me.

Even our boss, an energetic and level-headed female in her late forties, didn't know what to make of the man. She confided in me that reporting on him to her superior was an almost impossible task.

There was nothing to say about him, one way or the other. He just got on with his job, performing up to the standard required, but never went beyond that, never took any sort of initiative. I agreed with her that he seemed to have no substance, nothing to get hold of.

His self-consciousness, almost child-like priggishness, screamed of clueless inexperience. He looked uncomfortable when anyone swore. The man was thirty-five years old and I wondered if he'd slept with even a single female. A distinct blush crossed the stolid features whenever he was forced to discuss business with any of our female colleagues.

As for joining in the bouts of crude banter that erupted to make time pass less slowly - and a couple of our young girls were the worst of the lot - I'm sure he would sooner have stuck his head in the shredding machine.

Only one aspect of Clements stood out, made him seem both less and more of a mystery man.

PARTS

As with most offices, we have our slack periods. People at such times talk about things they've seen on TV or read in the papers. Soaps, the doings of celebrities, murder trials. The froth on the luke-warm drink of everyday existence. It was in the course of such debates that Clements flickered into life, coming out with almost the only spontaneous remarks I ever heard him make.

We would be having a general chat about some criminal or anti-social act that had just taken place in the big wide world when, without warning, Clements would suddenly join in. He never spoke more than a few sentences, before returning to his normal taciturnity, but they were always guaranteed to stun the assembly into temporary silence.

One time, we were in full flow about an outbreak of petty vandalism that was taking place locally, boys throwing stones at passing trains. A couple of the rascals had been caught in the act. Someone said they'd probably get off with a warning.

"I know what I'd do with them," Clements spoke up, fervently. "I'd strap them to the front of a train and take it at speed through a long dark tunnel. See how they liked that."

His interventions were always along the same lines, a suggested punishment to exceed the crime. Restauranteurs suspected of using rotten meat should be forced to eat the stuff every day for the next twelve months. Lorry drivers who fiddled with their tachometers ought to be made to drive through a minefield. Noise polluters to be locked in a room with a concealed stereo system at full blast.

The stridency in his voice always in stark contrast to his usual mutterings.

Immediately after each of his flare-ups he would put his head down and carry on working, as if it was the most normal thing in the world to rant that arsonists should be put on bonfires. The rest of us would just look at each other, several shrugging, a few of the girls giggling, one or two of the men muttering, "Weirdo!", before resuming our conversation.

It became part of the fabric of life in our office, a standing joke, and I suspect that some people went out of their way to spark a response from Clements.

While everyone else regarded him as a sort of village idiot, the man's behaviour made me speculate even more about what went on in his head. It was evident that he had strong feelings, with regard to certain things anyway, and equally obvious that he kept them under wraps most of the time. I wondered about the fires raging inside him.

I tried still harder after that to gain his trust, open a channel of communication with him, and achieved a small measure of success. Making sure I bumped into the man at the water cooler, I even managed to inveigle him into - short - conversations on topics unrelated to work. Once or twice I got the impression Clements was about to tell me more about himself, but he always relapsed into an awkward silence.

I began to wonder if the others were right and he was simply a waste of space. Which made it even more of a surprise when he came out with his remarks about me and Becky.

Becky was a colleague, a young woman in a miserable marriage, who had turned to me for support and comfort. Since she was pretty as well as unhappy, I was only too willing to provide my services. I think everyone in the place knew of our affair, but considered it none of their business.

All except Clements.

We were at the water cooler one day when Becky walked by and flashed me an intimate smile. I turned back to Clements and saw a look of ineffable disgust on his face. "You shouldn't be doing it," he said, heatedly.

I was too astonished to speak. "It's not right, she's married," he went on, with what I can only describe as a show of schoolboy disgust, just about stamping his foot. "You'll be punished, mark my words".

With that he walked off, leaving me with a jaw that stretched to the office carpet.

Our relationship, if it could be termed that, was never the same again. I began to time my trips to the water cooler to avoid him. On a couple of occasions I caught him looking at me in a strange kind of way, embarrassed and yet speculative, and I wondered if he regretted his outburst.

I couldn't bring myself to raise the issue with him; and Clements was certainly never going to prompt a discussion on that or any other subject. And so time went by. Months. Then a year.

Clements continued to indulge in his short-lived eruptions, while most people continued to regard his conduct as excellent if bizarre entertainment. Perhaps because of my personal brush with the man, however, I had begun to wonder if there was something about him we were all missing.

Saying that, it came as much of a shock to me as everyone else when we learned one morning, on arriving in work, that Clements had been taken into police custody. The astonishment was compounded a week or two later, after he was charged with murder. Although a few of the know-alls nodded their heads and said, "Told you so", even they lapsed into stunned silence as the facts of the case came to light.

PARTS

Clements had been killing people for some time.

The police had found human remains in the rambling old property where he lived alone. But the truly damning evidence resided in a collection of specimen bottles on a shelf in the building's cellar, a room which had apparently also served as a torture chamber. Each bottle, helpfully for the authorities, was labelled with the details of what it contained.

Clements had drawn attention to himself after a brush with a speeding driver as he cycled home from work one evening.

Catching up with the car at the next set of traffic lights, he had gone into one of his tirades, voicing murderous intentions towards all road hogs. Unfortunately for him, the motorist happened to be an off-duty policeman, who'd carted him off to the local nick on a charge of threatening behaviour.

I'm not sure what happened there, but Clements must have said or done something that made them suspect he was more than just a harmless lunatic. Anyway, a sergeant went back with him to the house, on some pretext or other, and immediately detected a sickly-sweet smell around the place. An investigation of the cellar quickly gave up Clements's secrets.

The bottles contained body parts, floating in formalin. Many of them were almost unrecognisable, but that was where his diligent labelling came in useful. It turned out the grotesque trophies all came from people who had offended Clements in some way down the years.

There was the hand of the postman who had forced a parcel through his letter box, thereby damaging several of his precious comics. The tongue, withered and misshapen, of a woman who had been a notorious neighbourhood gossip - the police suspected she had been spreading rumours about Clements.

One relic was the ragged foot of a boy who had kicked a ball through his window and then run away. Clements noted on the label that he had waited twenty months before murdering the miscreant, presumably to avoid attracting attention to himself.

The horror was overwhelming, the talk of the office for months, a variety of individuals shivering as they recalled how they'd teased him, speculating if they'd been next on his death list.

After Clements was sent down for life, though, things gradually went back to normal. Other sensations came along to monopolise our attention; gruesome crimes are much like buses in that respect. It's certain to be a long time, however, before any of us can think of Clements without giving an inward shudder.

PARTS

I believe I have more cause than any of the others to think I narrowly escaped the murderous attentions of our erstwhile colleague. It must have been some sixth sense that warned me about him, triggering the break-up with Becky not long after receiving Clements's reprimand.

But that doesn't help me sleep at night. I still have nightmares of being tortured in his dingy cellar, the sensation of overwhelming terror as he violates my body. I convulse awake, clutching my groin until it hurts.

1057989R0

Printed in Great Britain by
Amazon.co.uk, Ltd.,
Marston Gate.